A MINGLED YARN:

Scenes From A Family Saga

By Louise Williams

To Bear and NOZ

Heartfelt Thanks

Table of Contents

1981

There is no darkness but ignorance.

Shakespeare, Twelfth Night 4.2.42-3

A story has no beginning or end: arbitrarily one chooses that moment of experience from which to look back or from which to look ahead.

Graham Green, The End of the Affair

1952

PROMISE ME

It was early morning before sun up—Clare heard Sally Anne's muffled cry. "Sally Anne, is it time?"

Raising her head Sally Anne grinned and answered, "I think so."

The oscillating fan and the humidity caused both girls to shiver when their feet touched the floor. Dressing quickly and quietly, Clare grabbed Sally Anne's overnight bag and whispered, "Let's go get you a baby."

Sally Anne handed Clare an apple she'd picked up on the way out of their dorm room, and a photo of Mickey that she kept in a frame on her desk, asking Clare to keep it safe for her.

Clare thought it odd that Sally Anne had taken Mickey's picture from its frame, but she didn't question her. Placing the photo in her desk drawer, under papers, she figured it safe.

From Chestnut Hill College to the hospital was a short hop. With no air conditioning in her car, Clare drove Sally Anne to the hospital with all of the windows down, their hair flying every which way. The black Naugahyde seat covers stuck to their backs, and to make matters worse, Clare couldn't stop the vents from spewing hot air. The heat and humidity never relented that June day in 1952 in Chestnut Hill, tucked in the Northwest section of Philadelphia. The air was so thick that Clare thought she could take a straw and drink from it.

On the radio, Jo Stafford was singing, "You belong to me." In the middle of the song, the radio went static— Clare turned it off, but continued humming parts of the tune.

A mixture of excitement and anxiety rode in the chambers of Sally Anne's heart that day. Imagine her having a baby to hold—Mickey's baby. Hoping the child would be a boy, with Mickey's looks so she could have a reminder of him every day—although a girl would be nice too for so many reasons. She dreamed of Mickey and a little girl skipping and screeching over some private joke. Just as a happy thought occupied her mind, it would be replaced by the reality of the situation that translated to dread.

At a stoplight, she turned to Clare and, with a soft, deliberate voice said, "If anything happens to me, please don't tell Mick about the baby. Please—promise me that, please." Closing her eyes, she leaned back in her seat.

"Deceit never ends well. Why are you doing this? You love Mickey. You've told me often enough."

"I can't tie him down. He doesn't deserve that—he worked hard for his fellowship." She patted her rounded belly and continued, "Promise me, Clare, promise me."

"I think you're crazy, but I promise." *Must be the heat and hormones making her think like this.* Noticing a large red ball rising in the east, Clare murmured, "Another hot day." She couldn't remember if this was the ninth or the nineteenth day of this stinking weather.

Sally Anne twisted from a contraction; it felt as though her back were splitting in a million pieces. With her sleeve, she wiped the sweat trickling down near her ear. She wondered for the thousandth time if she were making a mistake not telling Mickey. She could almost feel the taut slender thread

2

between silence and speech. He would have insisted on staying with her and not going abroad. No, she couldn't do that to him. It would be selfish on her part. And yet she knew she was being selfish in another way— depriving Mickey of his offspring. A battle constantly raged in her head. Their baby was held hostage in that battle.

She kept sliding her locket back and forth across her lips, like a zipper, on a silver chain Mickey had given her for her birthday—this comforted her. Smiling, she remembered how shy he was giving her the locket, so afraid she wouldn't like it. She had called him a silly old soul and vowed it would never leave her neck.

Should I beg her to tell Mickey or leave her to her own crazy reasoning, thought Clare, slowing for a car that was having a problem, Clare looked over at Sally Anne, who had turned to her with frightened eyes.

"Remember your promise. If anything happens to me, you can't tell Mickey about the baby."

"I won't tell him, I promise, but he doesn't leave for two more days." Clare figured that it was more than likely a promise she wouldn't have to keep. Swallowing the last piece of apple, and pulling into the hospital parking lot, she said, "Baby time."

HOW CAN THIS BE?

Sally Anne didn't move. She grabbed her locket that had broken free of her neck and now hung from her hand. Slumping in her seat, she sagged sideways. Her face showed a spiraling pain as she clenched her teeth, while her eyes seemed to swivel sideways in their sockets.

Blood—blood was on Sally Anne's lap, her legs, and the floorboards.

Sticking her head out the window, Clare screamed, "Help, I need help! Get a doctor."

A young man, who had stopped on a sidewalk to light a cigarette, ran for the ER entrance almost knocking over a woman coming from another direction to the same door.

Clare grabbed Sally Anne's hand, but Sally Anne didn't grab back. She tried desperately to comfort her. "Everything will be okay—the doctor's coming— hold on—I'm here—Sally Anne, hold on!" Taking the locket from Sally Anne's hand, she dropped it into her pocket. Within a minute, a nurse tapped Clare on her shoulder, and she slid out of the car. A doctor was forcing his hands into disposable gloves as he hurried towards the car. The nurse helped the doctor ease Sally Anne across the front seat; she leaned in from the driver's side door, and the doctor from the passenger side.

Sitting on a curb, Clare prayed the *Memorare* aloud. "Remember, O most gracious Virgin Mary, that never was it known that anyone who fled to thy protection, implored thy help—she couldn't remember the rest of the

4

prayer so she used her own words. "Please God, let her live. Her baby needs her. Please God give her strength, please."

She would always remember this part of the day in a hazy way. The doctor turned towards her holding a baby as if he were beginning to waltz— his face told her the news before his words had a chance. The baby was handed to the nurse, who wrapped her in the folds of security. Still sitting on the curb, Clare put her head in her hands and sobbed. Her friend had exhaled her last breath, while her baby inhaled her first. Clare's mind was a roller coaster of thoughts and like the feeling she'd get from the up and down motion of a coaster ride, she felt nauseated.

Hearing the sound of footsteps, she raised her head and noticed two men in pristine lab coats coming towards the car with a gurney. Clare watched as one went in from the driver's side and helped the other on the passenger side slide Sally Anne onto the gurney, feet first. She was covered with a white sheet that turned into streaks of red, and was wheeled away.

"Obstetrical hemorrhage," the doctor said, as he helped Clare up from the curb.

Clare heard the doctor, but her eyes followed the red-veined sheet.

On the way into the hospital, he led her to an empty waiting room with dust motes moving lazily in front of double hung windows.

Why did I make that stupid promise? Best friends, as simple as that.

"We should notify her next of kin," the doctor said. He kept his hand on her arm a few minutes until she finally spoke. "How can this be—she was young and healthy."

5

"There was a uterine rupture that led to internal bleeding. She didn't suffer, because everything happened so quickly."

The traces of blood on the doctor's left sock made her turn away.

For the next two days, Wednesday and Thursday, he told her, the baby would stay at the hospital, barring complications. Standing, he said he would be back to check on her in a little while. The window air conditioner sent out a little stream of cool air. To take advantage of this small mercy, Clare changed her seat. Her thoughts were still riding the roller coaster.

When the doctor returned, she asked, "May I see my friend and the baby?"

Leading her first into a post-delivery section where Sally Anne was cordoned off by curtains, the doctor pulled one back. "Take your time a nurse will be along shortly."

Sally Anne was covered with a clean sheet. A ray of light coming from a curtain not quite closed sliced her face in half. Clare saw her best friend in a pose that could have been in Madame Tussauds's wax museum. Sally Anne's cheeks, normally rosy, were as white as milk glass, yet her beauty could not be denied even in death. Clare lifted her friend's hand and kissed it. "Sally Anne," she whispered and rocked back and forth, saying the name over and over again. A tiny speck of blood stained Sally Anne's neck. Clare took a tissue from her pocket, spat on it, and dabbed at the spot until it disappeared. *She will disappear, too.* "Oh, Sally Anne."

A short, comely nurse came in. Clare looked at her and said, "She's cold, she needs a blank-"—*no, that's not what she needs.* The nurse coaxed her out of the room.

Clare asked, "May I see the baby?" She followed the woman to the nursery. The wall color was a bright yellow, but the lighting was dim. There, in a crib marked *Girl-Crosby*, was a little head with wisps of blonde hair peeking out of a striped blanket. *So it's a girl.* Sally Anne's baby was fast asleep. Another blonde-haired infant was testing his voice with sonorous screams. "May I hold her?" she asked.

The nurse paused, met Clare's eyes, and handed the bundled baby to her and stood close to Clare. Grasping the baby to her chest she said, "Oh, Sally Anne," the baby felt so tiny, as if she were holding the Kewpie doll she had had as a child. It was then that Clare fully registered the gravity of the situation. She had to tell someone—Sally Anne's parents?

If only, the two words that once carried possibilities and now meant nothing. *If only she hadn't made that promise.* Mickey didn't leave for another two days. If she called him, she'd be doing exactly what Sally Anne hadn't wanted. Best to stick to her word—who was she to change her best friend's dying wish? *Surely, Sally Anne had the best of intentions.* Fiona, Sally Anne's older sister, would be the best person to call, but Sally Anne's parents should probably be told first. Her rocking back and forth caused the baby to twist and open her eyes. Over the baby's head, Clare glimpsed a couple holding their child and staring at her. Now sobbing, she handed the baby back to the nurse, collected herself, and asked about a pay phone. The nurse offered the phone at

7

her station and pointed to it. The corridor was half lit, and Clare stepped in coffee that had been spilled recently. Her right sneaker now looked as though Jackson Pollack had had his hand in the design. She wanted to scream but knew she couldn't—it was just a shoe.

Clare dialed Mr. and Mrs. Crosby's number. When Mr. Crosby answered in his usual stony voice, Clare hung up—too afraid of him. He had never been warm or welcoming to her, or anyone for that matter.

What was Sally Anne's sister, Fiona's married name? Her brain felt like a perforated sand bag. Nothing materialized. Jack, Jack what? Going through the alphabet one letter at a time, hoping to jar the name from her brain: Jack S, Jack T, Jack U, Jack V, Jack W, she stopped there, and *Walsh* popped into her head. "That's it!" she cried aloud. Heads turned. She couldn't make this call with five people standing within earshot. She went to find a pay phone.

"Hello, hello… hello, is someone there?" asked Fiona.

KEEPING THE PROMISE

Clare found her voice. Gasping she said, "Fiona, it's Clare— I'm not sure how to tell you this so I'll just say it." Taking a deep breath, which produced a dry mouth, she said, "Sally Anne died this morning giving birth to a baby girl."

"A baby girl?" Fiona asked confusedly. "What? I don't understand."

Clare repeated the terrible news until Fiona's shock gave way to a horrified understanding.

"Where are you?"

"Chestnut Hill Hospital. It's not far from the College."

Fiona and Jack lived about twenty miles west of Philadelphia. Fiona said Jack was at work; she'd call him and leave immediately.

Clare fidgeted. Minutes seemed permanently paused. A yellow sweater someone had left behind lay on a chair across from her. The wall was a pale Pepto-Bismol pink. It didn't help Clare feel better, and neither did the harsh overhead florescent lights in this waiting room. Lighting her third Newport, she kept thinking about the promise she had made —*what to do?* Putting the matches back into her pocketbook, she remembered Sally Anne's locket in her pocket, opened it, and took out Mickey's picture. She made her way quickly to the restroom. Her eyes scanned the room and found a trashcan. Tearing the photo in half, although very small, she shoved it into the can, making sure it was covered with debris.

9

She rinsed her face. Her usually peach-like complexion was still blotchy and made her freckles appear larger. Her strawberry blonde ponytail was half falling out of the rubber band— having pulled on it while the doctor had attended Sally Anne. Red capillaries ringed her teal blue eyes. Taking a deep breath, she went back to the waiting room. Should she break her promise? Sally Anne's baby could have a father. No, she had promised. They had been best friends since grade school. They once had hidden together when Mr. Crosby came looking for them because he had heard, while they had played a word game, one of the girls had said *Jesus*.

When Fiona and Jack arrived, Clare used the arms of the chair to help her stand.

Fiona was an Irish beauty with her silken skin, brown twinkly eyes, and tiny freckles across the bridge of her nose. Except for hair color, the sisters shared a close resemblance. Fiona was tall and willowy, with an open face, usually radiating kindness. Now, she looked as if she had thrown herself together after a long, sleepless night. Her dark hair shone in the sun as she passed the waiting room window; it highlighted her colorless skin.

Holding Fiona's hand was her husband, Jack, a few inches taller, with dark blonde hair, an aquiline nose, and a chin dimple. Both faces were awash with pain.

Clare hugged them and noticed Fiona's red-rimmed eyes and felt her shaking hands.

Jack turned to Fiona, and said, "I'll look after the paper work."

"Are your parents coming?" asked Clare.

10

"No, I want to be with my brothers when I tell them, you know how they are— we'll go to the house."

Clare knew all right—remembering Sally Anne's parents as word cannibals eating away at their children's love, strength, hope, and happiness through tight religious lips.

Clare and Fiona sat on a faded lime green sofa, which had one small hole in the fabric. Clare picked at the stitching on her pocketbook. She glanced at Fiona—a stream of tears bathed her face. Clare wanted to hug Fiona again, but wasn't sure she had it in herself to hug and lie at the same time.

Fiona returned her look and rattled off questions in rapid fire, "How long did you know that Sally Anne was pregnant? Where is the father? Who is he? Why didn't we know? Sally Anne wasn't like this. She didn't keep secrets."

Promise me. Clare's hands were clammy, and her head was spinning. Why had she ever accepted this burden? She knew why—she had made a promise, and wouldn't do to Sally Anne what a friend had done to her. Instead of a cross, Clare felt an albatross around her neck.

True to her word, but false to her heart, she said, "I didn't know w-w-who he was—Sally Anne wouldn't tell me. She seemed s-s- so busy this semester that I hardly saw her. I guessed she was pregnant a- a at the beginning of April." Clare looked down while she conveyed the lie but stuck to her story. "It wasn't that Sally Anne looked pregnant, as s-s- she didn't gain that much weight." *God, why am I stuttering?* That was something she hadn't done since fifth grade when was going through a lying phase about having

11

done her chores and homework. "She j… just somehow looked fuller."
Catching a small whiff of Fiona's perfume was unsettling, as Sally Anne had
worn the same kind, *Arpege*. *I need to get out of here. I can't face Sally Anne's
family knowing what I know.* Her lips were so dry that she searched in her
pocketbook for lip balm. It must have fallen out. Licking her lips, she thought
silence might be worse than an outright lie. Clare thought of *Macbeth*. Her last
exam yesterday had been on Shakespearean plots. This was a plot all right, one
of her own making. "Out, out, brief candle." Would she suffer from terrifying
dreams, also? Why couldn't she stop herself? *Why am I thinking about
Shakespeare?* She shook her head slightly, as if to shake her thoughts away—
yes, but Sally Anne was dead, and Mickey must never know.

"Clare—Clare?"

"Sorry, Fiona, this is all t-t-too much. I-I-I still can't believe what
happened." Reaching into her pocket, she grabbed onto the locket and
held it so Fiona could see it. "Sally Anne was wearing this when"—
looking down—she handed the locket to Fiona and said, "I'd l-l-l…like to
go home now."

Fiona opened the locket immediately. "Of course, Clare, and I want
to see Sally Anne and the baby. I'll call you about funeral arrangements."

As Clare stood, Jack returned with papers in hand. Again, they
hugged each other, and Clare left. Her father would take care of her car.

A taxi pulled up; Clare sighed and got in. *Should I go back in and tell
them about Mickey? Promise me, Clare.* She had kept her word, yet knew

when the owls were swooping through the dark branches at night looking for their next meals, her conscience would be eating away at her.

WHY ARE YOU HERE?

On the way home from the hospital, Jack and Fiona decided they would call the baby Elizabeth, the name Sally Anne had chosen for her Confirmation name. By the time they reached home, they'd shortened it to Liza. Fiona knew that a piece of her had died with Sally Anne—sometimes, the piece was lodged in her heart, or her mind, and even in her stomach. She prayed that time would help her expel this piece of death that maneuvered throughout her body, and that it would be replaced by memories of Sally Anne's life.

The heat had not abated. The windows were open in Jack's and Fiona's living room, but there was no breeze. In this attractive room, there were blue chintz fabrics, lovely watercolors, and carefully placed Chinese pieces. Above the fireplace was an old French mirror from Jack's parents. The strong scent of roses in a Ming vase filled the room. Fiona and her two brothers stood without speaking. Peter wiped his face with his handkerchief and lit a cigarette.

"Why didn't Sally Anne tell us?" Liam said at last. He was her outspoken brother—tall and built like a swimmer, with a smile that won people over easily, an associate professor in philosophy at the University of Pennsylvania; he was three years younger than Fiona.

Peter shook his head. He was as tall as his brother but had a head of thick black hair, and his eyes were a piercing blue that caused many people to look away when talking to him. He had a tendency to keep his own counsel.

14

Working as a lawyer, for the Archdiocese of Philadelphia kept him connected to his faith on a daily basis. He was four and a half years younger than Fiona—Sally Anne had been the baby of the family.

Passing through the living room with cookies in hand, Jack hugged Fiona's brothers, offered words of comfort and went upstairs to be with their children, Kate and Finn.

"We would have helped her," Liam said. "We didn't even get to say goodbye." He sat down on the edge of an armchair, shoulders drooping, spine slightly bent.

"Did anyone even know she had a boyfriend?" Peter asked. "Surely Clare knew." He hesitated, glanced at Fiona and blurted, "What made Sally Anne go against church teachings?"

Fiona flinched looking at Liam for support. Liam shook his head. "Father will eat us alive."

"Mother and Father will need support, too," offered Peter. His brother and sister turned from him.

The three of them were silent during the fifteen-minute ride to their parents' house in Liam's old Studebaker with its distinct odor of wet dog and sour milk.

In front of the large two-storied Colonial Revival sat two great American elms, one on each side of the walk, providing some shade for part of

15

the lawn. Liam pulled up and shut the engine off. They sat a few minutes. Peter lit another cigarette.

Liam said, "I'm still intimidated by them. Have you ever seen either of them cry?"

Fiona picked at a scab on her arm, making it bleed again. Taking a tissue out of her bag, she applied pressure to the wound until the bleeding stopped—blood, not something she wanted to think about. Distracted by Liam's cracking his knuckles, a holdover from his youth when he had awaited their father's return from work to be punished for some misdeed, helped her forget about blood. A fly clung to the ceiling of the car, too hot to buzz around.

"Let's get this over with," Fiona said. She was sick about Sally Anne, but sicker knowing how her parents were going to react to their daughter's death.

Getting out of the car, Peter said, "He just wanted us to obey the teachings of the Catholic Church, we can't fault him for that."

Liam edged closer to Peter, until he was within inches of his face, and said, "I swear to God, Peter, keep your mouth shut about the Church and our parents; no one wants to hear it." Peter backed away.

Fiona held Liam's arm as they started up the walkway. She caught the scent of roses close to the door climbing a trellis attached to the brick and remembered how Sally Anne had pricked their fingers with a thorn from these shrubs to become double blood sisters.

Standing in front of the dark green door, with its ornate knocker, and elegant fanlight, Fiona squeezed Liam's hand before knocking—knowing that mercy did not reside in this house.

Their father opened the door, looking sterner than ever— his face set in reinforced anger. His hair seemed whiter and his upper lip curled more than usual.

"What's this about? We weren't expecting you—why are you here?"

Peter spoke up, "Could you ask Mother to come down? We have something to tell you both."

Their father walked over to the stairs and yelled, "Mary, come down here."

No hug, no welcome, no have a seat. Fiona looked into the living room from the hallway; it had been off limits as they were growing up, except during Lent, when they had knelt there to say the rosary. More like a museum than a living room: the walls were a light, cold green, the windows were treated with traditional swags, an oil painting of the Infant Jesus of Prague hung over a Chippendale sofa. This had never been a lived-in house, more of a holding cell until they had moved out. Fiona was all nerves waiting for her mother and looked at the ivory holy water font at the bottom of the stairs.

"Hurry up, Mary," their father called up the stairs.

Fiona knew her mother's hands would be pressing her dress to her side— she always did this when their father yelled at her.

As her mother descended the stairs, Fiona regarded her carefully. For sixty-one she was still attractive, her dark brown hair hadn't turned gray, and she had kept her girlish figure, but there was now an invulnerable tightness in her face.

Stopping near the bottom of the stairs, Mrs. Crosby asked, with a hint of apprehension, "Why are you here?"

Liam found his voice first. "Mother, Father, perhaps we should go into the living room and sit down. We have sad news for you."

Their mother moved towards the living room, but their father held her back.
"Here is fine."

Fiona spoke up, "I think we all need to sit."

With a countenance that could freeze blood their father repeated, "Here's fine!"

Fiona said, "There's no easy way to tell you this."

"Just tell us," their father ordered.

"Sally Anne gave birth to a baby girl this morning. She had an obstetrical hemorrhage—the baby lived, but the doctor couldn't save Sally Anne." She paused, looked down, and said, "We don't know who the father is."

A ringing phone in the kitchen startled all of them, but no one moved to answer it —five rings later silence returned.

Their mother stood straight-backed, while their father walked into the living room and paced, fists clenched. The tall case clock in the living room played the Whittington Chimes. *The only joyful sound heard in this house*, Fiona thought.

Collecting himself, he returned to the hall and glared at his offspring for what seemed like a long time. Finally in a voice loaded with disgust, he declared, "Sally Anne wasn't raised this way. Were you raised this way?" All three looked down. Fiona knew it was better to say nothing once he started on a tirade.

"Sally Anne's name is not to be mentioned again in our presence— when she committed this sin, she left the Church, and left us."

Fiona looked at her mother, who still stood as straight as an arrow.

"She has humiliated all of us," their father coughed and continued, "She will not be buried in the family plot. Get rid of her and give that baby to an adoption agency!" He stared at them with flinty eyes. "Did you know about this—why, she must have been pregnant under our roof at Easter. Did you or did you not know about this?"

All three shook their heads, stunned into silence. Fiona wanted desperately to have her father hug her and shield her body from pain. Had he ever hugged her? No, not that she remembered.

Fiona looked at her mother who was pale, yet stoical—a specialist in the concealment of feelings.

In the total silence that followed, Fiona found the courage that her parents had trampled on since childhood, and in a clear voice she said, "Jack and I are going to adopt the baby. If you want to see Kate and Finn, then you'll have to see Sally Anne's baby, Elizabeth, whom we will call Liza. This is your daughter and granddaughter we're talking about; the child is guiltless. Please find it in your hearts to forgive Sally Anne."

"Please," Liam echoed.

Their father roared. "We raised the four of you to obey the Church's teachings. Forgiveness? You'd better hope she asked God's forgiveness before she died. If not, she's sleeping with the devil now and forever. We didn't raise our girls to be whores. What will people think? Now, go!"

As they were leaving, Peter squeezed his mother's arm.

Fiona wished to do the same, but their relationship didn't allow for that. She wanted to say, *Mother, it's okay to cry. Your beloved daughter has just died.*

To his father Peter said, "You have every reason to be angry— you raised us to abide by the tenets of the Church."

Beside Fiona, Liam seethed. Fiona put her hand on his arm. Peter's words made her think that maybe he had been branded at birth with their parents' beliefs.

20

STAR LIGHT, STAR BRIGHT...

Liam knocked into Peter's arm as he forged ahead down the front walk, throwing Fiona off balance. Helping her regain her footing, he turned to her and said, "Sorry, Fee."

Liam started the car, pounded his fist on the dashboard, and said, "We should be done with them; they didn't even cry. What kind of parent disowns a child for a mistake? Let them rot for all I care." He pulled into the street, still fuming, "Funny, their religion is so selective. What about forgiveness—no, they think *fornication*, and that's it. No more Sally Anne. It's as if she never existed. They lack the salve of forgiveness."

Fiona spoke. "They aren't going to change. Save your breath."

Liam turned, and said, "Sorry, Fiona, our sister is dead, and I'm not putting up with their religious crap anymore. You two can worship at their inflexible altar, but no more for me, thanks; as far as I'm concerned, they died with Sally Anne."

Fiona wondered what bond held her parents together. Surely, love wasn't a part of it. Her mother obeyed her father and that was that. What had drawn them together in the first place? Did affection ever pass between them? What happened on their wedding night? Had her mother been stripped of her feelings along with her clothes?

###

The siblings sat in Fiona's kitchen, a lemon yellow room with white trim. Jack had laid black and white linoleum tiles on the floor. There was an oblong chrome table with six chrome chairs upholstered in black vinyl, and the top of the table had a white- marbled design. A lazy Susan sat in the middle of the table. Three large watercolors of fruits and flowers were carefully spaced on the wall behind the table. A tiny, cobalt blue vase held one slightly wilted buttercup that Kate had given to her mother yesterday. The family spent many hours here. A small bulletin board leaned to the right overloaded with proof of a family's everyday existence: bills, photos of the children, a second place ribbon that Kate had won last year in the Peewee Swimming Contest, an invitation to a barbeque, a string of pink pop-it beads, a ticket for laundry which was on top of a folded piece of yellow paper, a holy card from the last funeral they had been to, a curled palm from Palm Sunday two years ago, and other things half hidden from view.

Liam said, "We need to pull ourselves together."

Peter lit another cigarette. "Sally Anne should have a Catholic Mass and burial, because that's what she would have wanted."

Liam and Fiona stared at him wearily but didn't reply.

"I'll call St. Bridget's to see if see if there's any way she can be buried in the Church, said Peter.

Liam opened a bottle of burgundy and poured while Fiona passed around biscuits.

"Remember when Sally Anne lost the telephone bill money?" asked Fiona.

Liam laughed. "Remember when she was named May Queen, and was leading the procession into church, a pigeon landed one on her dress, and she just kept walking?"

"How about the time she found the fifty-dollar bill on the train?" Peter said. "She turned it in. We begged her to split it with us. You know the conductor kept it."

"How is it possible," Liam said, "that we don't know who the father is?"

"What if he's married?" said Peter.

Liam glared at him. "Why must you think the worst—you're just like Father!"

"Clare didn't even know," Fiona said, "and you know how close they were. She seemed hesitant and nervous when telling me. I guess we just have to accept it." A cloud of doubt had inched its way into her mind, and it hadn't disappeared with Clare's explanation. *What didn't she tell me?*

"Maybe there's something in her dorm room," Liam said. "I'll collect her belongings and see if there's anything at all about him, his picture—something."

"She must have been pregnant at Christmas, too," Peter said. "She seemed quieter than usual. Other than that, we were all oblivious. Of course we were only there for a few hours. Although, looking back, I remember her wearing that big sweatshirt at Easter break when she came to visit us." He lit another cigarette and let the smoke curl its way around Fiona's kitchen.

Fiona took another sip of wine. "I think she didn't tell us so we wouldn't be seen as accomplices when Mother and Father found out—I'm sure she was scared."

"And ashamed," Peter said. When they gaped at him accusingly, he added, "It was a mortal sin."

Liam, as though sitting on a tack, jumped up, and grabbed Peter's shirt.

Fiona threw herself between them. "Not here, not now—we need to bury our sister." Liam backed off. They let Peter's comment float into the smoke from his cigarette. The smoke would clear, but the words would remain.

"Are you sure about adopting the baby?" Liam asked. "Linda and I could take her."

"At the hospital, when I held the baby, it felt right, and Jack thought so, too."

The light of day had disappeared when five-year-old Kate, wearing the same freckles as her mother's across her nose, and her father's chin dimple, came into the kitchen and asked her mother if they were playing a game in the dark.

"No, my darling. Why aren't you asleep? I thought Dad was reading to you and Finn."

"He started to, but he fell asleep, and Finn's asleep, too."

"Go upstairs and wake your father. I'll be up in a few minutes." Fiona turned to her brothers. "On Thursday afternoon, we'll meet with the funeral director and perhaps Father Riley. Friday afternoon, Liza's coming home, and the funeral will be Saturday morning."

After her brothers left, Fiona stood outside and looked at the night sky. "Goodnight, sweet sister." She imagined Sally Anne sitting on the handle of the Big Dipper, watching her movements here on Earth. *Star Light, Star Bright...*

SALVATION NOT PERDITION

Fiona woke to the sound of Finn yelling, "I can't find a shoe, and I want to go swimming!" Fiona donned a robe and headed downstairs and hugged Finn. "We'll talk about swimming later—give me a minute, and I'll help you find your shoe." Fiona sat down.

Kate climbed into her mother's lap and said, "I love you, Mommy." Fiona held Kate. *Leave it to Kate. She always manages to smooth the rough edges of my heart.* "I spy with my little eye a little boy's shoe under the radiator," Fiona said.

Finn raced across the room to collect the shoe.

Touching her cheek, Jack handed Fiona a cup of coffee and offered toast. She wasn't hungry, but took a sip of coffee, and they headed for the guest room. It had been decorated with adults in mind. It was to be Liza's room now. From an off-white ceiling, hung a brass chandelier. Two oils of seascapes hung, one on each side of the door. Fiona loved the crib at the far end of the room, which Jack had made in his garage workshop before Kate was born. That was the first time he had made spindles, which went around the sides of the crib. Fiona knew he had painted them with a coat of pride. As she ran her fingers over them, she could still see Kate's little fingers clutching them. Jack had taken apart the guest bed and put it in the garage that was half filled with furniture from his parents' house.

They made their way to the den, where Kate and Finn were playing a game of soldiers versus dolls. Fiona was disturbed at the force that Finn's

26

soldiers were using on Kate's dolls. After all, he was almost three. Jack caught hold of Finn's hand, bent down and said, "Whoa, partner. We never hit people, animals, or playthings."

Finn didn't look at Jack and tried to squirm out of his father's grasp.

"Finn, please look at me when I talk to you. Do you understand we want you to be nice to everyone?"

"Not if not nice to me."

"How were the dolls not nice to your soldiers?"

Finn ran a soldier along the back of the sofa and said, "They just were."

"Sit down, please. Your mom and I want to share something with you. He waited saying nothing until Finn sat down next to Kate. We're going to bring a baby home from the hospital. Her name is Elizabeth, but we'll call her Liza."

"May Liza sleep in my room?" Kate begged. "I have two beds, and she could use the other one.

"She's too little, Kate," Fiona said. "She'll need a crib, for now she'll sleep in the guest room, but you can hold her when she's not sleeping."

"I'll have my own real doll baby."

Jack and Fiona both managed to smile.

"Will she cry?" Finn asked.

"Yes, Finn, she will," Jack said.

"Can we play cowboys and Indians with her?" asked Finn.

Fiona sighed, "Not yet, she's too little."

"You don't look like Nancy's mom with a big tummy."

"You're right Kate, I don't." *She seems okay with that answer.*

"Come on, Kate, it's your turn to chase me." Finn ran out of the room, and Kate followed but turned back to say, "My own baby sister."

Fiona spoke first, as they walked back to the guest room. "I think it's best to begin adoption proceedings for Liza. We can postpone telling her till she's older. It's too much for a young child to take in. At sixteen she'll be able to understand better."

Jack mulled it over and said, "I'm for that. How do you think Kate and Finn will respond when Liza gets here?"

"Like any other children faced with a new sibling."

Surveying the room, Fiona lamented, "I wish I had time to paint it, put up a few mobiles, and get back the rocker that I lent to Linda and Liam. The striped wallpaper doesn't seem appropriate for a baby." Putting his arm around Fiona's waist, Jack said, "Darling, don't worry about the room, these blue stripes are soft, and I'll find those nursery-rhyme prints we used when Kate and Finn were little."

"Oh, Jack, I have an unsettled feeling—I can't describe it—I don't know what it means, and it scares me."

"Let's just take it one day at a time."

"If I lost you, Jack, I'm not sure..."

"Don't think about me now. Where's a sheet for the crib? I'll make it up."

At the linen closet, Fiona rummaged around until she found a crib sheet. Finn's initials were sewn in blue thread at the top of the sheet. Handing it to Jack, Fiona felt a tsunami of rage moving in to where wretched sadness had claimed its territory. She choked up, "Why didn't she tell me? I might have saved her."

The siblings arrived at the funeral home, but paused next to the car before ascending the stairs to the building. They felt heat rising from the pavement.

Peter said, "Father Riley doesn't want to bury an unwed mother in the Church. When he heard what I was asking, he took his time and told me that he was not in favor of burying a woman in consecrated ground, who had borne a child out of wedlock." Peter kicked the bottom step.

Liam glared at Peter and said, "And I bet you thanked him. I would have told that priest in no uncertain terms what a travesty his religion was, and then I would have shouted, *Futue te ipsum.*"

"Yes, we all know what you would have done, Liam," said Peter.

Fiona said. "Sally Anne was a devout Catholic until this transgression—it would shatter her not to have a Christian burial."

"I called ahead," said Liam. "But when I got to the College, they kept me waiting twenty minutes before they found someone who could open Sally Anne's dorm room. Her papers were all tidily stacked on top of her desk.

29

I felt underhanded going through her things. I didn't find any indication of a boyfriend. I did find baby booties in her sock drawer." Taking the booties out of his pocket, he handed them to Fiona and continued, "There was an overturned picture frame on her desk; it was empty. Clare must know who was in that frame—and I picked up her yearbook."

Once inside, Fiona looked around and said, "We should be in a church." The room reminded her of a small auditorium with folding chairs— no warmth.

Liam made all the arrangements. There would be no wake. Sally Anne's body would be cremated, and a short service would follow on Saturday morning. The cremation would take place that afternoon.

"May we place letters in the coffin with her?" Liam asked the funeral director. "And may we attend the cremation?"

Nodding, the funeral director started to leave but turned back, and said, "Most people don't attend the cremation, but it is allowed." Then he left them alone with Sally Anne.

Liam scowled at Peter and said, "When our parents die, I won't be writing them any letters."

Fiona bent down and kissed Sally Ann's rubbery cheek. She wanted to leave. *This can't be the last memory of my sister.* What could she replace it with? In May two years ago, her sister and she had driven to the beach and spent a lazy day letting the sun unfurl their bodies, so tightly bunched from an unusually cold winter. It had been a long time since the sisters had a chance to spend time together alone and to pick up where they had left off.

30

###

The cremation was set for four o'clock, giving them time to go to Liam's house to write their letters. Liam's golden retriever, Midas, kept putting his head on everyone's lap until Liam put him outside. Linda, Liam's wife, filled a kettle to put on the stove. No one talked. Fiona could hear Midas scratching the door to get back in.

Looking around the kitchen, Fiona thought how she had always liked this room: the slate-blue walls, the small but funny plates with fish performing different chores, such as baking, drying dishes and catching a man at the end of a pole were hung over the sink, warm pine furniture and every day clutter filled the room— it wasn't overpowering, it just meant people lived here. The faded blue and white checked chair in the corner was inviting.

Peter finished his letter quickly. Liam played with his pen, and Fiona closed her eyes for a long time before putting pen to paper— desperately wanting to say everything to her dear sister that she hadn't had a chance to say before her death. Finally, they folded their notes into cream-colored envelopes, went back to the funeral home at three-thirty, and put their letters into the casket.

###

The crematorium was a few miles away. Fiona sat in the back of the car weeping. It was another sticky June day. The sun caused the branches to shadow the windshield. She whispered, "How can Sally Anne be lying inside a wooden box on her way to be burned out of existence—how?"

Her brothers didn't answer.

They followed the hearse on a two-lane country road, carved through a hillside, with the roots of trees overhanging the road. Fiona could see ahead a nondescript stone building with white wooden doors. A simple brass plaque over the doors read, *Heavenly Peace Crematorium*. Chimney smoke from the last cremation still spun its way into the sky.

When they entered the viewing room, Fiona was surprised to find it so bare, with white walls and a tan tiled floor—four folding chairs were set against a back wall facing a tempered glass wall.

As the coffin came into view, Fiona stood, walked to the glass partition and touched it in a silent protest. Liam went to her and stood behind her with his hands on her shoulders.

Fiona turned around and saw Peter go out the way they had entered.

The wooden coffin was on a lift table that rolled up to a heavy hydraulic door. The door opened, the coffin rolled into the kiln slowly, and once it was in the kiln, the door shut immediately. Fiona stood motionless as the flames did their work on Sally Anne, *so that was it— nothing to see.*

They found Peter leaning against the car, his hand shaking holding a newly lit cigarette, and his face nearly as drained of blood as Sally Anne's had been. Fiona didn't need to ask if he were all right. Words made no sense; she just heard sounds. Fiona took his hand and guided him into the back seat. There was a faint scent of honeysuckle off in the distance.

The crematorium director, unwrapping a piece of candy, came up to the car window and told them they would be given the ashes after the service. Fiona thanked him and thought, *Please God, salvation not perdition.*

FATE'S SLINGS AND ARROWS

Friday, like the rest of the week, was another day for the weather record books: ninety-eight degrees, ninety-eight percent humidity. When Fiona opened the door to pick up the milk bottles, it was as if she stepped into a blast furnace.

During breakfast, Jack told Fiona, "I'll grocery shop and pick up some baby things, powder, lotion, and safety pins." He stopped and put his hand on her arm. "I'll make a list, and you can check it."

"And I'll call the diaper service and set up a pickup and delivery schedule. The house needs to be tidied, and a shirt ironed for Finn for the funeral." Fiona realized they were moving automatically through their tasks and until it was necessary, they wouldn't stand still. They clothed themselves in habit, and habit kept them going.

###

In the car Fiona put her hand on Jack's leg and said, "I'm so happy that Susan married Peter, maybe she can soften him." She hesitated. "Not all husbands would be able take on another child with no notice; I don't think I can ever love you enough— thank you." Jack took his right hand from the steering wheel and placed it on top of hers; she could still feel, because of Jack.

34

They signed paper after paper before Liza was handed over to them. Fiona stood next to Jack but didn't hear a word that was said. She was overcome with the strong scent of the lilies at the nurses' station, mixed with newly applied paint on the walls. Her hand in Jack's, she willed herself not to faint. When the baby was finally in her arms, Fiona held the bundle to her chest. This was a gift from her sister. Above all, she would love, guide, and protect this baby as she did for her own children.

The nurses on duty came to wish them well and say goodbye to their little patient. Fiona studied the baby's face. "Liza must have her father's features," she said to Jack. "I don't see Sally Anne at all."

"In time she might look more like her mother—think how much Kate has changed since her birth."

In the car, Jack started humming Brahms *Lullaby*. When they were approaching their street, Fiona asked him to pull over. "I don't want Kate and Finn to see what a mess I am." For herself, Fiona prayed for a quiet bravery—for Liza she prayed for her not to be a target for fate's slings and arrows.

Sitting on the front steps with Peter's wife Susan, Kate and Finn jumped up when they saw their father's 1949 sage green, woody station wagon round the corner at the end of the street.

When Jack opened her door, Finn tried to climb in to get a good look at the baby. "She small!" exclaimed Finn. "You're right Finn," his mother said. "So we have to take good care of her and help her grow big and strong like you." That being said, Finn pulled hard on Liza's toe, which caused her to cry.

"Finn, that wasn't nice. Why would you do that? Please don't do that again."

He turned back towards Kate and whispered, "She small."

Fiona thought it best to handle this incident later. *Surely he won't hurt Liza*, he's just upset that he's not the baby anymore.

"May I hold the baby, Mommy?" asked Kate.

"Of course, but first let's get her settled, and we'll go from there."

Susan, who had held back, came behind Kate and offered to take the baby so Fiona could get out of the car; Fiona tendered herself to Susan's grace.

Grief walked around Fiona's heart that night. Sleep, a small taste of death, opened its arms to her.

A SONG TO CUSHION GRIEF

Getting dressed for the funeral, Fiona tried on three outfits: first, a black sleeveless sheath, followed by a severe, black, tailored cut suit, and then another dress with a white skirt and black bodice. Checking her image in the mirror, she thought none seemed right. Finally, in her slip, she sat helplessly on the French provincial bed with her stockings in hand. Grief, now in permanent residence throughout her, had stolen her tongue, and she couldn't even ask for help. Her jewelry lay on the bureau, and the photo of Kate and Finn was slightly crooked on the wall across from her. *Maybe this room needs to be repainted from the lime green, which now seems dated, to a pale avocado.* She hung her head. Her mind flitted about; afraid if it stilled it would land in a hole of grief so deep there would be no climbing out of it.

When Jack entered the room, he took the stockings from her and began rolling one at a time up her legs and hooking them to her garter belt. Like a rag doll she leaned to one side. After the stockings, he found the black suit that Fiona had tried on and put back in the closet. He laid it on the bed next to her; he pulled her gently to her feet and began helping her into her skirt. When he finished buttoning her jacket, he took her hand and led her to the baby's room.

Fiona had dressed Liza earlier in a tiny pink cotton dress with white lace accents from Kate's babyhood. She had put on white baby booties, thought better of it and taken them off to replace with the yellow booties Liam had found in Sally Anne's bureau.

Before picking up the little bundle, Jack turned off the music box, which was playing *Eine Kleine Nachtmusik.* Together the three went downstairs.

At the bottom of the stairs, Finn was fussing with Kate, saying, "I don't have to tuck my shirt in, and that baby cries too much."

Standing outside the funeral home, Fiona whispered to Jack, "If I don't go in, it won't have happened." Taking her hand, Jack gently urged her forward.

Fiona sat through the service with Liza bundled in her lap. She could hear voices, but she didn't understand the words. *Where are you, Sally Anne?* Her eyes were fixed on the baby. At first she was hypnotized by the sound of Liza's breathing, but the odor of candle wax mixed with the scent of flowers began to overwhelm her; she tried to breathe rather than vomit. When everyone rose, she knew it was over. Walking out of the service, Fiona told Jack, "I wish I had asked you to sing for Sally Anne." To her his voice was silky and strong; it always seemed to cover her in a protective way.

In the semi-shaded garden outside the funeral home, the relentless heat bore down on Clare and Fiona. "I would like to be a part of Liza's life if you'll let me," said Clare.

38

Fiona tried to smile, but even her lips ached. "Of course, Clare, that would be wonderful." She stammered and continued. "Do you think there's a chance that maybe you could also try and find out who Liza's father is? I know he has to be a good man. Liza deserves to know who her father is." *I'll have doubts, Clare, till I get to the truth.*

Liam and Peter came behind Fiona, and Liam asked, "Clare, is there anything you can think of to help us find Liza's father?"

Clare, holding onto a dogwood branch with the last vestiges of flower bracts, knew that an iron curtain of lies was being built around herself, but said, "I'll try my best." Her face was flushed, and she repeated, "I…I'll try my best." The owl was swooping through the woods again.

Grateful that Liam and Linda had luncheon food ready for those who had attended the service, Fiona thanked them with hugs. She heard Liam say to Peter's wife, "It's been a seismic jolt." Other than that, she had no idea what was being said. Everyone was picking at the food but helping himself to the wine. Thinking it was time to celebrate Sally Anne, but not ready, Fiona sat quietly. No one uttered the repugnant remark, "She's in a better place"— for that she was grateful.

Jack spoke to everyone present. *Such a good man I married.* Fiona heard him say to Liam, "We appreciate you and Linda pulling this luncheon together." As Finn raced around the room, Jack grabbed his son's arm. When

39

he was eye level with him, he asked, "Please, Finn, not now, settle down."
Finn stuck out his tongue and crawled under the table.

Rather than forcing a scene, Jack faced the assembled, tapped with a spoon on a crystal wine glass, and waited till he caught everyone's eye. He nodded at Fiona and started singing, "O God Our Help in Ages Past..." One by one the bereaved started singing along. By the time they sang, "A thousand ages in Thy sight are like an evening gone..." many were sobbing. Fiona, overcome by Jack's thoughtfulness, let the song cushion her grief.

THE MAUSOLEUM CLOSET

After the service, the funeral director handed Fiona Sally Anne's pale blue ceramic urn. When Fiona asked Jack where she might keep the urn, he answered, "Up to you."

Fiona thought, *My walk-in-closet in our bedroom would work.* Clothes hung to the left and right of the aisle, with five shelves at the back. Emptying the top shelf, she placed the urn dead center. There was a low stool in the bottom of the linen closet, and she put it under the bottom shelf in her closet. She pulled it out, sat, and talked to Sally Anne.

Going back into the light of the bedroom, lying on the bed, she felt Jack take off her suit and leave her in her slip. Taking the afghan from the chaise, he covered her. Slowly, she slid into sleep.

Hours went by as Fiona pored over Sally Anne's yearbook. Luckily, at the end of the book each girl's name, class, and home address appeared. She looked at Sally Anne's graduation photo—how sweet and peaceful. Was the photo taken before or after her sister had found out she was pregnant? Each girl had a quotation under her name. Sally Anne's quote was from Pascale. "The heart has reasons, reason does not understand."

Fiona started with the A's in Sally Anne's Class. No luck there. They had either moved out of their family's home and married or remained single living at home. The parents were kind enough to share phone numbers of girls who had moved away from home. When questioned, some remembered seeing Sally Anne with a guy but couldn't remember anything about him. Others didn't remember seeing anyone.

Fiona was so discouraged by the time she got through the K's that she almost didn't finish. It took two months in all to catch up with the women in Sally Anne's class. One said, I think the guy's name was Ricky, but I can't remember a last name. Believing Clare, didn't seem plausible as her intuition nagged at her, yet she couldn't accuse Clare of lying— what if it were the truth? *No, Clare knows the truth. She is lying, and Liza is missing her father.* Has she put a plague on both our houses?

1958

LEAVE IT ALONE

In 1958, six years after Sally Anne's death, Clare married her college sweetheart, Sam Trini, in a small ceremony with only family present.

A year later, Clare had her first child, a baby girl they named Diane. Sam asked her, "Can you ever imagine having this baby without me? I want to be the best dad ever."

Touched by Sam's remarks, later that evening, Clare went to the study alone to call Fiona and confess. She noticed the book *East of Eden* that Sally Anne had given her as a birthday present years before, sitting askew in the bookcase. Picking up the book, she smiled to herself as she turned to the last page and the last word of the book, *timshel— thou mayest.* She knew the word gives mankind choice over actions. *Redemption is always a possibility. Maybe it's a sign.* Clare held the black princess phone, fiddled with the phone cord for a few minutes to straighten it, and finally picked up the receiver to dial. Hearing the first ring, she placed the receiver back on the cradle. *Leave it alone,* she thought, *just leave it alone. Do you really want to break your promise?*

POOL OF FRUSTRATION

At school Finn was doing well with other children. Once, however, he brought home a report card stating that he was a delight to have in class. Jack rubbed Finn's head and said, "Finn, this is great. We are so proud of you." Jack then found a pin and attached the card to the bulletin board in the kitchen.

Finn took it down immediately, and said, "It's mine." He stomped out of the kitchen. He was not a delight at home. He hit his sisters if he didn't get his way, and he took their things and hid them. Was a little ice cube of blood making its way to Finn's heart? When asking herself this, Fiona would immediately crush that idea and replace it with, *No, that's not happening; our love will keep his heart warm.*

One afternoon Finn had cut the hair from Liza's Barbie doll. "What were you thinking?" Fiona had asked him. "That doll wasn't yours, and you've hurt your sister." She took a deep breath and said, "Finn, I'm taking your toys away for a few days, until you can promise me that you'll never touch someone else's property without permission."

Finn stood still and didn't change his facial expression. "Can I go?"

What could Fiona do to make a dent in his belligerent attitude?

###

Jack asked Fiona, "Do you think a dog might help Finn to become more responsible and kind?"

Fiona answered, "We can hope!" So, for his tenth birthday, Finn was allowed to choose a dog; he picked an Irish Setter because he had recently seen the movie *Big Red*.

On the appointed day, the family drove to *Toora Loora* Farm in Central Pennsylvania to pick out the setter. As if a storm were brewing inside Finn, he jumped up and down, played with the leash for his puppy, and tried to put it on Kate's arm. Jack stopped the car, got out, opened Finn's door, and said, "Finn, please sit still, leave Kate alone or we're turning around, and we'll wait until you learn to behave to come back again." Leaning back in his seat, Finn settled down.

In the rearview mirror, Fiona saw her son look out the window and make faces at the passing cars.

A widower, Tom O'Reilly, bred the dogs, and greeted them at the front steps. "Come in the house, have a look at the dogs." Of course the puppy yips could be heard outside before he opened the door.

Fiona noticed that the house needed paint and the front steps were a bit tricky navigating due to rotting wood.

The room where the puppies were kept contained all sorts of memorabilia pertaining to Irish setters: there were framed photos, plates, miniature porcelain setters, ribbons won at shows, a rack with setter spoons, and even a shot glass with a setter painted on it. Shelves and shelves of these keepsakes covered the walls. Fiona saw one photo of a woman about Mr.

O'Reilly's age with a votive candle on one shelf; it was off to the side, while the dog memorabilia was front and center.

A pen was set up on a linoleum floor. A bitch named Rosey had whelped eleven puppies. As soon as Finn climbed into the pen, a soft, brown puppy climbed into his lap and licked his nose.

"Hey, I thought Irish Setters were red," said Finn.

Mr. O'Reilly stepped forward. "She'll turn red before the year's up."

Without much fuss, Finn handed the puppy to Jack and said, "I want this one."

Kate couldn't stand aside any longer —she climbed into the pen and cuddled a puppy. Fiona and Liza followed Kate's lead while Jack and Mr. O'Reilly settled the finances.

With check in hand, Mr. O'Reilly then walked over to Finn and said, "Son, take care of this dog, and she'll take care of you."

Maybe the dog should be called Hope, thought Fiona.

Sitting on their kitchen floor, Fiona reminded Finn that he had responsibilities concerning the dog: feeding, making sure she had water, cleaning up her mess in the yard, and keeping her fur brushed so it wouldn't tangle. "I know, I know," he said. *"She's mine!"*

Fiona wondered, *Will this dog stop the kernel of discontent growing in Finn?*

Fiona did notice that her son spoke to the dog through tender gestures, petting and whispering into her ear. Yes, a dog for Finn was a good thing.

"Rouge would be a good name for the puppy," said Kate. "In French, it means *red*." Everyone else picked up on it and so *Rouge* it was.

Finn said, "I don't care."

Fiona thought, *What does he care about?*

###

Making cookies in the kitchen with Fiona, Liza stirred the ingredients. The sun was going down, and a blue twilight crept into the room. Fiona flipped on the light switch. Standing side by side, with Rouge sitting patiently by her leg, Fiona said, "Rouge is hoping cookie dough will somehow make it to her mouth."

Liza faced her mom. "Why are Grandmother and Grandfather mean to me? They talk to Finn and Kate but ignore me—have I done something wrong?" She licked the spoon. "When they were here for Finn's birthday I asked Grandfather if he wanted to play checkers with me. He stood up and walked to the other side of the room. Grandmother turned away. I tried not to cry, I didn't want them to think I was a baby."

Taking the spoon from Liza, Fiona looked into her eyes. "You're not a baby. Have you ever noticed that they don't like me much either? They aren't happy people. I wish I could tell you why they act the way they do. I'm sure it has nothing to do with you. They are complicated people." *They weren't fit as parents.* Fiona took Liza's hands into her own. "I wish I knew how to answer that question. As a child, I was never allowed to explain why I had done something they disapproved of, even when they didn't have all the information." She squeezed Liza's hand. "I think you'll better understand a few years from now. Just know this, your dad and I love you. You can't worry about them. You can do nothing to change them, and they seem powerless to change themselves." Fiona was so angry she had trouble keeping her voice steady. Her wrath had never reached this fevered pitch before.

Liza didn't say anything else. They put the cookies into the oven, and while they waited, Liza sat on the floor with Rouge, who nestled her head in Liza's lap.

In the closet that night, Fiona took out the stool and sat. Rouge followed her in and sat beside her. Speaking to her sister, Fiona said, "They're hurting our Liza. I want so much to call them and tell them to stay away, if they can't treat Liza as they do Finn or Kate. They're so bitter." Rouge put her head on Fiona's lap. "I know what you used to say about forgiving, but I wonder now if you'd be so generous with them hurting your daughter. I miss you so much." For a few more minutes petting Rouge, she wondered how to handle her parents—this much she knew: she couldn't hang up her gloves until her parents accepted Liza. At last she stood, touched the urn, turned, and left the closet.

As Fiona shut the closet door, she could hear Jack snoring. He had been working long hours of late, and Fiona was careful not to wake him as she slipped under the covers.

Rouge started out each night in Finn's room but always ended up in Jack's and Fiona's. The dog came into the room, circled three times and settled herself on the floor next to Fiona's side of the bed. Lying on her back, Fiona dangled her hand to pet Rouge, still thinking what she should do about her parents. She could hear the wind rattle the windows on the third floor. The moon's light glistened on Rouge's fur. Fiona pulled the bed covers up wondering if it were possible to throw off the cover of her parents' religious intensity.

###

On a Saturday morning, a thunderstorm rumbled like drum rolls at a football game. Liza jumped into bed with Kate and whispered, "Wake up, Mrs. Burgee."

"It's okay, Mrs. Boobytrap, we're safe inside. It'll be over soon. Let's sing a song." So they sang their favorite song, *Apple Peaches Pumpkin Pie*, and when they had done that three times the storm abated.

Liza jumped up and stacked several favorites on their forty-five record player. When *My Boy Lollipop* came on, she grabbed two pencils from the desk and handed one to Kate. They sang loudly into their wooden microphones and danced round the room. Kate, looking out the window, shouted, "Liza, look, a rainbow." They hurried to the window and stood side by side while *It's Over* played behind them.

With a bright sun kissing their faces, Liza asked Kate, "When did we give each other pet names?"

"I think it was when you had the measles, and I was trying to cheer you up. I christened you *Mrs. Boobytrap*, and we laughed so much we had to stop, as you said that you were getting a tummy ache. So we stopped, but then you called me *Mrs. Burgee* and we howled all over again." She put her hand tenderly on Liza's back.

"Mom said that we have to clean this room this morning, let's do it before breakfast," said Kate.

Liza said, "Okay, but let's do it with this song playing,"— laughing, she put on *Kind of a Drag*. They sang while they straightened up.

Lying in bed, hearing the music from the girls' room Fiona smiled but concentrated on her son. The girls told their mom, "He laughs a lot at school." Yet Fiona knew he was quick-tempered at home, and he rarely included his sisters in his outdoor play. Fiona watched Finn scowl at his sisters if they came within twenty feet of him. Pranks sometimes consisted of taking their dolls and dunking their heads in Fiona's talcum powder. When she heard him tell Kate, "Your haircut looks like something a blind barber did," she called him to task. Fiona was proud of Kate, as she had not been drawn into his misguided musings.

Liza told Fiona that Finn called her a carpenter's dream, her body being a flat board. "He hurts me, Mommy." Fiona didn't like to think that her son seemed to have the instincts of a snake knowing when to strike. Liza, defenseless against his verbal attacks, stood cowed, her bottom lip quivering when Finn went after her with a tongue like an ice pick.

Finn told his parents that he had lost his report card. Fiona found it stuffed under his mattress, because of a small corner sticking out. When she asked him why he hurt people, lied, and generally made the girls' lives miserable, Finn replied, "I can't live up to them; they're perfect. I can't get the grades they get either, I'm just not like them, and Rouge likes you more than me." A dusky blue glow was coming in, and Fiona switched on a light. It was the first time she saw torment in Finn's features.

"Finn, they're not perfect. No one is. If you're getting the best grades you can, then that's all we ask. Only you know if you're working hard enough. As for Rouge—it's only natural that she favors me, as I'm the one who's with her all day. I've seen the way you play with Rouge, and I think she likes you better than the girls."

Finn shrugged and went to his room.

That night, Fiona swam in a pool of frustration trying her best to spiral into sleep.

She asked herself if Shakespeare held the answer. "Deal mildly with his youth:/for young hot colts, being rag'd, do rage the more.

1965

BIRTHDAY SURPRISE

In June of 1965, the day before Liza's thirteenth birthday, the entire Walsh clan was in the kitchen getting ready for dinner. Liza looked up from the counter, where she was working on a puzzle. This was her favorite part of the day; night trading places with day. Would she feel differently becoming a teenager?

Setting the table, Kate danced as she went around placing the forks; she stopped every so often to practice the mashed potato, a song and dance by Dee Dee Sharp. Kate loved all the different dances of the sixties: the locomotion, the shimmy, the swim, and the twist.

Finn was feeding Rouge and talking to her in a low sweet voice, almost as if the dog were a person who would answer back.

Her dad was opening a bottle of Chianti and talking about the escalating war in Viet Nam. "I'm worried that our boys might be dragged into this mess in Southeast Asia. No good can come from this war."

When her dad finished talking, her mom, stirring spaghetti, softly hummed the Temptations tune, *My Girl*.

Holding his lacrosse stick, Finn stood, turned to his dad and said, "I still don't see why I can't go to Stone Harbor with the team. I'm the one that scored the winning goal."

"Yes, you did, and a great goal it was but as I've already told you, you're too young to be in Stone Harbor un-chaperoned with boys as old as eighteen. Let's have no more of this."

There was a flash of lightning, and the lights flickered but came back on. Liza hoped the rain would stop tonight and not ruin her swim party tomorrow afternoon.

Scowling, Finn started playing with his lacrosse stick, pretending to shoot on goal; he changed direction and shot a ball into the trashcan across the room.

He's asking for it, thought Liza.

"Keep that up," their father said, "and your stick will be confiscated."

Finn glared at his father. Liza went over and touched Finn's arm, but he pulled away from her. *Why doesn't he like me?*

Her mother looked at Finn, worry creasing her face. In an obvious attempt to change the subject, she asked Liza, "What do you want for your birthday dinner? Pizza? Steak, perhaps?"

"Hmm, let me think." She kept a wary eye on Finn.

Finn smirked. "I've got a surprise for you, Liza."

"Really?" she said, amazed and pleased. Finn had never given her anything.

Finn smirked, "I've got a surprise for you, Liza."

"Really?" she said, amazed and pleased. Finn had never given her anything before except heartache. She felt like hugging him but didn't dare. "Should I try and guess?"

"You'd never guess in a million years."

"Did you pick it out yourself?"

"I didn't need to pick it out. It's not that kind of surprise."

55

Looking around the room, she saw her parents' and Kate's eyes riveted on Finn.

"I'm stumped, how about a hint?" she said.

"Nope, no hints!" He spun around, with his stick in hand as if ready to shoot for the trashcan again, but stopped mid swing and said, "Isn't it about time we told Liza she's adopted?"

Liza stepped back. "What?"

"You're adopted, and your father is unknown—you're illegitimate!" shouted Finn.

Kate's hand flew to her mouth. Even Rouge stopped eating and cocked her head at Finn.

Turning to her mother first and then her father, Liza read the truth in their pained expressions.

Her mother came behind Liza and held her. "Finn, what have you done?" She said it in a voice she'd never used before. It scared Liza, but if it scared Finn, he didn't show it.

Their father grabbed Finn's shoulder and in a tight voice said, "Go to your room, Son."

Finn glared triumphantly at Liza as he left the kitchen— she averted her eyes.

There'd always been a crack between them; now it felt more like a chasm.

Jack motioned for Kate to follow Finn; she obeyed. Then Liza and her parents made their way into the living room. Fiona eased Liza onto the davenport. Determined not to cry, Liza rubbed her eyes and offered a weak smile, as a sea of scrambled words sloshed around her head.

"Where to begin," her mother sighed. "Liza, it is true that I didn't give birth to you, but for all the world I am your mother. You've heard us talk about my sister, Sally Anne? She died giving birth to you. From the moment I first held you, I knew you were a gift that Sally Anne had given us." Her mother put her hand on Liza's knee. Liza looked down at that hand that was no longer her mother's. "Your dad and I decided we would tell you when you turned sixteen. We never told Kate or Finn, so how Finn found out is a mystery that we will be solving in a few minutes. He's angry with us about not going to Stone Harbor. He wasn't thinking about you—I'm so sorry."

Playing with the sofa cushion, and feeling waves rise and fall in her stomach, Liza was quiet for a minute. She felt as though Finn had somehow transmitted a disease no medicine could cure. "You're not my real parents— what about my father?" Where is he, and who is he? Why is he unknown? Am I really illegitimate?" Liza eyed her dad—now uncle. There was another flash of lightning, but she didn't turn away.

"Darling," he said, "We don't know who he was, and Aunt Clare didn't know either and when your mother died, Clare was with her. You are a legal and cherished member of this family. We don't know if your mother was married—we just don't know."

"Why didn't you tell me sooner?" She clutched the pillow to herself. The waves in her stomach were swelling to sickening proportions, and she closed her eyes hoping it would quell the queasiness.

"Sixteen seemed a good age to share everything with you. Perhaps we were wrong, but we did what we thought best. Ask anything, and we'll do our best to explain," said Fiona.

Liza had too many questions to know where to begin. Her mom took a deep breath and broke the silence. "Liza, I'm your mother, and I've never thought otherwise. Your dad and I love you as much as Kate and Finn. Clare is coming to your party tomorrow. You should have a chat with her about your mom."

"Am I like my mom—do I act like her?"

Her mom said, "You're very much like Sally Anne. You are sweet and kind like her— sometimes when you turn a certain way or laugh, I see your mom in you."

"Where is she buried?"

Her dad rubbed his forehead and said, "Maybe we should talk more tomorrow, so you've had time to digest all this."

"I won't sleep if I don't know where she's buried."

Her parents exchanged a look. "Very well," Fiona said. "Come with me."

"This wasn't how things were supposed to happen," Jack said.

Liza stood and from the kitchen caught a whiff of the tomato sauce that she might not ever enjoy again.

Her mom turned off the burner, which held the pot of spaghetti sauce. Following her mom upstairs, she passed a long window on the second landing. The storm had passed, and moonlight fell upon broken branches from the young maple in their side yard. Her mother led the way into her bedroom and then opened her closet door.

Was her mom going to give her an early birthday present? Liza stood at the door as her mom walked to the back of her closet, and from the top shelf she lifted a ceramic box and handed it to Liza. "These are your mother's ashes; they belong to you now."

Liza read the inscription on the box Sally Anne Crosby, May 16, 1932 – June 2, 1952. "Why ashes? Why wasn't she buried?"

"Your mother was cremated because your grandparents didn't think it right to bury your mother in the family plot since she wasn't married. Also, the Catholic Church wouldn't allow the burial in sacred ground of a woman who had a child out of wedlock.

"Maybe she married my father before she died."

"Maybe. We just don't know for sure."

"Is this why Grandmother and Grandfather hate me?"

"They were angry with your mother for having a baby with no apparent husband."

It was all beginning to make sense to Liza now, all those times that she heard her mom murmuring inside the closet. "You talk to my mother in your closet, don't you?"

Yes, I tell your mother everything about you and our family."

Her lurching stomach quieted as Liza spoke up. "I need time to think."

Liza held the box next to her throbbing heart and hoped her mother felt her hands wrapped tightly around her. *Is this why Finn hates me, too?*

Kate jumped up the minute Liza entered their bedroom. A lava lamp kept the room in a soft haze.

"Liza, do you want me to leave?"

"No, I want you to stay—are we still sisters? I'm confused."

"Of course we're sisters. It doesn't matter that we have different mothers and fathers—you've lived here since you were born," Her voice cracked a little bit. "That's what makes sisters. I remember the day you came home from the hospital. I have no doubt that you're my sister, and I hope you'll feel the same way about me, when you've had time to think."

Liza glanced down at the urn and then at Kate, "These are my mother's ashes and I have to decide where to put her urn."

They lay down on their beds opposite each other.

"Liza, give me your hand."

Liza took Kate's hand. With her free hand, she clutched her mother's urn.

They ended the day as usual. "Good night, Mrs. Boobytrap," Kate said.

Liza, exhausted, mumbled, "Good night, Mrs. Burgee." The last thing she remembered was the moon sliding slowly across the dresser mirror, lulling her into a deep sleep.

Touching his back, Fiona stood behind Jack as he knocked on Finn's bedroom door and asked, "Finn, may we come in?"

Fiona, knowing Finn's reply might not be forthcoming, urged Jack to open the door slowly.

Under his breath Finn replied, "You're going to anyway."

Fiona noticed he hadn't turned on a light in his bedroom, but the hall sconces dimly lit his face. Lying on his bed, on his side, with his arm bent and his hand holding up his chin, Finn said something else under his breath, but Fiona couldn't distinguish the words. His lacrosse stick lay in front of him on the bed.

Jack flipped on the light and said, "Sit up, please."

Finn took his time but sat up not looking at his parents but at his shoes.

With a shaky voice, Fiona asked, "Why, Finn?"

At first he was non-responsive, then he said, "I don't know," still glancing at his shoes. Finally, he admitted, "Searching for a stamp, I found Liza's adoption papers in Dad's desk drawer."

"My desk is locked on purpose so why didn't you ask your mom for a stamp? How did you find my key? You had to have been snooping."

Finn swallowed whatever he might have said and shrugged still not raising his eyes from his shoes.

"Are you sorry that you hurt Liza?" Jack asked.

Finn blew air from his mouth so that it ruffled his hair. He shrugged again.

Jack explained, "Finn, a family is a unit that needs to help and protect each other." It was a speech often repeated, and Fiona prayed that at some point in Finn's life, these words would come to mean something.

"You're grounded for two weeks," said Jack. "And you should think carefully about what you want to say to Liza."

Finn's room smelled like a locker room and looked like a garage sale, Fiona thought, *This is a pluperfect disaster* — she wanted to add— *and clean up this mess!* She thought better of it, as this wasn't the mess that needed cleaning up.

MOM, MOTHER, DAD, FATHER

Liza placed her mother's urn next to her cereal bowl and didn't look at Finn, but felt him staring at the urn. Even though the sun coming in strong through an east-facing window warmed her back, Liza shivered. She poured some Cheerios into her bowl. The milk was on the table beside Finn, but Liza walked around the table and got it herself. Sitting back down, she directed her conversation to her mom, who was buttering toast at the counter. "I've decided two things: I'll call you Mom and my biological mother, Mother. I'll call Dad, Dad, and my biological father, Father. That way no one will be confused. May Mother go back to your closet, since she's been there for thirteen years?"

"Of course, Liza, and you may visit and talk with her as I do."

"Thanks, Mom."

As Finn got up from the table, Liza thought he was about to say something, but didn't. To Liza his mouth always seemed like an oyster shell that needed to be pried open. He shook his head instead and left the house through the kitchen door, not quite slamming it.

Liza made her first visit to the closet that day. Tiptoeing in, she felt this to be a sacred place. Standing on the stool, she carefully placed her Mother back on the top shelf. *Better my mother is in here than under a mound*

63

of dirt. But where is my father? I'm going to find him—I have to. She wanted to be tough but felt her self-confidence was eroding slowly. Offering a silent prayer, she blessed herself, then stood on the stool again and kissed her mother's urn, waited a few seconds, climbed down and backed out into the light of her parents' bedroom.

In the kitchen a white wall phone hung beside the bulletin board. Holding the phone to her ear and petting Rouge, Fiona spoke, "Hi, Clare, it's Fiona. I hope you're still coming for Liza's birthday." Outside, a bluebird perched on a branch of a viburnum, while the shimmering light through the leaves gave the bird the appearance of standing in a strobe light.

"Yes, of course—just about to leave. Why?"

"Well, we've had a slight problem with Finn. He found Liza's adoption papers in Jack's drawer and told Liza that she's adopted so she has plenty to ask you."

"I'm not sure w-w- what to say since you know as much as I do." She quickly added, "Is there anything you n-n-need me to bring?"

"I don't think so, I just wanted to give you a heads up—see you soon." Fiona hung up the phone. *She only stutters when I mention Sally Anne. What would happen if I could peel back the thirteen years of storied layers to get to the truth of that day?*

STUNG BY SHAME AND MALICE

On the drive, Clare chained smoked. Even with her window open, the inside of her car had an off white greyish smoky haze swirling as fresh air tried to change places with it.

Should I break my promise? Sally Anne's baby could have a father— no, a promise is a promise. They had been best friends since grade school. She wouldn't do to Sally Anne what Leslie had done to her. The memory still hurt thirteen years later.

Many nights since high school, Leslie Wooster had loomed large in Clare's dreams. Leslie was the older sister of her first boyfriend, Fred. The queen of intrigue during high school, Leslie had walked in on Clare losing her virginity.

She and Fred had been lying together on the sofa in his den. She thought the room more of a men's club with dark paneled walls and the hunting trophies that lined a long bookcase. Fred had closed the drapes on the two floor-to-ceiling windows. She tried not to look at the mounted lion's head over the fireplace.

"My parents are gone for the day, and Leslie won't be back till after dinner. Haven't we fooled around long enough?" Getting up, he helped her to her feet. He unzipped his dungarees and was out of them and his underpants so fast it startled her for a second. It was the first time she had actually looked at his penis without being in a dark car in different states of undress. She thought, *This is going to hurt.* At the same time, she wanted to laugh at this strange appendage standing at attention before her, along with the argyle socks and tee shirt, which he was still wearing, that had patches of pink from something red that had run in the washing machine. She swallowed her mirth.

"Look how hard I am. This hurts. Help me out here. You know I love you." Pulling a condom from under the sofa, he put it on. "Clare, I've longed for this day—I love you so much." He undid the buttons on her blouse, and she felt shy with only her bra and skirt on. He unhooked her bra and freed her breasts to the cool air. His fingers played with her nipples. "You're so beautiful. Let me see all of you. Take off your skirt." She did as she was bid. He slid her panties down, and she stepped out of them.

As she kissed Fred tenderly, he moved her back onto the sofa, pulled his tee shirt over his head, slung it quickly behind himself, and then straddled her. The first thrust made her gasp. Just as she was beginning to move in sync with Fred, the door opened and there stood Leslie.

Fred hesitated at first he then jumped up. Clare shielded herself with her hands and turned her face away. He yelled, "Get out!" He got up and continued yelling, "What the hell, Leslie?" slamming the door on her. By then Clare was up, too. He went back to her. "It's all right, come on, lie back down with me." He patted the sofa. "Come on, she didn't see anything. God, I was just about to...didn't it feel great?"

By this time, Clare had shoved her bra into her pocket; she was buttoning her blouse with shaky hands. "I can't. I'm sorry." Leaving, she noticed his tee shirt hanging by a hair on the lion's head.

"Clare, come back here. If you leave, that's it! We're over!"

66

She didn't look back. On her way out of the house, Clare saw Leslie reading a magazine in the living room. She was still shaking as she walked into the room. "Please don't tell anyone."

Leslie turned her head and looked Clare up and down. "Don't worry, your secret's safe with me."

A week passed, and true to his word, Fred dropped her. As for Leslie, Clare thought *maybe, just may*—but the following Wednesday, at a crowded lunch table, Leslie said, "You'll never guess—I walked in on Clare in her birthday suit, having sex with my brother on the den sofa."

Clare was sitting at the next table, her back to Leslie. She looked down, not meeting anyone's eyes, stung by shame and malice.

"Poor Clare. She must have been so afraid that she'd lose my brother by not giving in. And I happen to know Fred dropped her because she did." Clare could feel Leslie's eyes burning a hole in her back. "Of course it was for her own good."

What a colossal lie, thought Clare.

Clare had stayed home from school for a week, claiming flu. Two guys from the football team called to ask her out. Sally Anne was the only friend she could talk to, and yes, she would keep her best friend's secret. She owed her that.

###

Pulling up in front of the Walsh house, Clare saw Liza looking out the window. She was in the vestibule as Clare entered the house. The child gave her a quick hug, and as they stepped into the living room, Liza was right on Clare's heels.

Fiona laughed, "Liza, let Aunt Clare at least put down her bags before you begin your interrogation."

Clare tried to deflect what was coming by handing Liza her birthday present, a red leather diary with a little gold key. Clare remembered burning Sally Anne's diary the day after the funeral. She was tempted to read it but decided not to—Sally Anne would never have read hers.

Finn was standing in the doorway between the living room and dining room, watching Clare and Liza—Rouge by his side.

Liza opened the present, exclaimed over it, and expressed her thanks. Then she put the diary on the end table and turned to Clare. "I know now that I'm adopted. You were with my mother when she died. Can you think of any way we could find my father?"

"You must know who her father is!" Finn said.

Clare could feel the blood draining from her face and once again she was conscience stricken. *Sally Anne's dead and Mickey never knew she was pregnant...* I just d-d-don't know." She was knotting her dress. "Your mom was s-s-so excited about having you—bursting at the seams to tell me h-h...how wonderful she felt about you." *No reason to tell Liza of her mother's anxiety and fears.* She cleared her throat and continued, "She would love you with her whole being. She would k-k-keep you safe." Except for hair color,

68

Clare thought Liza resembled her father, but Jack was her father now, and he was a good father.

Liza leaned back into the sofa, sighed, and shut her eyes. Clare put her hand on Liza's arm, "I'm Sorry, Liza."

Clare saw a puzzled Fiona watching her and wanted to crawl under the davenport. Did Fiona remember her stuttering in the hospital when she first started this lie? This lie that was growing and soon wouldn't have boundaries. There would be no containing the mess she had made. A ball and chain around her heart kept her anchored to the lie. The promise—that's what she had to focus on. Avoiding Fiona's eye, she turned to ask Jack how his work was going. Jack responded, and the conversation about Sally Anne was abandoned for another time.

When cake was served, Finn looked across the dining table at Clare and declared, "I just bet you know something you're not telling us."

Jack intervened, "Finn, you could try the patience of a saint. Sorry, Clare, I'm sure you've told us what you know."

As presents were brought to the table, Clare breathed deeper.

Liza made a fuss over each present. When she finished opening the present from Kate, four different colored headbands, Fiona stood, walked to the end of the table where Liza was sitting, and handed her a small box wrapped in a flowered paper with a green bow. Fiona kissed the top of Liza's head and went back to her seat.

Liza shook the box a little and looked back at her mom.

"No guessing, just open it."

Ripping the wrapping paper from the box, Liza took out a black and white photo.

Fiona smiled and said, "That's your mother when she was thirteen."

"Really?" She stared at the photo for a minute. "My mother was so pretty. Thanks, Mom." She started to get up.

"Liza finish looking in the box."

She lifted a silver chain with an oval locket from the box. "But this is your chain, Mom; you always wear it."

"No, it was your mother's. I just wore it until it was time to give it to you, and now it's time."

Clare remembered taking the chain from Sally Anne's still hand and could also call to mind the stricken look on Sally Anne's face. Clare started coughing and couldn't stop.

Pouring water into her glass, Jack said, "Take little sips." She swallowed and smiled.

Seeing that Clare was fine, Liza continued, "Oh, Mom, it's the best present ever, thank you." She rose, went to her mom, hugged, then kissed her and said, "Would it be okay if I cut the photo to put my mother's face in the locket?"

"That's a splendid idea."

Having set the wheels in motion thirteen years ago, Clare knew after this dinner there would be no turning back.

###

Finn never really apologized for his adoption outburst. He mumbled something that Liza didn't understand as he passed her in the hall a few days later. *If he would just repeat what he said, maybe...* but she was afraid she might not want to hear what he was thinking. He pretty much left her alone after that. *I could just go up to him and say, "Finn, please love me."* Of course he would ridicule her. Why did she want so desperately to be loved by her brother, when there seemed to be nothing there to cement the relationship?

The night of her origin eruption, Liza lost something she didn't know she owned, a complete sense of self. Though she loved Fiona and Jack with all her heart, her adoption became an unexplainable stone in her chest that would weigh her down at the oddest moments. *Why didn't my father want me?* That thought left her weary. Each night after her prayers and her goodnight to Kate, Liza would whisper into her pillow, "Father, where are you?"

71

NIBBLING AT THE EDGES

"What should we do about Finn?" Jack asked Fiona. "He seems to have a heart that's setting like concrete, a little more each day. I just keep hoping." Jack was sinking further into the sofa cushions. They could hear Rouge walking around upstairs in Finn's room.

Standing by the mantle, Fiona picked up a photo of Finn. I think we treat him the same as the girls—don't we? He does get into trouble a lot, and the girls rarely do, but that's not their fault. I guess we should keep holding him accountable and telling him that we love him." Tapping her fingers on the mantle, she continued, "Maybe his behavior is normal for a boy stuck between two girls." Her voice trailed off, "I keep wondering if we're not meeting Finn halfway?"

"We can hardly turn our backs on his hurtful actions. Perhaps counseling?" asked Jack.

"Perhaps, let's sleep on it." A stream of barely controlled fear saturated her dreams.

Dr. Sanders was a child psychologist, who had been working with teen boys for eleven years. His office was in a high rise building in center city Philadelphia, with a commanding view of the city's art museum and the Schuylkill River. Rowers could be seen on the water. The room was sleek with modern leather furniture and dark grey walls, and Dr. Sanders's desk was marbled-topped with chrome legs.

When he stood to greet them, he towered over Jack. He had a deep voice and a pleasant face.

Listening carefully to Fiona and Jack's concerns, he thought Finn's problems might be associated with unresolved sibling rivalry. Finn had been the baby and had gotten most of the attention until Liza came along. They hadn't had the nine months to ready him for Liza, so his behavior changed to get the attention he was missing. The doctor would need to meet with Finn, however, to confirm his hypothesis. A meeting was set up for the following Wednesday afternoon.

"You've been nibbling at the edges of this problem for a while," Dr. Sanders said as they were leaving. "Let's see if we can get to the core. I'm looking forward to meeting with Finn."

On the way home Fiona said, "Is our hope an illusion?"

On Tuesday night, Fiona and Jack told Finn they had made an appointment for him to see a psychologist regarding his behavior at home. "There's nothing wrong with me." Finn countered, "You should send Liza and Kate for being so perfect."

"They aren't mean to you, but you are mean to them," said Fiona.

Turning to his bedroom window, Finn said, "You're wasting your money, because I'm not talking." He picked up his lacrosse stick, which lay on the floor and fingered the strings of the pocket.

"If you share your feelings with Dr. Sanders, maybe you'll feel better about your sisters," said Jack.

Finn's defenses were now on high alert.

"Why do you think you're here, Finn?"

Finn shrugged. Determined not to answer any questions, he certainly wasn't coming here every week. *I just want everyone to leave me alone.* Besides, he was missing basketball practice. He felt as though every question posed by Dr. Sanders was a piece of bait that would ensnare him in a trap. *What business does this man have to pry into my inner thoughts?*

The hour passed, and the doctor had not gained his confidence.

When Fiona came to pick him up, the doctor asked Finn to step into the hall.

"Unless Finn talks, I can't help him. Since he has no problems at school, I suggest you make more time for him apart from his sisters," the doctor told Fiona. "Sibling rivalry doesn't always work itself out. Don't be too hard on yourself. It may take time, and it may take until he's an adult. Sometimes it takes an unusual event for a child to turn towards his siblings instead of away from them."

Fiona thanked the doctor. He added one other thing, "You and your husband are always welcome to come in should you feel the need to go over anything."

Fiona thought, *Our son's heart is becoming unsoldered; I don't know how to help him put it back together.*

POWERLESS

In 1965, five days after Kate entered Georgetown, Fiona had her yearly checkup with her OB-GYN. Fiona thought the doctor was taking a long time examining her breasts. Staring at the ceiling, which had a poster of a Monet's Poppy Field, she was amused that every year there was a new poster.

When the doctor stopped and told her she could bring her arm down to her side, he added, "I'm feeling a tiny lump in your right breast, which I don't like. Have you noticed it?"

"To be honest, no. I've been tired lately, but I've also been busy."

"It's small, but we'll need to take some tests to be sure. I'll have my nurse set up an appointment for a mammogram.

The mammogram results showed a growth in her right breast and another in her left breast.

When she returned to the doctor, he told her where to go in the hospital for an incisional biopsy. "This afternoon if possible," he said. "You will be cut in both breasts, and we'll send the tissue to a pathologist. We'll see what comes back and decide from there."

"How long will it take till I know?"

"Four days, but if we're lucky, and the lab isn't backed up, possibly three. There's a good chance that it will be benign."

On the way home, her insides were a maze of anxiety and fear, but her mind told her to hold fast to life.

Three days passed with no word on the biopsy. Fiona prayed for the best but imagined the worst. She thought about not being ready to take her leave just yet. She thought of Dylan Thomas and his invocation, *Do not go gentle*— it became her unspoken rallying cry. Fear circulated with every heartbeat; it made long stops at the brain and then went round again. She was powerless to stop it. Sometimes she stood still and stared until the phone rang, someone knocked at the door, or Rouge barked for various reasons. These sounds would jolt her back to reality.

The call came while Fiona was doing laundry. She had just made piles of each person's clothes. Finn's was always the biggest. The phone sat on a table under the hall window. As Fiona answered the phone, she noticed how bright the sun was. Her expectations were raised. "Hello," she said, her eyes widened and her mouth was suddenly in the shape of an O. Was she supposed to thank the doctor for this feared information? *No, you've made a mistake.* Although the doctor's words were said with a kind voice, the biopsy results were unequivocal: both breasts had cancer. She mumbled something and agreed to meet with him the following day at three o'clock. Her first thought was of her sister. She didn't want to join Sally Anne on the shelf. Two women she knew had died of breast cancer in recent years. She wanted to live for the children and Jack—*Do not go gentle!*

Walking back to the kitchen table where she had placed the piled clothes, she took her arm and in one fell swoop knocked all the clothes on the floor. Her heart was pounding and her mouth was dry. She sat down at the table and put her head down. The quiet in the room allowed her to hear a drip of a faucet on the second floor. Neither Jack nor the plumber ever seemed to fix that drip.

Rouge left her blanket in the corner and sat next to Fiona with her head in her lap. They stayed like that until the clock chimed three.

"Oh Rouge, Liza will be home soon. I'd better clean up this mess, rinse my face, and stay calm till I talk with Jack." With that she walked over to the kitchen sink and washed her face, drying it with a paper towel. Then the clothes went back on the table, and Fiona poured herself a glass of water. The glass slid out of her hand and splintered into a thousand pieces on the tile floor. Her hand had a slight laceration, but the blood was copious.

"Get back on your blanket, Rouge, so I can clean up the mess." The blood had unnerved her. She imagined Sally Anne and all the blood seconds before her death. While stanching the flow, she quivered and found it hard to concentrate. Her body and mind were numb as she swept up the fragments. *The closet*, she thought...

Making her way slowly up the stairs with Rouge in tow, she entered, pulled out the stool and sat quietly. "Sally Anne, help me. How will I ever find the strength to handle this?"

She heard Liza racing up the stairs and calling, "Mom?"

With the weight of her dread held back, she answered, "Yes, darling. I was just checking in with your mother."

"What happened to your hand?"

"I dropped a glass and cut myself cleaning up. I didn't realize how late it was getting. Help me put the laundry away. This day somehow got away from me."

Waiting till after the dishes were done, and Liza and Finn were in their rooms doing homework, Fiona looked at her husband and cried, " I have breast cancer, Jack."

"Oh, my darling," he said as he drew her to him. Then silence overtook them.

Fiona knew that sometimes quiet guards wisdom.

In bed she laid her head on Jack's chest and listened to his beating heart; this was their conversation. The news triggered a tidal wave of passion. She wanted to burrow inside of Jack. He couldn't get close enough to her. And so they made love and slept. She didn't want to untangle herself from Jack's arms as the morning light crept into the room and covered them.

Both brothers took the news badly. Each had the same reaction. "What can I do?" She knew they were thinking, *We can't lose another sister.*

"Please don't call our parents. I'll deal with them."

"I agree," said Liam.

Peter balked, "I believe the commandment, honor thy father and thy mother."

She cringed, knowing he would call their parents and tell them of her illness. She needed calm and not them. *What does my illness have to do with honoring our parents?*

Later, when she asked if he had called them, he said, "Yes, but I told them you weren't up for visitors."

She didn't ask what they thought about her illness; she really didn't want to know because a small part of her heart smoldered when she thought of her parents, and she didn't want it turning into a roaring fire that would destroy her.

Fiona saw her family circle the wagons, determined that this crisis would see a better ending than that of her sister.

In her mind, having a mastectomy, though traumatizing and disfiguring, was better than the alternative. She tried to master her doubts and fears during her stay in the hospital.

The girls had made one hundred origami flowers, with which they decorated the hospital room while Fiona was in surgery. Their aunt Susan helped them.

"Won't Mom be surprised?" asked Liza.

"I hope so!" exclaimed Kate.

Fiona forgot about her pain for a lovely minute before the anesthesia wore off, as she looked around the room. Her first words were, "My girls."

A week later, when her bandages were finally removed, Jack, who had been waiting in the hall, came in with yellow roses and notes from Kate and Liza and Finn. He shut the door.

Fiona read Finn's note. *Get better.*

Jack sat on the edge of the bed, lifted Fiona's hospital gown, and kissed her disfigured breasts.

"Dad's singing, let's go," said Kate, who was home for the weekend from Georgetown. The girls left their bedroom and sat as close to each other as they could on the oriental runner outside their parent's bedroom. Tree branches were casting shadows on the Palladian window at the other end of the hall. Jack's countertenor voice carried into the hall even with the door shut. Liza knew he was singing their mother's favorite hymn, *Be Thou My Vision.* When Liza heard her father sing, *High Kind of Victory, my victory won*, she changed the last part to *Mommy's victory won.* Hope was medicine for the onlookers.

Liza looked at Kate with moist eyes and spoke softly into her sister's ear. "This is my favorite hymn, too."

Kate took Liza's hand. "It's nice to be home for a few days."

They thought the song was over and were starting to get up when the door opened, and their father motioned them to come in.

Fiona extended her arms to her girls. Sitting on the bed, all four of them sang the hymn one more time.

Afterwards, a deep stillness fell upon them. "Let's just stay here," said Liza.

Fiona turned towards the door. *Where's Finn?*

SMALL CLAW

While Fiona was going through chemotherapy, Liza visited the closet daily, praying that her mom would recover. She was shaken to the core facing the possibility that she could lose another mother. Her first words were always, "Mother, look over Mom—let God know we need her." She sat on the stool, holding her mother's ashes as she spoke. Sometimes she said nothing. The closet provided a warm comfort. At times she gathered the hems of her mom's dresses and cloaked herself in them.

On days when Fiona had a little strength, Liza would accompany her to the closet, and Fiona would sit on the stool with Liza on the floor against her knees. Liza thought they were probably thinking the same thing. If Rouge tried to wriggle her way in, too, they would have to leave the door open all the way for air.

One such time, the three of them were sequestered in the closet when Fiona touched Liza's face, "My darling, should anything happen to me, please be good to Finn; I worry about him." It was the only time her mom voiced the possibility of dying—it was as though a small claw reached inside of Liza and pulled out her heart and stomach through her belly button.

Liza trembled at this. Fiona holding her daughter's shoulders quickly said, "It's time to put all negative thoughts behind us. Besides, I want to be around for grandchildren."

Liza responded with a kiss on her mom's hand, while Rouge licked Fiona's face.

Each weekend Kate would take a train from Washington to Philly and then change trains to Bryn Mawr. She would commandeer the kitchen and make casseroles and the like for the week ahead. Every Sunday she went over the prep work with Liza so the house would run as smoothly as possible without their mother's hand to guide things. Kate also became a master at making Baked Alaska, her mom's favorite dessert. The first time her mom was able to eat in the dining room was a joyous occasion. After dinner was finished, Kate entered with the flaming desert. Fiona put her hand to her mouth. "Oh, Kate, how wonderful."

During this period, Liza began writing. She wrote poems and narratives about her family. Fiona treasured them. She told Liza she read them over and over till a new installment came. Dad, Kate, once in a great while Finn, and Rouge sat on the bed with Fiona, and Liza sat in a chair across the room under the bay window. Kate, Finn, and Liza's portraits were now hung around the room. After she wrote each story, Liza read to them. These were uncomplicated, simple family accounts that chronicled their lives, or events that had touched them. These stories or poems reached into the heart of a

83

loving family. They exposed the gentle affection and respect each had for the others—except for Finn.

One Sunday afternoon in her parents' bedroom, Liza read aloud a piece she had written.

Finn walked in the room when Liza was half way through the story. He didn't sit down. He leaned against the doorjamb and left the second it was over.

Finn's Fall

Yesterday, Dad received a phone call that every parent dreads. Finn was suspended from school. Dad was to meet with the Principal, Mr. Myers, and the Athletic Director, Mr. Talley, before picking Finn up. Finn had asked Mr. Myers to call Dad and not Mom, as he didn't want her to feel worse than she already did. According to Finn, seven lacrosse players picked the lock and broke into the gym so they could shoot hoops. As if that wasn't enough, two of them decided that a peek into the Athletic Director's office as well as his filing cabinet would be kind of fun. After all, what could be the harm? Slowly, the two egged others to join them until all were implicated. Finn had agreed to the break-in of the gym, but he was reluctant about the AD's office. He was last man standing but felt the need to remain part of the team. He took the necessary steps to join his fellow reprobates.

Mom was doing well that day, so Dad held a family meeting. A sullen Finn trudged into the kitchen and sat down. He didn't look at any of us. Dad opened with words that really hit the core of each of us. "Finn, you have broken trust with us."

Mom countered with, "Finn, look at me? Why?"

Finn lifted his head, eyed his mother, and said, "Well, everybody else did it."

Mom replied, "We are not everybody else's parents. Do you realize that this could go on your college transcript?"

Dad took Finn's hands in his. "You have emptied your bank account of trust with this family. It will take perseverance and honesty at all costs to fill it up again."

Mom asked Finn how he proposed to deal with what he had done.

After a long pause, Finn thought that apologizing in person to the AD would be the best thing to do.

And so when we make mistakes we move on with our parents' guidance.

The End

When Fiona passed the girls' room later, she asked if she could enter. The girls sat up straight on their beds. Fiona saw admiration in their eyes. *Oh, may I never disappoint them.* Kate asked her how her parents would have handled Finn.

Fiona took her time formulating a reply, "He would be made to feel sinful, and would be punished severely and then he would be taken to confession to make sure he was right in God's eyes. Also, he would be scared of the wrath of my father. Finn would have been treated like a leper until the next sibling fell from grace. Again girls, you must remember that overly strict parents raised my parents."

Fiona touched each girl's cheek. "That's all they knew. They modeled themselves after their own parents." Fiona felt such a strong surge of love for these two girls that she continued, with a catch in her voice, "My father, a metallurgist, had a word for dishonest people. He called them *pinchbecks,* which in metallurgical terms, means two alloys are used to imitate a better metal. An alloy of copper and zinc is used to imitate gold. We knew his meaning as *spurious,* or *false* and that was the last thing that you would want to be called. We would not be granted forgiveness and would just move on with a lot of heavy baggage."

She looked out the window and saw that spring was climbing down from the top of the tulip poplar, "Once, I remember my mother saying, 'Put that in your sack of sins!' I was determined that when I had children, they would know they were loved, no matter the infraction." The three sat quietly for a few minutes. Then Fiona turned to Liza and said, "It was a good story you wrote today, but I think it best not to read stories aloud that you write about Finn. It's like posting a snapshot of him naked on the bulletin board in the kitchen."

The next day Finn sidled up to Liza, pinched her arm forcefully and said, "You just had to write about me and my behavior didn't you—butt out of my life and write about yourself or the saintly Kate."

"Finn, I didn't..." her words drifted into the hallway as Finn turned on his heel and disappeared into his bedroom, slamming the door behind him.

Standing in front of his door with her fist raised, she wanted to knock, but she knew he wouldn't answer, instead she screamed, "Why are you so mean?" Not sure that that had been the right thing to do, she leaned against Finn's door and said, "Sorry, Finn."

"Go away Liza. Leave me alone."

Liza didn't know what to think. It was as if her hands were tied behind her back and her tongue were twisted. She went to the closet and sat quietly for a few minutes and rubbed her arm, which was already showing bruise marks, she let her thoughts wander. Finally, she spoke, "Mother, your mother and father hate me, and so does Finn. ...and where is my father? I don't know what to do. I don't want to tell Mom and Dad about Finn, as they have their hands full with him already." Her head rested between two of Fiona's dresses as she leaned against the wall. The clothes carried the faint scent of *Ambush*, Fiona's favorite perfume now. Liza kept repeating, "Mother, help Finn to like me."

Liza thought about her other mother, certain that she was pleased at her being Fiona's daughter now. At the end of the story she had written about

Finn's fall from grace, she remembered her mom's eyes glistened. Rouge was quick to lick her face, which elicited laughs all around. Liza wondered if her mom cried alone, and if Rouge were in the habit of giving comfort in this way.

Liza fell asleep that night with a plea in her heart: *Make Mom better.*

Chemotherapy continued and the treatment left Fiona feeling nauseated and exhausted.

Sometimes she asked the girls to sit with her. "I'm so tired. That's what this treatment does to me, but I want you girls to know I have faith in this process and that I'll do everything I can to get better." Yet she was thinking, *Faith and doubt seem married at times.*

Kate took her mother's hand and said, "Mommy, we know you will."

"My little women, you and Finn and Daddy are the ones I live for. You are my best medicine."

Knowing her family did everything they could to distract her from discomfort, Fiona felt blessed. She smiled when Jack set up a daybed in the sunroom. Three walls of windows overlooked a brick patio surrounded by dogwoods and azaleas. She loved Jack helping her down in the morning and settling her with Rouge. Fiona would curl up like a cat in the sun. Never leaving her side, Rouge was able to fit her sixty-five pound body on that daybed with Fiona, who said, "I like having Rouge's gentle breathing against my back."

"You two have a language all your own," said Jack.

When the family was scattered throughout the house, and Fiona wasn't capable of summoning one of them, she would ask Rouge to bark—it was her shrill bark that got their immediate attention. No one hesitated. Fiona watched them trip over themselves to get to her. Along with the phone ringing, the background noise of the TV, and voices floating around her, she felt connected to life. "It's my fight, and I'm ready for all it implies." *Do not go gentle...*

Sitting with her mom in the sunroom, Kate asked, "Are you afraid, Mom?" Fiona adjusted her pillow and swallowed. "Yes, Kate, sometimes. But mostly I try to think about the future, seeing the three of you married and my growing old with Dad." She knew she leaned on faith a lot, but wondered was it strong enough to hold her?

###

"Do you think it would hurt Dad if I looked for my biological father?" Liza asked her mom. She loved Jack and considered him her dad, but she yearned to know who her real father was, and if he could love her.

Fiona thought a minute and replied; "I think your dad would do anything to make you happy. He loves you, I don't think it would hurt him."

"It's just that I don't know how to begin." Morning light saturated the sunroom.

"Neither do I, my darling."

"Can I get in bed with you, Mom?"

Fiona lifted the cover with all her strength. "Of course. Rouge, down you go."

Liza was careful climbing in. Fiona kissed the top of her head. *She didn't come through my loins, but this child came through my heart.*

Fiona voiced something to Jack that had been nagging her all these years. They were in bed and had just turned out the light. A full moon was peeking from behind the poplar tree in the yard, casting lacy shadows on the wall. "Clare and Sally Anne were so close. Surely, Clare would have known whom Sally Anne dated." Fiona turned on her side towards Jack, "The only other thing I can think of is that Sally Anne was raped, that would be a reason for her to keep Liza's father's identity to herself. Liza doesn't want to hurt you, but she wants to find her father. Would that bother you, Jack?"

"Of course not. I'll do anything to help her. Even if she finds him, I'll always love her as my daughter. But what if Sally Anne were raped? Would this information help Liza? Would we want our beautiful girl filled with such heinous knowledge?"

"How did I ever deserve you?" asked Fiona.

The idea that Clare almost certainly knew the father was never far from Fiona's mind, yet she didn't feel she could ask Clare about this again. If she found out who the father was this splinter in her heart might dislodge itself.

###

Losing her hair from chemotherapy, Fiona managed to keep her dignity—at least that was what she hoped she was doing. Something in her told her dignity concealed her fright and whenever she gave into it she would have a shaking spell. When she felt irritable, she would try to pray till she felt more at peace with herself. She bought a wig and each morning Liza would say, "Mom, let me fix your hair for you." Fiona would smile at Liza and nod. It was the best she could do. Some days a dark dust settled somewhere within herself which she could never quite find to sweep away.

When the girls heard a retching sound, they ran to their mom, as did Jack. When all was cleaned up, Fiona would ask, "Where's Finn?"

"Finn is hiding in his room with his eyes shut and his hands over his ears and sitting on the edge of his bed, rocking back and forth," said Jack. "I asked him if he were okay. He got up and shut the door. I saw tears on his cheek." Jack caught his breath and said, "I don't think he knows what to do, but I do think he cares what is happening to you."

Fiona with her hands to her heart whispered, "My poor son, if only he would share his thoughts with me, it might lighten the darkness in his heart."

ONE DAY HE'LL SAY YES

When Finn was walking through the sunroom, Fiona said, "Finn, join me, tell me about school."

"It's okay," he said standing by her daybed.

"Have a seat Finn."

"I'm good standing."

"Are you worried about me? Do you have any questions you want to ask me?"

"Gotta go, I forgot I have a science report due, and another chapter to read of *The Great Gatsby*." He flew up the steps before she had a chance to ask him to stay a minute longer. *What to say to open his heart and thaw his frozen emotional self?*

"Do you think we should talk with Dr. Sanders, again?" Fiona had asked Jack more than once. Sitting on the chaise in the bedroom with a glass of water, she asked the question again.

As Jack undressed down to his shorts and tee shirt, he answered, "I'm not sure. I think we know what the problem is. I'll see if he'll do a round of golf with me."

He scratched his head. "Is that okay with you? I hate leaving you when I have a chance to spend the day with you."

"That's fine, Finn needs you as much as I do. Anyway I feel stronger every day." Fiona wondered how long Finn could walk along this precipice and keep his footing. She drew her robe closer around herself. Sing to me, darling.

"Anything in particular?"

"*Earth Angel* would be nice."

Jack smiled, took hold of Fiona's hand and started singing, "Earth angel, will you be mine?" Fiona closed her eyes and let Jack take her out of herself.

On Saturday, when Finn came down to breakfast, Jack asked, "How about a round of golf, Finn? We haven't played together for some time."

Fiona was standing by the stove with her fingers crossed behind her back. *Say Yes, Finn, just say Yes.*

"Can't, already have plans." Grabbing a piece of toast, he sailed out the door.

"You tried, darling; one day he'll say yes.

1968

SURELY WITH TIME

Now living in New York, Clare visited the Walshes less and less. On her last visit, Fiona mentioned Sally Anne. They were sitting in the sunroom with the sun trying to shine through windows that were in desperate need of a cleaning. "Clare, you never mentioned if Sally Anne were upset being pregnant? Surely, she must have been so scared."

Clare wasn't sure which way to answer. She felt it a trap. "I've told you all I know; I...I didn't know she was pregnant for months. Can we l...let this matter drop? It was sad enough to go through it." *If I give her more information she'll know for sure that I know who the father is. Best to stop talking.* Clare finished the tea in her cup.

Graciously, Fiona let the matter drop, poured more tea, and turned the conversation to movies.

On the same day as Fiona's question, Liza took Clare to the closet and wondered aloud, "I want to find my father. I love Dad, but I can't stop thinking that if my father had been with my mother perhaps she wouldn't have died."

Clare wanted to help but by now knew it was too late. Even with the ever-present needle pricking her conscience, she had to tell herself that this was what Sally Anne had wanted and what she herself had promised. Guilt raced around her innards. *Surely with time... Does this closet make sense? Traipsing in and out of this airless space.* Vowing not to return to that closet,

97

she told Liza "If anything, anything at all comes to me to help you find your father, I' I'…I'll do what is needed." Clare never knew how to muffle the sounds of the lies she told once her brain got hold of them.

UNPACKING THE JOY

Liza wanted to attend the Junior Prom with Finn's best friend, Steve. Although Liza was two years younger, she was only a year behind Finn and Steve in school. A few inches taller than Liza, Steve had an athletic build like Finn but unlike Finn his face had a warm, open expression. When Liza was around, Steve always asked her little things that made her feel special: was she playing any sports? How had she enjoyed Sister Mary Martin's English class? Once when she had her hair cut shoulder length, Steve told her he liked it.

Finn and Steve were so different; Liza never understood how they had become friends except for the old adage *opposites attract.*

On a Wednesday afternoon three weeks before the Junior Prom, Steve found Liza in the sunroom reading. The windows were open and the scent of lilacs was in the air. Liza hadn't noticed Steve standing in the doorway. He cleared his throat. She looked up.

"Liza," he hesitated, but then spoke rapidly, "I was wondering if you'd go to the prom with me?"

"Sure." Her heart had never beaten like this.

"Great, I'll fill you in on the details later. Finn and I have to finish some Chemistry problems together. I'm glad no one else has asked you." Smiling, he turned, and took the steps two at a time.

Liza wanted to scream, "I'm going to the prom with Steve." Instead she unpacked the joy in her heart as she danced around the room holding on to a not-so-imaginary partner. She almost knocked over her mother's Ming vase. She caught it in time, kissed it, and returned it to standing position.

Liza called Kate at school and told her about going to the prom with Steve. "I can't believe my luck!"

Kate asked if she could hold on for a second. She was just saying goodbye to her boyfriend, Andrew. Liza could hear a few terms of endearment before Kate picked up the receiver again. "Liza, you just don't get it. You have no idea how lovely you are. You should hear how Andrew's friends have talked about you. I hope when you do realize this it won't change you."

After hanging up with Kate, Liza looked critically in a mirror at herself for long time. Washing her face, combing her thick hair, and brushing her teeth before leaving the house was her normal routine. This wouldn't change. She was more concerned about the prom and Steve. Clasping her hands to her chest, she wondered, "What if Finn tries to stop my going?"

Oh, the preparation! Fiona and Liza made a Saturday trip into Philadelphia by train. Fiona's cancer was in remission at last, and she took great pleasure in this shopping expedition. They walked from 15th Street Station to Market Street. Liza could hardly keep herself walking alongside of her mom. Her feet wanted to skip ahead, and her brain was a tickertape of intoxicating ideas that kept changing every few seconds.

Fiona promised Liza that they would go to Wanamakers to buy her dress. Liza fell in love with a pale pink, sleeveless empire dress, with a lace bodice, a chiffon skirt, a satin sash. When Liza came out of the dressing room, she twirled for her mom and exclaimed, "I love this. Do you think we can afford it?" Her mom stood behind Liza as they both faced the mirror. "Yes, for your first date and first prom, I think we can afford it." Liza hugged her, "Thanks, Mom, I hope the prom will be as much fun as today, and I'm so happy you're strong enough now to be with me." Satin shoes were to be dyed to match.

They had lunch in the Crystal Tea Room on the ninth floor. Liza kept looking at her package with the dress in it that leaned against her knees. In between bites of chicken salad, she smiled. Her mother smiled back, "I remember my first date with your dad. I was excited as you are now." Patting her lips with a napkin, she continued, "we went to the movies—saw *Spellbound,* an Alfred Hitchcock movie." She looked off into the distance and said, "And that's what I was and still am with your dad."

The prom itself was even better than her dreams. Not by design but by a run in Liza's stocking.

Steve in a rented black tux waited in the hall at the bottom of the stairs as she changed her stockings.

"She'll be down in a minute." Fiona said. "She just had to get something," and then added, "You look so handsome, Steve—I'm so used to seeing you in sweats or jeans."

"Thanks, Mrs. Walsh. Has Finn left yet?"

"Yes, he left to get Sophia a little before you came. I was hoping he'd bring her back here so I could get a picture of the four of you."

Straightening his bow tie for the hundredth time, Steve kept his eyes glued to the stairs.

When Liza turned on the landing where they could see each other, Steve grinned and said, "Wow!" She didn't remember the rest of the steps. He took her hand to walk to the car, she couldn't tell whose hand belonged to whom. She was sure that they melted into each other. *This must be love.*

A multipurpose room, which was the gym with a stage about four feet off the floor at the far end, was decorated island style for the dance theme, *Island of Love.* Cardboard palm trees were taped against the walls around the room; a large Tiki bar was placed in the center of the room with soft drinks and snacks. The rumor that rum was being put into cokes for "more island favor" was making its way around the room.

Whoever thought of the many electric fans creating a tropical breeze didn't consider the big teased and sprayed hairdos that a few girls were still wearing. Some of the girls were moving towards the straight hair look fostered by the hippie movement. Many coifs were tangled messes after three passes in front of a fan. Several girls met in the girls' room, trying to recreate the original effect, and decided it was time to take action and they unplugged every fan.

According to Donna Bessinger, the girl who seemed to be present for every crisis, there were seventeen fans in all. Small wonder a circuit breaker didn't cut off.

Someone (Finn Walsh) dimmed the lights, and a chorus of "Groovy" went round the room. The lights weren't faint for long. Sister Anna Marie jumped up on the stage and went behind the curtain, and the lights came up quickly. She made her way to the microphone and told the assembled, "The prom will end if the lights are lowered again."

Steve and Liza danced nearly every dance. His hand on her back when they slow danced felt natural. When they fast danced, Steve smiled at her. Liza was almost too afraid to talk in case the spell would be broken. Unable to keep the grin from her face that night and the following days by just thinking about it, she wanted to keep this memory safely locked in her heart where no one could steal it.

When they arrived at the front door, Steve took her hand and asked, "May I kiss you?"

Blushing, she said, "I was hoping you would." Her first kiss— inhaling his breath and tasting his lips—she had had no idea it could be like this.

How perfect was everything in her world?

###

After breakfast, when Finn went to Sophia's, and her dad went to play golf, her mom asked Liza how the evening went. Liza found her insides stirring again at the thought of Steve.

Fiona continued, "Is there anything you'd like to talk about—anything at all?"

She squirmed in her chair. Her mom's words about the sexual side of things when she got her first period hadn't left her, but her mom had left out the stirring part. The talk hadn't been totally clinical. She could still hear mom talking about her love for Dad and how sex was important in a relationship, but not until she was old enough to handle the emotional part that comes with that commitment. Like most teens before her, Liza believed parents just didn't understand. How could they possibly know about the firecrackers of her soul that ignited every time she thought of Steve?

"Nope, we had a great time, and I think we'll be seeing more of each other."

"I'm sorry your mother couldn't see how beautiful you looked last night."

"You're my mom, and you saw me." She kissed Fiona and sailed out of the room.

Steve was in her heart when she closed her eyes each night and was still there when she opened them each morning. And while her heart was filling, her mind came back to *A Midsummer Night's Dream,* current reading for her English class. "The course of true love never did run smooth." She would sigh when she thought of it and reason that it didn't apply to Steve and her.

UNDER CONTROL

Finn was dating a junior girl, Sophia Reed and in the beginning, Finn, Sophia, Steve, and Liza sometimes double-dated.

Liza liked Sophia but never saw the soft side of Finn with her. When Liza was present, he was matter of fact. Once, she asked Steve his take on Finn. Steve didn't belabor the issue, "Finn and Sophia are made for each other. Also, Finn's different when family is around—when you're not here he has the best sense of humor. Everyone thinks that, and you can count on Finn; he'll be the first to offer help if you're in a pinch."

What was it that made Finn so cantankerous with his family? At school Liza saw him laughing and smiling with his friends. He was a conundrum if anything, and one not to be readily solved. Sitting in the kitchen, she asked him, "Would you be upset if I asked Sophia to go shopping with me?" She was dumbfounded by his reply.

"Keep Sophia out of your personal life. Okay? I don't want you prying into my life with Sophia." With that said, Finn called Rouge who followed him to the basement.

Liza was anxious about Steve, Finn, and Sophia going off to college the year after next and leaving her to fend for herself. It was like always having a mosquito buzzing around her head in the darkness of night. *Why could nothing stay forever?*

106

In the sunroom a few weeks after the prom, Fiona sat with Liza working on a jigsaw puzzle. Liza could smell the gardenia plant in the corner. Rouge in a shaft of sunlight was lying at Fiona's feet.

"Liza, darling, I see how attached you are getting to Steve. He's a pretty nice guy to get attached to, but I worry, however, that he's older, and he'll leave for college and things will change drastically for him."

Rouge started dreaming and whimpering while her tail thumped at a fast rate.

"Chasing squirrels no doubt," said Fiona. "Anyway, Steve will experience things that you can't appreciate till you're away at school. I don't want to see you hurt."

"You don't have to worry, because I have everything under control." The shaft of light started edging snail-like onto the carpet in front of Liza. Questions like this always allowed a small inkling of doubt to take a short romp around her brain before she could catch it and stuff it with all the other things that had no business being there.

In the closet Liza whispered to her mother. "Mother, Mom thinks I'm getting too attached to Steve. She doesn't understand that we love each other— I know we've never used the word *love*, but I can see it in his eyes. I'm sure he loves me." She fingered a long blue silk dress that Fiona wore for special occasions. "I can't imagine a day without him. It was bad enough when Kate went off to Georgetown; with Steve leaving, I don't know how I'll make it through each day." Lingering in the closet, until Rouge barked to let her know that Steve was downstairs, she had to contain herself not to run down the stairs and into his arms.

She knew Steve wanted to attend Brown, and Finn, Princeton. Although that would be an academic stretch for Finn, his athletic prowess was in his favor. Lacrosse coaches from several schools were calling to talk with him, hoping that their calls would make a difference in his choice.

The Viet Nam War and the draft by lottery lurked in Finn's mind. He wondered who knew the truth of what was going on in country? Television showed boys his age whose faces were masks to hide truth. He wondered if what he had read was true, said by Aeschylus a Greek tragedian, "Truth was the first victim of war?"

And his mother kept insisting that Canada was an option.

Finn called Sophia. "My parents are always nagging me about how I should live my life— you're the only one I trust. Maybe I'm adopted too, and that's why I never fit in with my family. They'd be better off if I died. They already have two perfect daughters; they don't need me." He felt his heart cuffed by his emotions.

"Finn, don't ever say that, please. I wouldn't be better off, and I doubt that they would be either.

NO RESOLUTION

The summer of 1968 the Walsh family decided to spend it in Cape May, New Jersey. They did the usual beach things: swam, beach-combed, and sat on the sand reading for hours.

Jack took the train from Philly to the Shore after work on Fridays and returned on Monday morning. Fiona and Rouge would meet him faithfully every Friday evening.

The first night after they settled in, Fiona asked Finn to stay a minute after dinner. They were sitting at the table on the screened porch facing the ocean. "Your dad and I really like Sophia, but we're hoping you're not getting too attached." Watching a ship far out making its way north, she waited for his answer.

Standing up, Finn said, "I'll take care of Sophia, and you take care of Dad."

Standing, also, Fiona touched his arm and said, "I care about you."

"Why are you always touching me?" he snapped. "I don't do drugs, I don't smoke, I don't get bad report cards, I come home on time, what's your gripe with me? Is this family ever going to leave me alone?"

"I love you."

Turning his back on his mother, he headed for the beach.

The sun was setting, and its mirror image bobbled on the water, while the sand looked as though diamonds had been sprinkled about. Fiona's heart bobbled about in her chest. Had Finn slapped her it would have felt the same as the words he had uttered.

###

When Jack arrived, he knew immediately something was wrong and asked, "Fiona, what is it?"

"It's Finn; last night I tried to talk with him about Sophia, to say how much we liked her, but we're hoping that they aren't getting too involved." Plovers skittered at her feet. "He as much told me to mind my own business."

She sat down in the sand and put her arms around her legs. Sitting next to her, Rouge was a sentinel at her side. Fiona glanced up at Jack, "Sometimes, I feel as though Finn's words chip away at the heart of my heart when I start conversations with him; he answers as little as possible. It's as if anything personal he shares could violate his code of behavior."

Jack sat down on the other side of Fiona. "The one thing Finn does is to make sure he attends any family meeting or function that is required of him," Jack said. "He thinks we have nothing to complain about and should leave him alone, but I see darkness in his eyes."

###

A trip to Dr. Sanders's office seemed necessary for Fiona and Jack. After they gave an account of Finn's latest interactions with the family, Dr. Sanders explained that Finn might not really know why he's angry. It might

111

take years before he opens up. "You seem to be doing the right things, you tell him you love him, you ask him to do things with you without his sisters. You are not bad parents. Finn has the war on his mind, a girlfriend, college, and other things you're not privy to." The doctor tapped his fingers on the arm of the chair, "Until he talks to someone, there can be no resolution.

The rented shore house was a rambling, weathered bungalow on the beach with a wrap-around screened porch where most of their living took place. Unless it was raining, they ate, played cards and board games, took naps, and read there. Before each Monopoly game, Finn would pipe up with, "Games are for cheating, life is for real."

Though she didn't like this saying, Fiona felt she had to make a concession for Finn's sake. She believed his game-playing rule fed into his behavior that lacked kindness.

On the south end of the porch was a long picnic table with benches on each side, where as many as fourteen could be squeezed in to share a meal. The opposite end contained six single bed cots. Rouge started out on her own cot but sometime in the middle of the night, she climbed up with Fiona. This cot was smaller than the daybed Fiona had shared with Rouge at home. How Fiona and Rouge slept comfortably on that cot together was a mystery to the rest of the family.

Air conditioning at the shore didn't exist, so the sleeping end of the porch was reserved for hot nights, as there was always a breeze coming off the ocean. They fell asleep to the scent of beach roses and the sound of the surf. After much discussion the family decided that when they slept there they would read a book aloud. After choosing *Don Quixote*, they sat on their cots and took turns reading. Everyone agreed Jack was the best reader.

Getting settled was always a problem because someone would yell, "Wait, I forgot to brush my teeth." Or "Whose turn is it to read?" They remembered the quests and how they were right in the middle of the adventure. "Somewhere in La Mancha..."

Finn was the only one who passed on reading, and he didn't comment or seem to wonder about different aspects of the story. In fact, he was usually asleep before the reading was finished. There were nights when he wanted to scream, "This is so damn boring!" He knew if he did this everyone would stare at him as if he were a leper. *Why do I feel so apart and alone in this family? I wish I knew. Why can't we read, The Last of the Mohicans, not this journey of a middle-aged man on an unlikely quest? Why do they go on about symbols, themes, plot, or motifs? Why can't they just read and keep their thoughts to themselves?* Instead it was easier to think about Princeton and his chance to escape all this family nonsense.

BECOMING

To Liza that summer was magical. Looking from the outside, most people wouldn't notice anything extraordinary. Magic isn't always overwhelming. She thought it could happen within and spread from head to toe silently. Yes, sexual desire was at play here, but it was more than that. They learned from each other, tested ideas, and opened doors to the world around them. Emerging from the childhood cocoon, they hadn't taken wing yet. They could feel themselves *becoming*, and they liked it.

Kate and Andrew preferred being by themselves, but sometimes the six of them talked until first light. Time-honored subjects, as well as new topics came up for discussion.

"Does God exist?" asked Andrew.

"I think He does," said Kate.

No one else chimed in.

Finn said, "Everyone should read Ayn Rand's *Fountainhead*."

"Why?" asked Kate.

"Because the protagonist isn't willing to give up his vision for what architecture should be— he's willing to struggle rather than give in to what most people thought about design."

"I guess that's good as long as it isn't at the expense of others," replied Liza.

Instead of answering, Finn ran his fingers through the sand.

Steve, who loved astronomy, asked, "I wonder if the U.S. is really going to orbit the moon in December."

Liza asked if Ice Station Zebra or 2001: A Space Odyssey was the better movie?

Of course the one topic that garnered the most attention was the bloody, unending war. They still liked building a fire on the beach and toasting marshmallows. During one such evening, Steve asked the group, "Anyone think the war is justified?"

"Not to me it isn't," said Liza. "What's the point? I don't get it."

Steve answered his own question. "My family is against it, and I must admit I'm not sure what I think cause I'm scared I'll get my head blown off. What purpose would that serve?"

Andrew remained quiet.

Sophia turned to Finn, "What do you think?"

The wind had picked up and sparks were flying, so everyone moved back a bit. Quiet reigned for a long minute. "I don't know how I feel about it," answered Finn. "I guess I'll know what I think, when and if the time comes. Who wants to skinny dip?" With that said, Finn jumped up and yanked his clothes off as he ran into the water yelling how great it felt, glad that he didn't give up his personal anguish and tell them that his thoughts belonged to him, so stop prying. In the same moment he wanted to tell them Viet Nam made mash of his insides when he thought about it. Finn found the chilly water a welcome relief from the war talk. The guys followed him.

The moon being so bright caused Liza to yell, "Turn away till we're up to our necks in water."

Liza thought about her brother that night. Nothing was easy for him. *How can I share my thoughts with him?* Scared for him because she had heard fear in his voice for the first time, she pondered whether he opened up to Sophia. Maybe she would talk to Sophia, if the opportunity ever presented itself. Her parents' low voices in the next room caused her to ask Kate, "Are you asleep?"

Sitting up she answered, "No, I've been thinking about Finn."

"Me too."

"He seems so alone and fraught with anxiety over the war. I'm scared for him."

Keeping her back to the wall, Liza asked, "Do you think we should tell Mom and Dad?"

"No, I think they know what he's going through and have tried to talk with him. My guess is they're relying on the power of prayer. I, however, would rather they rely on Finn's common sense to make an appearance."

With a stifled yawn, Liza said, "Goodnight, Mrs. Burgee."

"Goodnight, Mrs. Boobytrap."

RAGING HORMONES

Some nights when the moon surfed the water, and fingerlike breezes moved soundlessly over their exposed arms and legs, their own hands wandered purposefully around their partners' bodies, lifting every nerve ending to the skin's surface.

Sitting on a log at the edge of a dune, Liza took Steve's hand and told him, "I want to be your Dulcinea." For a long moment he looked at her, then he smiled and kissed her.

Liza wanted to make love with Steve, but unless he told her that he loved her, it wasn't going to happen. The entire summer she wrestled with using birth control. "I don't know, Steve, it's a big step." This was one quandary she wasn't sharing with her Mom, who had told her, "I feel you're too young to handle all that having a sexual relationship entails."

Liza wondered how many girls have uttered this phrase: "You know I want to, but I'm afraid of getting pregnant." Steve made it clear that he wouldn't pressure her, but many makeout sessions were a prelude to what they both wanted. The thought that was uppermost in her mind was if she went ahead, she would have a better claim on him when he left for college.

Where was her mother? Why had they left her mother's urn at home? Liza had so much she needed to share with her. She would just have to close her eyes and imagine she was in the closet, spilling her feelings.

Inexperience and raging hormones have always been overpowering ingredients for misfortune. It may have been the sexual revolution, but most of the girls Liza talked with wanted a committed partner.

One afternoon, Liza talked to Sophia on the wrap around porch. They were sitting at the table playing spit, a card game. It was a windy day and they could hear the waves crashing the jetties. "Sophia, I'm thinking about going on the pill, but I guess I'm waiting till Steve tells me he loves me."

Sophia looked at Liza as though she had two heads. "I'm on the pill, but your brother has never said that he loves me. He hasn't made any promises either. But we're tight." She threw her head back to move her lustrous black hair out of her face. The way the light shone on her soft brown eyes, they flashed specks of gold. "In time he'll come around, as he's closer to me than anyone else, that much he did tell me." She shook her head again, "It's just a matter of not pushing him till he realizes that he can't live without me."

Liza knew better than to say anything; she couldn't help but think that Sophia didn't really know Finn at all. She imagined that for Finn sex was sex, nothing more, and nothing less.

###

In the middle of heavy petting one night on the beach, Steve stopped, took hold of Liza's hands and whispered, "If anything happened, I would marry you."

Liza sat up on the blanket, which was hidden in the dunes. "What does that mean? If I don't get pregnant, you won't marry me?"

"Don't be silly. We each need to go to college. I was just trying to comfort you. I want you to realize that I would take care of you sooner if you became pregnant— I do love you." He had said the magic words.

"Oh Steve, I love you, too." Her insides were fizzing like champagne. "Give me a little more time. I need to think about this. Our love for each other changes everything." She really wanted to feel him inside of her now. Maybe she should talk to Kate, or Sophia, or maybe she should get on the pill and not worry.

As he touched her breasts and kissed her neck, Liza murmured, "Do you have any protection?"

Steve reached in his back pocket and pulled out a condom. They were both somewhat shy removing their clothing. Sitting upright, he looked at her. "You are more beautiful than I imagined." Smiling self-consciously, Liza reached out and pulled Steve to her.

At first she worried that she wouldn't know what to do. But when pleasure she didn't know existed overtook her, she stopped worrying and let herself respond naturally. She was sure her skin was porous because Steve was touching her beneath the surface of it. She was surprised when she groaned as his breathing quickened. When they finished, she felt sore between her legs but wanted to experience it all over again.

Why had they waited so long? There was no turning back. They lay on the blanket a while longer, quiet and happy. Steve twirled her hair through his fingers while Liza ran her fingers around his chest.

The blanket—she had better get rid of the blood stained evidence. She turned to Steve and said, "What about the blanket?"

Ever the gentleman, he said, "Don't worry, I'll take care of it."

As they walked towards the cottage, Liza knew she would never forget this night; the smells of salt water, beach roses, grasses, and Steve's sweat, along with the play of the moon on his tanned body were her keepsakes.

When they reached the cottage, Steve said, "I love you," while he tussled her hair. "It was worth the wait."

She wondered if anyone had died from too much pleasure. There was no way for her to reign in her feelings for Steve. Falling asleep, it dawned on her that she was following in her birth mother's footsteps, and her father—*Oh Father, where are you*?

She thought of the blood on the blanket, she thought of her mother's loss of blood, and "Blood alone moves the wheels of history…" a phase used often by her history teacher quoting some leader, now nameless.

In bed that night, Liza's hand reached up to finger her mother's locket. It was gone. She looked around her room and didn't find it. In the morning, she ran to the spot where they had made love looking at the ground the entire way. Plowing her fingers through the sand, she didn't find the locket. *It's been swallowed up by the tiny grains and sent to sea.* Liza sat down. Looking out at the swells coming to shore, she realized she was riding a torrent of loss. Her one tangible connection to her mother was now gone.

Although she didn't believe in superstition, she wondered if the loss of the locket was a sign of bad things to come. As she sat in the baking sun, pondering her misfortune, she caught the scent of the near beach roses, thought of the previous evening, and became dizzy with delight. That sentiment was replaced in time by trying to assuage the tiny trace of guilt she felt for following in her mother's footsteps. Explaining to her absent mother that Steve proclaimed his love for her, she went on to say that they would be extra careful. She understood now that her mother must have loved her father a great deal, even though for some reason he hadn't stayed. *How dare he treat my mother this way? If I ever find him, I have a few things to say.*

Revealing her happiness to Fiona would be great, but she guessed that no one ever shared her first time with her mom.

As for Finn, he didn't understand the constraining need of girls to have commitments. Running on the beach one day, with Rouge, and Steve, Finn told Steve, "If Sophia wants sex she can have it." *But she can't have my heart.* He questioned himself sometimes if he had a heart. *Solitary* was a word he had used to describe himself in a short autobiography he had written for English class.

Steve stopped running, cast a sideways glance at Finn, and said, "That's between you and Sophia."

Rouge took after a wounded sandpiper, which squealed like tires on pavement. She carried the bird in her soft mouth and deposited it in front of Finn. She didn't molest the bird, but the bird wasn't moving. Literally, scared to death.

Shaking his head, Finn decided not to admonish Rouge—although she had never been hunted, her natural instincts had taken over. Steve scooped sand into a pile and Finn laid the bird in the hole and covered it, while Rouge whimpered.

"You never know when your time's up," said Steve.

SHORE JOBS

Steve and Finn had been lucky enough to land jobs together that summer at a juice bar, squeezing oranges from sun-up to sundown. Steve told Finn, "I think we're exempt from scurvy for life." Finn liked working beside Steve. Steve didn't judge him. Or, at least he never made pronouncements about Finn's behavior.

At a small shop on the boardwalk, Kate pulled and aerated candy to become saltwater taffy. The shop had doors that slid back so customers could see the whole process. After pulling, Kate shaped it by hand, rolled it on a wooden table, and then cut it into two-inch pieces.

The Libouton family from France, who had rented a cottage for the summer about a quarter-mile down the beach from the Walshes, hired Liza as a mother's helper. Mr. Libouton had business dealings with Jack's firm. They had three extremely different children. Marie, eight, was a tremendous help to Liza. She would guide her in handling Nicolas, six, and Françoise, four.

Nicolas kept his thoughts to himself and didn't like any type of food touching another type of food on his plate, while Françoise was a live wire with a short circuit. Her capacity for movement was measureless.

Each morning, Liza arrived at their cottage at nine, after the children had breakfast, ready for a day at the beach, they would be in their swimsuits. Building castles and animals in the sand was a favorite pastime. They walked the beach looking for treasures and played in the water. While they taught her everyday French, Liza read to them in English —these three children were easy to love.

She tried to keep her eyes on them at all times. One overcast Monday, she stood at the water's edge with Marie, watching Nicolas swim. Françoise, twenty feet behind them played in the sand. Now eleven o'clock, the beach filled with mothers, nannies, children, and a few men on vacation. When she turned around to check on Françoise, the little girl was gone. Liza scanned the beach but didn't see her bright red swimsuit. She grabbed Nicolas from the water and yelled at Marie, "Help me find Françoise." They ran up and down the beach, asking if anyone had seen a two-and-a-half-foot girl in a red suit. With a racing heart and trembling knees, Lisa felt the urge to vomit but knew she couldn't. She had to keep Marie and Nicolas calm. She never looked towards the ocean. She willed Françoise not to be delivered on the underside of a wave. She had to be on solid ground. *How on earth do parents keep track of their children each day for years?*

As they made their way back to their towels, Liza was trying to think how she could explain this horrible mishap, when she saw Françoise sitting on her towel. The first words out of Liza's mouth were, "Where did you go?" In an adept movement, Françoise slid under the towel and disappeared from view.

"Why didn't you come when you were called?"

With a smile that melted any annoyance and fear Liza had, Françoise said, peeking from under the towel, "I wanted you to find me."

She had another dilemma. Should she tell the Liboutons or not? Many people had been searching with them. Surely, the Liboutons would hear of the incident and might lose trust in her for not saying anything. Surely, one of the three children would recount the tale at dinner that night. Liza walked past her own cottage on her way to the Liboutons and stopped to talk with her mom.

"Difficult situations, my darling—meet them head on."

When Liza entered the Libouton cottage, Mr. and Mrs. L. were both there, sitting on the screen porch on wicker rockers, having a drink and reading *Le Figaro*. White plastic shades kept the sun at bay.

Liza's throat was so dry that she had to excuse herself and get a drink of water. She returned to the porch and sputtered out the day's event. Mortified at not having done her job, she twisted her hands behind her back, waiting for the worst admonishment of her life. Mr. Libouton laughed and said, "Isn't Françoise a clever child?"

Understanding immediately what Liza had gone through, Mrs. Libouton said to Françoise, "Don't scare Mademoiselle Liza, and come when you are called." She asked Françoise what she had to say about the incident.

Françoise muttered, "Nothing."

Mrs. Libouton said they would speak about it more with her— "Françoise must understand not to hide unless you are playing a game." Mrs. Libouton hugged Liza as she was leaving and said, "I'm so happy you are taking care of our children."

1969

ABSORBING EVERYTHING STEVE

By the new year, Liza was deeply in love and on the pill. Sophia had given her the name of a gynecologist in Philly. She thought her mom and dad wouldn't find out since Philly was a big city. Sleeping with Steve, Liza thought it was everything she hoped it would be. Making love came as a release and a relief. Sitting in his car, with the radio on and Simon and Garfunkel singing *Bridge Over Troubled Water*, Liza said, "In bygone days, this must have been the honeymoon phase." She ran her hand along his sleeve, "I can't get enough of you. I go to sleep every night wet with desire and happiness."

Steve admitted to his wet dreams. "I'm crazy about you." Snow fell like little pieces of splintered glass under the streetlight.

Many times that year, Liza visited the closet. She was coming to terms with her relationship to Steve, "Mother, things are different for me since I'm on the pill." She played with one of Fiona's shoes, and then she picked up her mother's urn and held it on her lap and said, "Everything's okay." She knew she was really trying to convince herself. She didn't remember ever regretting her decision, as all reason disappeared whenever Steve even brushed against her or looked at her from a distance. Yet a sliver of doubt seemed to get tangled up with her confidence.

###

When Steve's parents were away one evening, and his sister was staying at a friend's house, he invited Liza over to watch a movie. When the movie finished, Steve took her by the hand to his parent's bedroom: a large room with oil landscapes hung on dark green silk wallpaper, the four-poster bed with a canopy looked like something out of a fairytale and was covered with a deep red paisley bedspread. Liza had never seen anything so sumptuous.

"Oh, Steve, we can't, not on your parent's bed."

Steve's reply was to unbutton her blouse and slide his hands around her back, pulling her to him. She was nervous, but she couldn't refuse—she didn't really understand why she couldn't resist? Feeling playful and fearful, Liza bent over, waved her hair in his face, and giggled. She thought she heard the door open and in one swift move she was totally under the covers, next to Steve, trying not to make a sound or wet the bed. Françoise flashed through her mind hiding under her towel... *What if it's Steve's parents?* Steve jumped up and said, "Sirius, what are you doing in here? Go outside, be a good dog."

Liza exhaled, laughed aloud, and begged, "Let's go to your room."

Occupying "their" booth at the Pizza Palace, Steve took Liza's hand and said, "Liza Walsh, will you be my date for the senior prom?" The place was jumping, and the jukebox turned up as high as it could go. *He just asked*

me to the prom. Will he come home from college next year to be my date for
my senior prom?

"Let me see. I'll have to think about that for a second." She looked down at her slice of pizza and then raised her eyelids to Steve. "Of course I will, did you even doubt that I'd go?" Going around to his side of the booth, she kissed him and said, "I was so nervous about our first date— worried about everything from my hair to whether or not you would kiss me goodnight. This prom will be special, as I can be myself and not worry about the details."

"You think you were nervous? I kept rubbing my hands on the back of my trousers hoping you wouldn't notice how damp they were. I hate thinking this will be our last prom together." He took a bite of pizza and washed it down with 7UP.

She was proud holding Steve's hand and liking the idea that she was his girl now. *A Steve sponge, that's what I am now, absorbing everything Steve.*

###

The decorating committee learned from last year's fan fiasco and settled for *Moonlight Sonata*. An oversized moon hung from the gym's rafters, along with a cascade of stars. The center of each star and the moon had a small battery powered light attached. The set design crew from the theater department covered the walls with cardboard trees. Liza and Sophia thought everything struck the right chord. Even the guys thought it cool. Romance was in the air.

In the middle of a slow dance, Steve asked Liza, "Please close your eyes and stand still." Reaching in his pocket, he placed a warm chain over her neck with his class ring dangling from it and said, "May we always be together even when we are apart."

"Oh, Steve…" Her heart was performing a drum solo, she couldn't wait till she told her mother and her mom of this turn of events.

There was one moment in the girl's bathroom when Liza was hit with a cold dose of reality. As she entered the room, she heard a girl saying in a whisper, "Someday, someone will like you." It happened so fast that as Liza turned the corner of the protection screen, she saw a senior girl, Marion Wallstor, who had been working the food and drink table, crying, looking in the mirror. She had come without a date to the prom. She was attractive but uncommonly shy, dressed in a blue silk, boat neck dress with beading around the waist.

In a split second decision, Liza did not speak. This girl didn't need her pity. It was the first time she considered what it would be like to go through high school without a boyfriend. She wanted so much for Steve to ask Marion to dance one slow number, but that wouldn't be good; it would in essence be a cruel move on her part. When Liza left the stall, Marion was gone. Liza wondered if Marion's desire was like a whip that constantly cracked her heart. When she entered the closet to tell her mother about

Steve's ring, it had lost some of its shine, because Marion's face in the mirror remained with her.

###

Alcohol was ever-present at parties and before each and every one of them, Finn would take Liza aside and say, "You have a one-drink limit, because I'm not taking care of you." Something in his command gave Liza the feeling that maybe Finn did care about her. But when she thought about it longer, she figured he would get in trouble from Mom and Dad if she were caught drunk.

At one party, she thought she'd like a second drink. If she timed it right Finn wouldn't see her. What would be the crime? She went for a second beer. Finn materialized out of nowhere, took the beer out of Liza's hand and turned to Steve and said, "Take her home—she's had enough."

Liza turned scarlet and was about to protest when Finn stood six inches from her face and in a hard voice filled with anger behind clenched teeth ordered, "Go now, Liza."

Steve stayed quiet.

On the way to the car, Liza felt the night covering her. She turned to Steve and demanded, "Why didn't you stick up for me?"

"I thought I'd better not come between the two of you."

"Take me home!"

When they pulled up to the front of the house, Liza got out of the car and ran inside. No goodnight, no kiss, and no terms of endearment. Going in the house, Liza roared past her mom and said, "If Steve calls, I'm asleep."

Steve called once, and Fiona answered, "Liza is asleep. It's probably best if you call tomorrow."

Liza waited two days and called Steve. "I'm sorry, Steve. Can we put this episode to bed?"

"Absolutely."

By now, it was too awkward if they continued to double date, the couples went separately to parties and events so that they had privacy.

Finn and Liza shared a two-toned green '65 Ford Fairlane. Since Steve had his own car, a Nash Rambler, passed down from his grandfather, Liza basically gave Finn free use of their car that year.

Although the Rambler wasn't exactly made for sex, they managed to learn the geography of the car and position themselves accordingly. Liza's side had a few bruises from the gearshift.

"I hate all this lifting and lowering of clothes. I just want skin on skin," Steve said. "This car leaves a lot to be desired."

"Couldn't agree more." Through the forming fog inside the windows of the car, Liza saw bats swirling in the sky, they scared her. She remembered the time as a child when one swooped close to her and a wing lightly brushed her cheek. She held Steve tighter.

Touching the right spot, Steve diffused her memory. They continued their lovemaking. Upon reaching a climax, Liza realized her arm was stuck in the steering wheel. At first they laughed, but it took ten minutes of thought and twisting to free her aching arm.

"Can you imagine what the scenario would have been like if we needed someone to saw the steering wheel to free my arm while my bra and tee shirt were wrapped around my neck?"

"I think I would have gotten a saw and freed you myself, because I would never let any one find you like that."

Liza loved that Steve had the essential ingredient of a gentleman, kindness.

###

On Saturdays, Steve's parents visited his father's mother for lunch and his mother's parents for four o'clock tea. Thus Liza and Steve spent most Saturdays in his bedroom. He bribed his sister, Christina, with everything from movie money to car rides to keep her from telling about their afternoons. She was only twelve and worshipped Steve. He took the time to listen to her prattle on about the inner-workings of preteen girls, and she beamed as much as Liza did when looking at him.

Liza memorized every inch of his bedroom: the two single maple beds, the desk, dresser and bookcase. Kate and Liza's bedroom had maple twin beds, too. Surely this was a sign that they were meant for each other.

Papered with a tan grass cloth, the walls were decorated with pennants of sports teams and colleges. Closing her eyes she could see the Brown University, the Phillies, and circus pennants on the wall above his bed. Over the desk was a bulletin board with several photos of Steve and her, two varsity letters for swimming, ticket stubs from movies they had seen together, and sporting event programs collected over his high school years.

Steve had mapped out the constellations on the ceiling. He told her once, "I want to explore everything about our planet and galaxies."

"Is that how Sirius got his name?"

"Yep, Sirius is the dog star."

"And I thought it an ordinary star. How clever you are."

Another time, he used the word *enthralled.* If she lay down on his bed before him, she could luxuriate in his scent, and learned quickly that foreplay can happen without touching, as any one of the five senses had the ability to trigger excitement.

Liza thought of the time she and her mom were shopping in the mall, and she had seen a man ahead of them with a sweater that matched one of Steve's. She was taken aback when she blushed and became aroused thinking of Steve in the sweater.

Without warning, euphoria would take hold of her and stay with her throughout the day.

TORN HEARTS AND SHREDDED THOUGHTS

In 1969, men were drafted for service by the use of a lottery. There were 365 blue capsules, each containing one date of the calendar year. The capsules were drawn and opened, one by one, and assigned sequentially rising numbers. When the lottery was held, the first capsule contained the date September 14; so all men born on that date from 1944 through 1950 were called to duty. The last date drawn was June 8, which was assigned number 365. There was a second lottery for the 26 letters of the alphabet, to determine the order of priority, by last name, for each date of birth.

Finn's birthday was the second capsule drawn and W was assigned *three*. There was no doubt that he would be drafted. Timidly, Fiona reminded Finn that they'd drive him to Canada.

Sunlight flooded the living room as Finn in a low, cold voice said, "I can think for myself. I don't need you to run interference. I'm going to Sophia's."

Reaching for his arm, Jack said, "Son, wouldn't you like to talk this over with us first?"

"Not really."

"This may be the most important decision you'll ever make in your life."

"Yeah, but it'll be my decision." With that said, Finn turned on his heel and left.

"Jack, you don't think he'd go, do you?" asked Fiona.

135

"Let's hope Sophia will say the right things."

Liza ran after him, calling "Finn, Finn, wait up. Don't do anything foolish."

"Oh Liza, don't you become like Mom and Dad. Let me do what I need to do in peace."

"I only want to let you know that I care," with that she went towards him to hug him, but he walked away. She wondered how Finn ever became a mental prisoner in solitary confinement.

###

Back inside, Liza saw her dad with moist cheeks trying to read the paper. She stood for a long second in shock. She backed out of the room before he was aware of her and went upstairs. "Mom, I think you should go downstairs to Dad."

Fiona went right down, while standing at the door, the only thing that Liza overheard was her mom saying was, "Finn is now a pawn of chance."

Why was her dad crying? Liza was sure that Finn would finally understand the risk and go to Canada. Maybe just the idea of him going was torment for Dad.

Finn came home early and walked past everyone sitting in the kitchen eating mint chocolate chip ice cream and went straight to his room. "Goodnight, Finn," they called after him and then waited a few seconds, ever hopeful that he would return the sentiment. Liza believed her mom and dad went to their room with torn hearts and shredded thoughts.

The following evening, all was quiet when Finn came into the kitchen for dinner. Liza was doing homework at the table, their mom cutting up carrots, and his dad swinging an imaginary golf club, half humming and half singing *Can't Help Falling in Love with You*. Finn knelt and played with Rouge on the floor. Liza thought this unusual, as he normally didn't stay in a room with them unless he had to, and he never arrived early for dinner. Nevertheless, she felt good about his being here.

The afternoon light had turned a leaden color, making everyone's face have an ashen hue. Liza pulled down the retractable light over the table and switched it on. Faces now had a soft glow.

Finally, Finn started talking, "I went to the draft board this afternoon and signed up. I'm not going to Canada because being a draft-dodger will just cause difficulties down the road." Everyone tried to talk at once, but Finn held up his hand and said, "What's done is done. I can't let down all the guys who went before me. It's for them that I fight. I've signed up because it's my duty, like it or not. You all act like Liza's mother is the only dead person that matters. I'm here to tell you that you're all blind to the outside world."

There was a deafening silence. Liza thought the blood racing through her body was beating so loudly in her ears that she covered them till she could calm down.

For the second time in her life, she heard Fiona echo words that became indelibly etched in her mind. Her mom held Finn's shoulders and looked him in the eyes and said, "Finn, what have you done? Did you stop to think that you might have gotten a college deferment?"

If he thought he had made a mistake, Liza could tell he wasn't going to own up to it, but she was sure he heard his father's voice that had urged them so often to "finish what you start." His enlistment was in motion. There was no turning back— Finn was not going to Canada.

As Fiona finished speaking, Kate called. Liza answered the phone and told her what had transpired. Immediately, Kate asked to speak with Finn. He took the phone and said, "You heard right; I signed up." Kate said something else, and Finn said, "There's no more to say. I'm so tired of everyone trying to run my life." With that he hung up.

Fiona and Jack somehow seemed older than they were before Finn's outburst. Their faces were maps of pain, sorrow, and confusion—they had no words to help Finn. Their insides were bruised.

Liza hustled to her bedroom and kept telling herself that it would be okay. Finn was smart and would take care of himself just fine. What she really felt was anger towards Finn, and she wondered if keeping anger bottled up could finally kill her fragile relationship with him faster than the tough words she wanted to say.

When Fiona called everyone for dinner, all but Finn sat down. Everyone was wrapped in thoughts about Finn and the war. Please pass the salt, or the like was the extent of their conversation.

To be an elite Army Ranger, that's what Finn wanted. He had the notion this might help his family understand him. Finally, in their eyes, he'd be a hero. He'd be as perfect as Kate and Liza. *I'll work till I drop to achieve this. I will become a ranger.*

Beneath his mattress he hid brochures. At night, he pulled them out and read them over and over as they were thrilling to him. He drew sketches of himself doing terrain assessment, tactical and special security missions, recovering prisoners of war along with capturing enemy soldiers for interrogation and intelligence. Even more drawings of himself tapping North Vietnamese Army and Viet Cong wire communications along the Ho Chi Minh trail lay in his closet. All of these charcoal sketches were kept in tissue paper in a shoebox.

The part that really made him desire this covetous position was the Ranger Creed, consisting of seven parts. The main one that hooked him was: "Readily will I display the intestinal fortitude required to fight on to the Ranger objective and complete the mission, though I be the lone survivor." *Someday they'll understand me.*

139

###

The next weekend Kate arrived and all except Finn were in the kitchen having cold cuts on rye bread with potato chips and pickles. While Fiona poured Cokes for everyone, she said, "I wish that cardinal would stop flying into the window," she said. "He's going to hurt himself."

"Maybe," said Jack, "it's mating season and my understanding is that they see their own reflection as a competitor and attack their own image."

"My God, even birds fight their own species," said Fiona. Once again, the cardinal's body thumped at the window. Fiona pulled down the shade, changing the bright light in the room to a filtered one.

Kate started, "Finn's reasoning is altruistic."

Jack retorted, "I think he can't see the forest for the trees."

We're all trying to get inside Finn's mind, which has become a gallery of abstract cubes, each a different variation of an angry red, thought Liza.

"Please support Finn's decision as I don't want him leaving unsettled. I want him to deploy with love," urged Fiona. Rouge was lying at Fiona's feet, whimpering through a dream.

"It'll be okay, Mom. Finn can take care of himself. He's smart and needs to do this to prove something. I'm not sure what, but I think it's important to him," said Liza.

"Maybe he'll be able to relax when the war is over—maybe the shroud of his secrecy will be lifted."

140

Fiona couldn't leave it there and said, "Is this the courage of his convictions, or his inability to back down from a dreadful decision?"

"At this point, semantics aren't the problem—you're right, we need to stand with him," said Jack.

They agreed to honor his decision and to be present to him as they had been for Fiona when she was sick.

Ralph Vaughn-Williams's *The Lark Ascending* started to play on the radio. Jack put his finger to his lips and closed his eyes. The shimmering strings held them spellbound while the violin reached notes so high that they could hardly hear them. Liza knew this to be one of her father's favorite pieces. It was followed by news. Fiona jumped up and turned off the radio.

They ate their cake in silence.

Calling Steve, Liza let everything out. "My parents are miserable. I think Finn's being stubborn. Why can't he be a loving son and brother?" She played with the phone cord while looking out the window at two squirrels chasing each other up, down, and around the sycamore tree. "Do you think Finn's just being idealistic?" On the verge of ranting, her voice was high-pitched and loud. "Can't you talk some sense into Finn?"

"It's not my place." She heard the fear in Steve's voice and remembered that he had told her, "I'm becoming more and more against the war, yet I probably won't be a draft dodger."

"So you'll go?"

"I wish I knew— I've been over it a thousand times and end up in a bigger quandary."

Liza was now annoyed as much with Steve as with Finn and told him she had to hang up. They each said goodnight. No— "No you hang up," echoed again and again.

In the closet, Liza lifted her mother from the shelf and sat on the stool. A gust of uncertainty stirred within her. "Mother, this closet isn't big enough for any more ashes. Please ask God to keep Finn safe and sound."

While Liza was in there, Fiona came in and asked if she could stay with her. Liza nodded. Neither spoke, but Liza was sure their prayers were in the same vein.

It was rare that Finn and Liza found themselves alone in the house. Finn, with Rouge beside him, was lying on the living room floor reading Patrick O'Brian's *Master and Commander*, first in a series about the British Royal Navy in the time of Nelson. A stream of light crossed both their bodies while an open window caused the curtain to flutter and the scent of peonies to saturate the room.

Liza couldn't keep everything bottled up any longer and kicked his book lightly with her toe and said, "Finn, talk to me."

Staring at Liza for a long minute, he said, "I'm just about as scared as I can be without shitting myself. It's my decision, like it or leave it. You can tell the rest of them that they need to live with it." Rouge sat up beside Finn. "None of you has a clue about the world outside this house. Your world is that death closet that you go in and out of."

Not being able to bite her tongue any longer, Liza cried, "Finn, will you never realize how much we love you? Why are you so hostile to us? We're not the enemy."

As he crossed his arms over his chest, darkness enveloped him. If only she could shout, *DON'T GO, FOR GOD'S SAKE, PLEASE DON'T GO!* Not wanting to violate Fiona's wishes, she didn't. "It's your choice, but I hope you know what you're doing."

"You're dammed right it's my decision! I finally have some control over my own life."

"You're willing to risk your life to prove that you're in control?

His face changed its expression before he said, "I'll test the water first; I'm not a fool."

"How does one test the water in the middle of combat?"

Not answering, Finn petted Rouge and shook his head—as if to say, you just don't get it.

Standing silent for another minute, Liza realized that this conversation was over. She started to reach for him, but Finn gave her a sullen look. The shifting sun made it seem as if Finn had a halo atop his head, which caused her to smile. She told Finn that she and Steve were going for pizza and asked if he and Sophia wanted to join them?

Finn's usual shrug surfaced, and Rouge jumped up and followed Liza to the door. Patting Rouge on the head, she said, "Sorry, girl, you can't come." With a dejected look, Rouge trotted to the kitchen door to wait for Fiona to return.

As Liza turned away, Finn reached for her and was glad she hadn't seen the gesture. His demons pulled at him from every direction. He just didn't understand why he felt so alone in this family. He knew everyone loved him. He hoped that war would change things. He wasn't sure how, but he hoped.

###

On her way to meet Steve, Liza thought about what had just happened. Probably the longest conversation they had ever had. Is our family the enemy and not the North Vietnamese? *Loving Finn's a one-sided proposition.* Could he be missing a piece of his heart when it came to his family? She knew he needed a miracle, but she also knew he didn't believe they existed.

When she heard Finn's voice, Liza turned and saw that he and Sophia were about five steps behind them at the Pizza Palace. Sophia must have changed Finn's mind. "Oh, great, you're here," said Liza.

Liza knew that this gang of four would soon be disbanded. Finn in the rugby shirt that he had bought at Princeton looked like a college guy. Steve was in madras bermudas and a polo shirt, while Sophia, always elegant, wore a pale blue sundress. Liza clicked a mental picture of them that she hoped she could retrieve periodically.

"Who wants to hear *I'll Be There*?" asked Sophia.

"Good one," said Steve.

"Are you packed yet for school, Steve?" inquired Finn.

"Almost. Wish I could take Sirius with me."

"Yeah, I wish I could take Rouge."

"It will be a sweeter homecoming when they greet you with licks," mused Liza.

And so with twists and turns in the conversation, at a small pizza joint, the afternoon faded into dusk, and the gang separated. Liza wondered if this time next year they would be together again.

The day of Finn's induction into the army was cool; a red sunrise announced the morning. It was the first week of July. Fiona woke everyone to have breakfast together. Kate was home from school; she was taking extra

145

classes to graduate early. Jack took the day off. They would all make the drive to Fort Dix. An aroma of coffee and bacon wafted up the stairs, inviting all to eat.

Finn was last to the table and first to finish. His mind was a jumble— what had he gotten himself into? Why couldn't he leave his family with love, or kind words? He didn't know how. He just didn't know how! He had treated them so badly for so long that he felt compelled to play his part as he always had. He would fuss over Rouge. How he wished he could take her, a silent partner; he might feel safer with her. At least she'd be in the car today.

"I don't know, Finn, if the Eagles can win the division this year."

He's just trying to ease the tension, thought Finn. "I know."

Fiona rushed around to make sure everyone had enough food.

She's probably praying that some unexpected occurrence will transpire to keep me home after all, thought Finn.

Kate said timidly, "It won't be the same without you being home."

Wanting to answer, Finn thought, *"Probably it'll be better is what you really mean."* He didn't say it, however, realized at this point he didn't need to prove himself to anyone.

Shielding his eyes from the sun, that had worked its way across the table, Jack said that it was time to go.

Everyone climbed into the station wagon, including Rouge in the way back. Fiona fiddled with the radio and tried to find a music-only station. They all had heard a snippet of the numbers of war dead. She jerked the knob and produced static before she finally found a station playing the Beatles' *Let it Be*. Kate and Liza sang along softly, while Finn looked out the window.

Finn wished that Sophia were with him to be a go-between with his family. He just wanted to get the hell out of the car and shut the door behind himself. Sophia and he had said their goodbyes the night before, with Sophia trying desperately not to cry. Finn had made it clear to her that she should see other people, and they could see how they felt when his tour of duty was over. He liked Sophia because she didn't nag him about anything. She didn't seem to want to know if he loved her. She kept things simple.

When the car pulled up to the induction center, Finn said, "We can say goodbyes here, since I'll be home in a few weeks anyway." As each hugged him, he accepted the hugs and tried to loosen his stiff arms. *Why were they always doing things like this? Why can't they say goodbye and be done with it? Why can't I feel for them? I wish I knew.*

###

Leave was a three-day pass.

"It's his shaved head that bothers me most," confessed Fiona. "The last vestiges of his childhood have been stripped away."

Visiting with Sophia, Finn had left the door to his bedroom open. There were two darts in his dartboard. One was a bull's eye; the other was hanging off the bottom of the board. Sitting near his closet, there was a pair of sneakers with socks falling out of them. Fiona picked up the diary from his desk—it was open—almost as if he wanted someone to read it. *A possible cry for help* ran through Fiona's mind.

Holding up his hands and backing away from her, Jack said, "I don't think we should read that."

"I want to know what is going on with him."

Jack didn't stop her. He left and went downstairs.

Walking around the room, she picked up his belongings one by one and then put them back exactly as she found them: his class ring which she tried on, a varsity letter for lacrosse, his robe on the back of the closet door, a pen that advertised, The Pizza Palace, a picture of Sophia turned upside down, a stick of gum, some change in a dish and other bibelots of living. Finally, she picked up the diary and turned the pages.

When Fiona read, *I hope I've found a place where I can be my true self,* she closed the diary, sat on Finn's bed wondering how had they gone so horribly wrong that Finn would choose army life over a family who loved him. She couldn't share this with Jack, and she knew that by not telling him, he would understand that whatever was written would be a knife to his heart. She also knew that Jack wouldn't ask.

Motionless on Finn's bed, Fiona sat for a long time trying to make some sense of his writings. Taking his pillow and holding it to her chest, she feared for Finn. A murder of crows outside the bedroom window amplified her feelings.

###

Only once later when Finn, Sophia, Liza, and Steve were together at the Pizza Palace did Finn tell tales of what went on during those first weeks.

Finn laughed and said, "One recruit tried to hide a hundred Snickers bars in his duffle bag. The sergeant found them during inspection and made him eat every one." He laughed, "You can imagine how sick he was, but he still had to march and go through the drills like everyone else."

Liza turned to Finn and said, "I don't find that funny."

Finn retorted, "Of course you don't."

A *Time* Magazine arrived in the mail the weekend Finn was home. He was in the living room reading *Slaughterhouse-Five*, as Jack walked in with the magazine and sat down. The cover story, *What Price War*, caught Jack's attention.

Finn knew the story. Not only was it about his unit, but also he was quoted in it several times. He remembered telling the reporter, "I have no choice but to serve."

The story also dealt with a suicide in Finn's squadron. In a note the young man had left, he said he found the thought of war a disease that had overtaken his mind like a cancer. He would be no good to his comrades in arms. He needed to have peace so as to end the chatter of brutality that swirled constantly in his head. Finn had been surprised when he read this part earlier.

Jack turned the pages and put the magazine down with trembling hands.

"This is all part of war. You should get used to it," Finn said.

"War is something that no one should ever get used to," Jack said.

Thinking about what Jack had just said, Finn could feel his heart beating in sync with the tick-tocking of the tall-case clock. *At least I'm in sync with something.*

Liza came into the room and suggested they all go to a movie; *Butch Cassidy and the Sundance Kid* was playing at the Bryn Mawr Theater. Finn opted out.

Sitting alone in the kitchen well past midnight, he ate butter pecan ice cream—he had a spoonful and then gave Rouge a spoonful until the pint was finished. Why wasn't Sophia here with him? He hated going to the movies with his family. It was simple enough; he wanted to be alone because his heart was drifting on a sea of fear.

It was the end of August and Finn was home again. Fiona and Jack often stole sidelong glances at him. They tried to keep the laughter flowing, and his time home was over just as they were finally reaching the rhythm that made their family different from that of any other family.

When it was time for Finn to leave, a quiet came over them. They were awkward. "Well, Son, I think it's time."

"I'll be home again before I'm deployed."

Finn picked up his duffle bag in the hallway and muttered, "Bye," as he rushed out the front door into a thunderstorm. Outside another recruit was waiting in a battered blue pickup. Under a soaking downpour, Finn hunched into his field jacket and ran to the vehicle. Rouge in her excitement gave one shrill bark.

Settled in the truck, Finn saw his mother looking out the window. He raised his hand tentatively and dropped it quickly. Fiona put her hand to her heart and then blew her son a kiss.

NO PROMISES

Playing with Steve's hair, Liza finally asked him, "Do you think it's best we separate so you can enjoy college fully?" He shifted on the sofa. He rubbed the back of her neck. Not really wanting this to happen, she thought if she said it first, then he would see what a generous and loving person she was. Liza was floored when Steve said, "I don't know—time will help us solve this one way or another."

Chewing her fingernail, all she could think was, *He has doubts about us. Maybe I shouldn't have slept with him. No, that's crazy. Of course he loves me. He said so last night.*

She almost said, *I'll apply to Brown too, so we can see if it works*, but thought better of it. Now she was anxious about Steve and Finn. Both were out of her control. So she snuggled up to Steve and wrapped herself in his familiar scent.

###

The day Steve left for Brown, he stopped by the Walshes' house. Liza answered the door, "Steve, I thought you were gone." She put her hands around his neck and kissed him. He kissed her back and then stepped into the hallway. The sidelights from the front door cast yellowy green block paintings on the navy wallpaper.

"I have something for you. It wasn't ready till this morning." He handed her a gold bracelet with one charm, a little vial filled with sand. "Such a tender remembrance." Not wanting to see him leave, she kept hugging and kissing him.

"Wait a sec," she said and took the stairs at a fast pace. Since he hadn't given her anything last night, she thought it better to keep what she had gotten him safely hidden in her purse. Upon returning, she handed him a little silver box. Inside, a silver key chain with his initials engraved on the medallion lay in a wad of cotton. Liza smiled and said, "Every time you unlock your dorm room, think of me." *What a stupid thing to say. Why didn't I let him figure that out himself?* Come Christmas she would have the perfect gift for him. So they parted with a kiss but no promises.

Less than a minute had passed since Steve had left, when she was up in her room composing a love letter—second-guessing every word took too much time. Words failed her. Rumpling the paper in her hand, she threw it into the trashcan—over and over again.

Why is it, Liza thought, *when we try too hard, we usually overreach, and the results are flawed?*

NO ANSWERS HERE

With a drawn face, Finn came home carrying a standard army issued duffle bag. He told Rouge that anything he could fit into it and still be able to carry the bag was allowed. "Get in, girl. How great it would be with you by my side." Liza was sitting on the arm of a chair in the living room while Finn was sprawled on the floor.

She handed Finn a laminated picture of Rouge with a lock of her fur bubbling up on the back. "She'll be with you in spirit."

Finn looked at the photo and then at Rouge. He tucked the photo into the inside pocket of his jacket. Liza smiled.

Kate, who was home from school and had been standing in the doorway, handed him a bracelet of knotted white string that she had made for him. Standing now, he put it on and began rocking on his feet. He was in motion like the trees outside the bay window.

Fiona walked down the stairs slowly, entered the living room, and gave Finn a letter, "Please don't read this until you're in Viet Nam." The letter joined the photo of Rouge.

Later Liza asked him about his training. He provided a laundry list of practical survival skills, with a few highlights thrown in: how to shine your boots, make your bed, stand at attention, salute; learn the rules of war, land navigation, first aid, in-ranks inspection; how to throw hand grenades and maintain an M16 rifle. She was shocked at the length of his answer but happy to have a response not covered in barbed wire.

A partly cloudy day, with the sun making short appearances every so often, accompanied them to the train station. Standing in a huddle, they tried to make conversation, but it was stiff. Liza made a lame attempt at a joke and when no one laughed, Finn said, "You don't have to stay; I'll be fine by myself."

Fiona took a chance, held Finn's arms, and said, "Yes, but we won't be."

His one concession, he quickly touched his mother's hand.

He wished he had the gumption to tell his family that he loved them, but it seemed impossible to him. Anyway he'd just be mouthing words. *Stay the course* was all he could think. He stood with his hands in his pockets. *What's wrong with me?*

Jack pressed his Tissot Swiss watch into Finn's palm and asked him to give him his Timex. Jack's watch had a compass, and he told Finn that he could always find his way home. Finn didn't know what to say; it was too overwhelming. He stood as if he were at attention. *Why, Why, Why do they do these things?*

About five minutes before the train arrived, Finn and Sophia stepped away from everyone and said their goodbyes in private. He wasn't sure what else to tell her as he tried to express his feelings last night; he didn't want to tie her down. She should date and when he finished his tour of duty they could see where they stood. He let her take his hand—that had to be enough.

Finn requested they all go no further. Grudgingly, he did the round of hugs and saw that each of them wore a tight smile. When he got to the top step of the railroad car, he turned and said, "I don't understand all this fuss. I'll be home before you know it."

When Finn was finally alone for a minute on the train, he thought that maybe he did need help and when he came back from Nam he would try and get some. All would change when he was a Ranger. He looked around the train car filled with soldiers. *No answers here.*

###

Liza didn't say anything; she just sat quietly rocking in the closet.

Jack and Fiona must not have realized that Liza was in there as she heard her mom say, "Oh Jack, I feel as though a piece of me died today."

"Fiona, darling, he's so strong willed. Somehow, I know he'll survive. This war might teach him compassion. Remember what Dr. Sanders said, 'It might take an unusual event to change things.'"

"Mom, Dad, I'm in the closet," called Liza.

"It's okay," said Fiona. "Your dad's right, Finn's strong and will come back to us."

1970

DISTANCE

During winter break that year, Liza had started looking at colleges. Jack was the one who took her to see the schools that piqued her interest.

With the help of the college counselor at St. John's, Liza had three different schools in mind: Bard, a small residential college on the Hudson in New York; Stanford, the leading research and teaching university in California; and The Catholic University of America, a liberal arts school in Washington, DC. The counselor always made sure there was a Catholic college included in a student's list.

The sun was brilliant the morning they flew into San Francisco. They were on time and had no trouble renting a car. Liza switched on the radio as her father drove the brown Chevy Monte Carlo. When she heard the words Viet Nam she quickly changed the station to classical music.

"Dad, did you enjoy college?"

"I don't remember all that much; I just remember your mom and wanting school to end, to get a job and marry her." He adjusted the rear view mirror. "Yes, I guess I enjoyed it. I played Rugby, which was a club sport, and sang in the Glee Club. I got decent grades…so yes, I enjoyed it."

Liza thought about this for a while and didn't resume talking. She didn't feel like being chatty.

When they arrived at Stanford's campus, she was astonished at the sandstone and tile buildings not seen on the east coast. Liza found the red tiled

159

roofs warm and welcoming. After the tour, they ate in the dining facility and walked the entire campus.

Standing beside the rented car, her dad said, "So, what do you think?"

"I don't want to be this far from you and Mom, or even Kate."

She knew her dad thought the same thing, but he said, "The distance might be a welcome change for you."

"Let me think about it." *There's no way I'd enroll here.*

Although she liked Catholic University on a later visit, it just didn't feel right; so she went with her gut and chose Bard.

DINING ON A BITTER HERB

Letter writing between Liza and Steve slowed down as Steve's freshman year progressed. He told her for his part he had a lot of work due all the time. At Christmas when he came home they picked up where they had left off only Liza thought something wasn't quite right—something she couldn't put her finger on—something that made her intuition move towards the resentful herb of jealousy. When the break was over, and Steve was headed back to school he told her that he loved her.

After Christmas letter writing disappeared on his part—on her part it was clockwork. She tried to give him the benefit of the doubt; she tried to be upbeat and loving. He wrote a postcard at the end of March, which consisted of four words, "See you spring break." What to make of that? Again her intuition was dining on the bitter herb.

The fabric of her soul was knitted with prayer. Prayer had the power to conquer—at least that was what the nuns said. Time to put it to the test. After each novena she would calm down but within a short time her thoughts would go haywire. She tried to be patient, but patience was almost as bitter as jealousy.

Answering the phone on the way in the house on a cool April afternoon, Liza knew it was Steve before she answered. Was it okay if he came over? "Sure can, can't wait," —said a little too cheerfully, with high hopes mixed in.

Coming through the door, trying to greet her with a smile, but not reaching for her— her worst fears were confirmed. *He's moved on.*

They sat on the terrace facing each other. Rouge was rolling around on the grass. It was overcast but warm.

Not being able to stand it another minute she asked, "Are you seeing someone?"

He nodded but didn't explain; she didn't need an explanation—and she really didn't want to hear about his new love.

He scooted to the edge of his chair and reached for her hands. She sighed feeling the warmth of his touch and looked him in the eye.

"Liza, I wish the same for you."

Trying to be civil she asked about school life and his summer plans. He was headed to Appalachia—she saw his lips move, but she didn't hear anything after the word Appalachia. "The course of true love never did run smooth."

Sleep was hopeless with tears endless. Her mind was like a rolodex— flipping cards with Steve, her mother, and her father's photos on them. When she would reach for one of them, another would take his place. Each gone forever.

###

The end of her four years in high school was not remarkable; she remembered more about the National Guard killing four students at Kent State and the loss of Steve, than her walk across the stage to receive her diploma.

###

A package came from Bard to help Liza get ready for September. Her roommate was to be Sarah Dabney from Richmond, Virginia. After talking on the phone for almost an hour, Liza took to Sarah and invited her to visit her family before school began.

They stayed up talking late into the night. Liza saw a lot of Kate in Sarah. When her parents and Liza took Sarah to the train, Sarah's parting words were, "I think we'll do just fine together." She handed Fiona a wrapped box and disappeared at the top of the train steps. It was a small crystal Orrefor's candy dish.

Fiona and Jack thought as Liza did and felt relief for her and for themselves.

Liza hadn't realized how much energy they had spent on her.

###

Freshman year lifted some of the edges of the murky veil of grief from missing Steve, and allowed Liza to see with more clarity. She and Sarah arrived a day early so they could shop together and buy the necessary bedding,

163

curtains, and other furnishings for their room. Two single beds, two desks, two small closets, and a bulletin board above each desk crowded into a small cubicle. The best part was having two windows because it was a corner room.

They chose pale green and pink plaid bedspreads with pale green curtains to match. After they made their beds, hung the curtains, and unpacked their clothes, the two girls lay on their beds and talked about the year to come.

"My first and only love, Pete, told me since he'd be in Oregon it would be best if we saw other people. I had no idea he was going to tell me this." Sarah sighed. "I almost told my parents I wasn't ready for college because of him."

"I sort of know how you feel. This May my boyfriend told me he had found someone else—just like that.

Although they were tired from their shopping, they had enough energy to walk to Red Hook for pizza.

They found out that they had both been raised Catholic, and Sarah still had a strong commitment to her faith. Liza, who was angry with God, told Sarah, "I believe if there is a God, then he certainly works in mysterious ways. Where does believing get you?" *Sure didn't help me get Steve back.*

Sarah smiled and replied, "God is an anchor in my life. I don't know how well I can explain it. There's has to be something better than man. God just makes sense to me."

Is my faith polluted, and do I have the wherewithal to clean it up?

After being still for a minute, they decided it was time to head back to school, where they found more girls in their dorm. The already high noise

164

level was now punctuated with shrieks, as some of the students found a friend from high school or saw someone remembered from orientation. Male students were helping the females move in. Of course their motives weren't totally selfless. The women were eyeing the men, and the men were making mental notes about the women. Some four-year romances were formed that night. Liza wondered if her next love walked these halls. The more she thought about it, the more she thought she should date a few different men.

September mornings on the Hudson had been nippy since she arrived. On the first day of classes, Liza was journey proud. That anxious feeling she had before she took a trip—it was a mixture of excitement and anxiety. Waiting for Professor Michael O'Flarity, who taught her creative writing class, Liza studied the large Greek Revival windows. The room would darken and then lighten when clouds passed swiftly by, as if a child were playing with a light switch.

Some girls in front of Liza were talking about O'Flarity before he came into the room. She could hear snatches of conversations.

"He's a looker. I saw him yesterday in the Library. I heard he has an illegitimate child," said the girl in the red sweater.

"Is he married?" asked a gorgeous redhead.

"Someone told me his wife died. He's grieving and lonely,"—this added by a girl with horn rimmed glasses.

165

"I could cheer him up. Anyway my roommate said that he has his eyes on Mademoiselle Gelot, the French Lit professor," said the gorgeous red head.

When he came through the doorway, Liza figured his height to be six feet; O'Flarity's height was similar to her dad's. A dark-haired Richard Chamberlain from *Dr. Kildare* came to mind. When he said, "Good morning," she felt the undercurrent of excitement ripple through the females in the class. Pheromones were flying. She saw the way the women sat up with arched backs and felt it a rather vulgar display. If O'Flarity noticed the women ogling him, he gave no indications. *I'll bet he's used to this.* Liza saw one male student raise his eyebrows to another male student, resigned to the idea that female attention wouldn't be coming their way in this class.

O'Flarity's blue jeans, white wrinkled button-down collar shirt open at the neck, and navy sport coat were not what she had been expecting. *So different from the nuns!* When he took the class roll, he eyed her and tilted his head slightly as though being caught off guard. She ran her fingers through her hair. He caught her eye once more for a fleeting second when his instructions about the class were over, and his lecture began. Finding it almost embarrassing to look at him, she felt his clear blue eyes had a charming power that disarmed her. Lowering her head, she tried to concentrate on her note taking. His voice, however, was raspy with a medium to low pitch that caused her to hear only its resonance and not his words. *What is wrong with me?*

VULNERABILITY

After seven months in country, Finn chose Hawaii for his R&R. He was trying to assess his life. Why, why, why had he been so cantankerous with his family? Why was he so angry around them? Not understanding why, somewhere deep inside himself he felt betrayed when Liza took his place as the baby. Things had to change.

He took the first two days to do nothing except swim and soak up the sun. The last three days were for composing a letter to his mother and father trying to explain how the war helped him see things differently.

The turning point happened on a routine night patrol when Larry, a new recruit like Finn, heard a rustle in the tangled overgrowth about two hundred feet in front of them, and there was enough moonlight that they saw a slight movement. Immobilized, Finn could see the whites of Larry's eyes. Larry signaled that each would go the opposite way and surprise the intruder from behind. They knew they could be fired on at any moment. Maybe more than one person was watching them. Finn never felt his mouth so dry, nor sensed a fear so strong that burrowed into the core of his body with each carefully placed step. He saw the jet-black hair and a uniform through the vines. He pointed his rifle but didn't put his finger on the trigger. He waited. He could hear the Blue Eared Barbet bird and the Tokay Gecko lizard calling out to their mates. They would go still for a few seconds and then the animals would call again. There was another slight movement in the snarled vines. He then heard the shot and a guttural sound from the bushes.

167

He arrived at the spot the same time as Larry. It was a child, shot in the head, wearing a military jacket. Most likely it belonged to his father, brother, or uncle. It wasn't even a North Vietnamese jacket. Larry fell on both knees and held the boy with one hand trying to keep a hanging part of his brain attached. Through his sobs, he kept saying, "What have I done? What have I done?"

Another guy, Ed, on patrol came towards them.

Finn heard him and quickly met him before he got to the scene of devastation. "Just a wild dog. You can go back to your post," said Finn. Ed turned back, and Finn went the opposite way.

They both knew that there was a village a few miles south. Larry picked up the light and lifeless child and started walking towards the village. Larry's uniform was soaking up the child's blood. Finn followed, a razor blade of despair slicing through his heart and mind. They never gave a thought about leaving the perimeter of the camp unguarded. And for some reason a guardian angel went with them.

When they arrived at the village, it was well after midnight. There was only one old man outside sitting on a bench staring into space. When he saw Larry's bundle, he rose and extended his arms. The child was handed over, and the old man cradled the child, and looked up at the two men. The old man's eyes were the shells of eyes in a sorrow-masked face.

Finn and Larry never talked about what had happened that night—nor did they ever look directly at each other again. On the way back to camp, they walked single file. Finn kept seeing his mother at the window and she had blown him a kiss. It struck him that it could have been his body that would be carried to her. He hadn't even the wherewithal to wave back to her. He had to make amends. He tried to explain how war sharpened feelings. He had always thought of himself as a sturdy oak. He realized now that he was the weed at the base of the tree. Vulnerability: he was learning the meaning of the word as he wrote. Could his family forgive him?

1971

A NOTE OF JOY

It was snowing when Finn surprised his parents. They were reading in the living room waiting for Kate and Andrew to join them for dinner. "I'm so glad we put a down payment on the same beach house we had before," said Jack.

"Maybe Finn will join us for awhile. I read his letter every day Jack— Dr. Sanders was right. It took an unusual event for Finn to come back to us."

Finn tried the door, and found it locked. He knocked and his dad answered. Not saying a word, he stepped inside and hugged his father through a veil of tears. Hearing nothing, Fiona called out, " Who was that Jack?"

"It's Finn."

She couldn't get to the hallway fast enough. Finn's arms around her torso gave her a feeling she would never forget.

When Finn found his voice, he told them he loved them. They didn't question him. They answered in kind. They had their son back. They could breathe easier—was there really anything that needed to be said?

Rouge came in the kitchen door shaking the snow off herself, while Liza, home for the weekend from Bard had taken Rouge for a walk. Rouge pulled at her leash and barked. "Mom, Dad look what" ... It was at that second that she saw Finn. She let go of the leash. Rouge got to him first, and jumped on him. Finn wrestled with Rouge for a minute, then stood and embraced Liza. She didn't want to let go. All the prayers she had prayed worked. He had come home in one piece.

Finn opened the door for Kate and Andrew. A note of joy escaped Kate. Her hug was like Liza's and her parents' before her, one that erased the anguish that had settled in their hearts because of Finn. They had their family back.

In the blackest part of night, Finn wrestled with the child crouching in the tangled growth. He replayed every second, along with the sounds and the smells of that night wanting to find out if there were something he could have done to prevent what happened. He usually woke in a cold sweat. Knowing he couldn't walk backwards into the future, he lay quietly until sleep reclaimed him.

Daytime was easier for Finn, as he was trying to plot a strategy for his future. He thought of the time when an army ranger was all he wanted to be. That dream was left behind in Viet Nam. He never wanted to hold a gun again, be in uniform again, look at buddies dying or dead on a ground so far from home, smell a rotting jungle or meticulously place one foot after another to avoid landmines.

172

Med school seemed the way to go. Unlike high school, Finn was determined to work hard and be proud of his work. It was another way to say thank you to his parents. Princeton had given him a deferment, and he would enroll in September.

1972

MAJOR SCAR

Getting out of her car on a false spring day in February, Fiona took a deep breath. A day like this always gave her hope that the real spring would bloom outside and within herself, too.

Jack opened the kitchen door, took the bundles from her, and placed them on the table.

She was confused; she hadn't been gone that long. *Why was Jack home so early in the afternoon?*

Wrapping his arms around her, he quietly told her that a drunk driver had killed Finn. He didn't get to say more because Fiona pushed back from him and opened her mouth, but there was no sound. She collapsed like a roof unable to hold the weight of snow any longer. Jack dropped to the floor and took Fiona in his arms.

When she came to, Jack said, "We need to be here for each other and the girls. Imagine, making it through a war only to be struck down by a car." They stayed on the floor, plunged into the valley of death with plenty of evil in their hearts. Who was this person who had taken their newly found son? Fiona wanted desperately to scream at this drunk person. What right had he to take her precious son?

"We'd best call the girls, and I'll go and identify Finn."

"Not without me—he made it through that bloody war for what— for what?" she screamed.

Liza would take the first bus she could get to NYC, and then take a train from there.

Hanging up the phone, Kate was on her way.

Seeing her dead son's face, Fiona felt a tempestuous sea of pain crash into the lining of her heart. A major scar was forming. A murky darkness took a seat in her heart that day, and she knew she would never be able to remove it.

Back at the house, Kate and Liza sat in stunned silence. They stood when their parents returned. None of them knew what to do. On her way upstairs, Fiona vomited her lunch. Jack went to her and helped her to their bedroom. Kate got a sponge, a bucket of water, and Mr. Clean to remove the bits and chunks of the unrecognizable splattered food. She thought of Finn being splattered on the ground.

Kate and Liza could hear the sobs from their parents' room, which triggered meltdowns in them. They held each other until their shirts were stuck to their chests. When they went to their room neither spoke—each hunkered down under her covers.

The coroner had given Jack a manila envelope with Finn's belongings: the watch that Jack had given him, the knotted bracelet from Kate, his mother's letter, which he carried every day, the picture of Rouge from Liza, his wallet, the letter to Princeton that he was on his way to mail; it was

176

dirt stained with tire tracks, and a picture that Sophia had taken of the Walshes at the shore. On the back Finn had written in lower case letters, *my family who loves me.*

BREAKING RANKS WITH GOD

Planning the church service was difficult. Liza knew both her mom and dad were questioning the existence of God. They were performing tasks by rote, going through the motions.

The first time they saw Sophia was at the church service. Fiona asked her to sit with the family. Steve, Andrew, and Clare also walked in with them.

The church was packed with Finn's classmates that were still in the area—and a few army friends. Seeing all these young people temporarily helped Fiona's damaged heart.

Steve held Liza's hand so tightly that she thought he might break a finger. Yet she didn't take her hand away. It provided a sensation of pain and let her know she was still living. The feel of his hand took her back to the junior prom when she had fallen in love with him. The feeling didn't last long when she remembered why he was holding it.

When the priest gave his final blessing and Liza crossed herself, touching her forehead first, *In the name of the Father*, touching her heart, *and of the Son*, her hand fell stiffly to her side. She could not bring herself to complete the sign of the cross. What sense did it make?

Affectionate tokens were placed in the casket, along with letters that each family member wrote to send him off. *Off where—* that was the question on Liza's mind. She also wondered if a person's life came down to a small group of keepsakes.

Neighbors had descended on the house with food. The Walshes were exhausted from crying all night and at the service. Liza remembered only snippets of that day.

Rouge never left Fiona's side as she thanked everyone for their kindness, support, and prayers.

Liza walked into the kitchen and found Kate in the pantry leaning against a shelf, trying to pull herself together. "Liza this is too hard. Every time I try and talk to people, I can't control the waterworks." She took a deep breath.

Hugging Kate, Liza whispered, "I know, but we need to go back out there for Mom and Dad."

As they walked into the dining room, they saw two lacrosse team members laughing and eating chocolate cake. Kate said, "God, I hope they're remembering a great story about Finn."

Liza tapped Kate on her back, "Look at Sophia, she's just walking around in a stupor. I'll go say something to her."

With empty eyes Sophia looked at Liza. "We had just decided to be together again."

She watched her dad slipping from person to person. His voice quaked and he kept rubbing his forehead. When he glanced her way once, she gave him a weak smile.

Liza went over to her grandparents and asked, "May I get you something to eat?" They didn't answer her. What to do? She cleared her throat. *Maybe they didn't hear me.*

Fiona heard her and glared at her father and in a low voice hissed, "Since you can't treat Liza with courtesy, I think you'd better leave. Should you want to see any of us, you'll have to apologize to Liza. She is one of our children and, need I remind you, a child of God."

Mr. Crosby, with his head down, made his way towards the front door, took his wife's hand, and said, "Come, Mary, it's time that we left." He cleared his throat. "Where did we fail our children?"

Mrs. Crosby didn't answer but gave Fiona a pained look. She wondered if perhaps her mother were beginning to see that God wasn't as rigid as they were.

Peter avoided Fiona and left with his parents, tugging at Susan's sleeve to follow him.

Liza watched her uncle Liam smash the cake he was holding onto an empty plate on the table and went after all of them; she followed. Liam said, "Susan, could you return to the house for a minute?"

Peter held onto to his wife's hand and said, "She's not going anywhere."

"What is wrong with all of you?" Liam said. "What has Liza ever done to you? She is a baptized Catholic. Who do you think you are? You play at being God." He jiggled the coins in his pockets. "Fiona and Jack's son has died, and you act holier than thou. Peter, you're on the fast track to becoming a carbon copy of them. Are you going to raise your son the way we were raised, with no love?" He put his hands up and backed away. "This time when you leave, don't expect to see me or my family until you are capable of demonstrating love and compassion."

Liza wondered if the holes in her relatives' hearts were so big they'd never close.

When she thought about it later, after most friends had left, Fiona wasn't sure how she had garnered the strength to rail at her father. What she had done helped some, but it also hurt some. She could feel her heart's anguish beneath her breastbone. Families should be the all of love, not the source of contention. Does that family exist? She would like to think *yes* but knew deep down that there was no such family.

The priest, Father Riley, now middle-aged, overweight, and walking with a cane, was last to leave, saying what he must have said a thousand times before with a name change, "Finn rests in the arms of our Savior. He is home at last."

Home? No, he wasn't home. Liza wanted to scream, *He's in a coffin and going to be cremated.* She would have liked Father Riley better had he said it was a terrible tragedy and that he would pray that they had the strength to cope. She remembered one of the first questions she had memorized from *The Baltimore Catechism #2*, "Why did God make us?" The answer, "To know, love, and serve Him in this world and be with Him in the next," didn't ring true now. Would a perfect God be so narcissistic? Surely, He wouldn't need or want His flock to live only for Him. *If He did create us, what obligations did He have to us?*

Without any declaration or premeditated thought, she broke ranks with God that day.

When the house was theirs again that night, Liza said, "I'll turn out the lights Mom. I'll be up shortly." Rouge followed Fiona and Jack up the stairs.

If Liza sat for five minutes or fifty, she'd never know. She was agitated. When she roused herself and climbed the stairs, she heard her dad singing with a vibration in his voice to Fiona. She sat down outside the room and sang along almost in a whisper, *Amazing Grace! How sweet the sound…*

Kate wasn't in their room. Liza searched and found her in Finn's bed, with his cover pulled over her head. For a split second Liza was jealous. She didn't bother with the light in her bedroom; instead she slid out of her dress and her stockings, which landed somewhere on the floor, and crawled under the covers. Sleep overtook her immediately.

###

In the weeks to come, Liza cried not just for Finn but also for her dead mother and her lost father—and Steve. Seeing him at the funeral set her back a bit. She also worried about her mom and dad.

Fiona asked Liza to help pack up Finn's things. "We'll give his clothes to The Salvation Army, and his sports stuff to The Boys and Girls Clubs." The sun was so bright it seemed to bleach the room. After caressing the handle of Finn's lacrosse stick, Fiona finally put it in the sports box. She found his diary in a desk drawer, along with five unopened condoms. She took the diary to the closet and threw the condoms in the trash. Holding his favorite plaid lumber jacket against her face caused Fiona to weep. In his closet there were two shoeboxes. One held a bunny he took to bed with him as a child, wrapped in tissue, as if Finn had put the bunny to bed. The second contained drawings of a soldier in different combat missions. Both went into the closet with Sally Anne and Finn.

"Liza, put the dart board in the box, please."

Fiona went to the window and stood watching buzzards make lazy circles in the air.

"Mom, what should I do with Sophia's photo?"

Fiona turned around, "Why don't you keep it, Liza." *This is the way my son's life ends, boxes now full of what once was important to him. These*

things will be used by others, who won't have seen his hand wrapped around
his lacrosse stick playing as hard as he could, or his softness talking to Rouge.

When they had finished, the room looked as if no one had ever
inhabited the space.

###

Finn's urn sat next to Sally Anne's ashes. In some unknown way,
they would keep each other company. That closet became Liza's confessional.
She could get things off her chest. She always had a clearer picture of both of
them when she entered than when she was outside that sacred space. The
closet became a touchstone, and she needed it then. Unseen scars were making
inroads to her heart.

One shelf, two urns.

###

Once when her mom was going into the closet as Liza was leaving,
she told her mom, "I feel close to my mother and Finn when I step inside and
hold them."

Fiona replied, "I know, my darling, I feel the same way. It's as if they
hear and in some unknown way, they tell us to hold fast to the memory of
them."

184

"Sometimes I think I'm betraying Finn if I have thoughts that I want to move on."

"I know this; we must mourn in order to do that. Let the sadness work its way out of you," her mom said.

"Do you think it's working its way out of you, Mom?"

"The trickle is so small and so sticky with sadness, I don't think there is time enough to be all gone."

Liza left her mom alone in the closet.

Fiona picked up Finn's urn. She wanted to smash it and hold it simultaneously. Her anger over Finn's death had not abated. After she rambled on, telling him about Liza and Kate, she picked up Sally Anne's ashes and asked her to look out for Finn. "You now have my child, and I have yours." *I wonder if there is life after death, and if the dead communicate with each other— I hope so.*

The weeks didn't pass by. They wore on. Liza was back at school. Her parents were sleepwalkers during the day and insomniacs at night. They didn't talk much or eat much. They thought it was a good day if no one stopped them to see how they were doing, or if they could get in and out of the grocery store, or a bank before they were given the knowing looks of sympathy.

PERIOD OF QUIET

Home for a long weekend, Kate and Liza sat in the kitchen having a cup of tea. After a period of quiet, Liza said. "I feel so alone at school sometimes." Rouge was scratching the door wanting out. She stood and opened the door. "Finn made it through battle only to be mowed down by a drunk driver. Nothing makes sense."

The teakettle whistled again as Liza had forgotten to turn off the burner. Kate got up and took care of it. "We've all been dealt a severe blow. And freshman year is difficult—so much to get used to." She blew on her tea. "How do you think Mom and Dad are?" asked Kate.

"Mom seems locked up inside herself."

"She's locked in a prison with Finn—let's hope time truly heals."

Rouge barked to be let back in. A blast of fresh air came in with her.

Liza thought "moving on" was a funny term as she looked ahead, because her rear-view mirror was always in plain sight. In the beginning, Liza had a feeling of someone coming from behind and stabbing her in her ribcage. As time passed, it was more a pinprick to her heart. The worst part was having Finn return to us, loving us, and then having his life snuffed out." The Walshes were now the walking wounded.

1973

LATENT FEELINGS

Liza was determined to take every course O'Flarity offered. Sitting in his advanced writing course, a year later, the more Liza tried to erase O'Flarity from her mind, the more he lingered like a cobweb high in the corner that reappears even though it was swept out the day before. She decided to take a chance and see what his reaction would be if she wrote a passionate piece about a college girl and a professor. A few days later he stopped her when class ended and asked to see her. Her hopes were high and her insides were in a flutter.

Sitting behind his desk, O'Flarity motioned Liza to come in. She made a quick survey of the room with its dark green painted walls, oak bookshelves, and stained woodwork. There was a fireplace that had been blocked up, and Liza thought, *Too bad, a fire right now would be perfect.*

O'Flarity pointed to a maroon leather chair and Liza sat down. Coming from behind his desk, he sat on another leather chair facing her, crossing his right leg over his left. With her paper in his hand he asked, "Liza, why did you write this?"

Liza cheeks were burning; she searched his eyes and answered quietly, "Because I have feelings for you."

It was O'Flarity's turn to redden. "Oh, Liza, even if I did have feelings for you, some things are not meant to be. Surely, you understand this. You are a wonderful young woman and your writing shows promise. For now you'll just have to accept this." His hand seemed to be coming towards her, but he moved it upward and ran his fingers through his hair.

"I'm sorry, Professor O'Flarity." She took her paper and walked slowly out of the room. *Please, please come after me.* Could she ever face him again? Angry with herself and O'Flarity, she ran back to her dorm room praying Sarah wouldn't be there. Why had he said, *Even if I did have feelings,* and *for now you'll just have to accept this? For now*—was there a hidden message in his words? Determined to be cool with him, she would show no signs of her feelings ever again. *He had had his chance, and he had almost succumbed. I'm sure he almost touched my face…and yet… he did say, "Even if I did have feelings for you, and for now…"*

Michael walked around his office trying to make sense of Liza Walsh. *My God, I almost touched her. I could fall into her eyes.* In all his years of teaching he had never had an unseemly thought about a student. The room seemed hot so he checked the thermostat. It was fine. Undoing another button on his shirt, he admitted to himself that some students were beyond attractive, but he knew not to touch forbidden fruit. Besides he was intimate with Nancy Gelot. He turned on his radio, sat down at his desk, and tried to grade some essays. He fiddled with his pen and wrote *Liza* on a separate pad next to an essay. When he saw what he had written, he crumpled it up and threw it into the trashcan.

189

###

For her next assignment, Liza wrote a piece about Finn's death. Not naming Finn, she concentrated more on the emotional upheaval that a family endures when a death occurs. Once again O'Flarity asked her to stay a minute after class. With her heart beating loudly, she wondered could he have changed his mind about her?

"Liza, this is a well told story; I know how it feels to lose a loved one." As he sat down on the edge of his desk, he knocked over an empty coffee cup onto the floor.

She backed up as he reached for it. She hoped he didn't see the disappointment that she carried inside.

"I think your story powerful and encourage you to keep writing as an option for a career."

With inflamed cheeks her voice was almost a whisper when she said, "Thank you." The cold wind was a welcome relief as she walked on to her next class.

How did she feel after that conversation? Confused. She didn't want to find out that he was a caring person. This just made her want him more. In November he read one of her pieces aloud in class. She turned scarlet when he complimented her perfect use of hyperbole. She tried not to think about him, but he was creeping into her thoughts on a daily basis.

Every once in a while around campus, Liza would see Professor O'Flarity, and he would ask her how her writing was getting on. If she needed him to look over anything, he would be happy to oblige. Occasionally, she took a new piece of writing for his critique. The room lacked oxygen when she was in his presence. She tried to be dignified, because she knew that dignity sometimes had a propensity to hide feelings. Gradually, he became her mentor and friend.

One time, however, she caught him looking at her in the odd way he had done that first day of class. She thought he lost his train of thought. She saw the faintest hint of a blush on his face. There was no impropriety on his part or Liza's, yet she could feel the sexual tension when they were together.

If she saw him across campus, she would make a quick detour so she would have to walk past him, just to say, "Hi." Once she found him in the dining hall eating a sandwich by himself. She went over to him and asked if he minded her sitting with him.

"Not at all." No sooner had she sat and taken a bite from her sandwich than three other women from her class appeared and sat down. After saying "Hi" to Liza, they talked at O'Flarity without pause, and she never had a chance to speak. She was angry that he didn't shoo them away. After all, Liza could have been having a conference with him. She was determined not to be one of the panting girls.

###

One winter day, cirrostratus clouds were forming a halo around the sun. As Liza and Sarah walked towards their dorm, O'Flarity crossed their path.

"Are you ladies ready for the snowstorm?" Professor O'Flarity asked.

"It will be fun as long as we don't lose power," answered Liza.

"And have you finished your short story?"

Liza's cheeks were red from more than the cold. She smiled shyly and said, "Almost."

When they were out of hearing distance, Sarah turned to Liza and quipped, "Well, who has a crush on whom?" It was Liza's catching of her breath that betrayed her feelings this time. Her answer was a pathetic, "Don't be ridiculous." She was gratified that Sarah didn't pursue the subject, since she had no control over these latent feelings.

A QUANDARY

Working the lights for most of the productions, Liza joined the Theater Arts Club. She never had the confidence to seek an active role, but she enjoyed unconsciously learning the lines as rehearsals progressed. Once or twice she got to prompt an actor who had forgotten his lines.

On one occasion in Lower College, when the actors were rehearsing Eugene O'Neill's *Anna Christie*, Liza was asked to step in for Anna, as she was back in the dorm fighting the flu. The play reminded Liza how difficult it was to change one's life. Their circumstances were profoundly different. Anna was a former prostitute who falls in love and has difficulty turning her life around. On the other hand, Liza remembered the dark days after Finn's death, and the difficulty she faced trying to bring herself back to the living. She didn't have to reach far inside herself to make Anna believable. Having already memorized the play, and with no audience, she could hold her stage fright at bay. The other actors and stage hands gave her a rousing ovation at the end of the rehearsal, and the director said, "We won't have to worry if Alison is sick the night of the play as Liza is also ready for the part." When he said that, all Liza could think of was a line from the play, "Gif me visky, ginger ale on the side, and don' be stingy, baby." She'd need more than a drink to carry the lead.

Reciting for Sarah was one thing, but she had nightmares for weeks about having to take Alison's place as Anna on the night of the play. The audience would become a field of horror, each seat filled with snipers ready to shoot down her performance. Because Alison returned to good health, her nightmares never came to fruition.

###

Swimming every day, allowed Liza's mind to float as much as her body. One Friday afternoon when she was finished doing laps, a male student swam over to her and introduced himself. "Hi! I'm Simon Watts. It seems you like swimming as much as I do."

"It's relaxing." Like a morning glory's tendrils, Liza's mind was reaching into the future instead of being in the moment. *Is this a person I could have a relationship with?*

He seemed nice enough and asked her if she wanted to go into Red Hook for a casual meal later. Returning to her room, she wasn't sure why she had said yes, but Sarah was overjoyed at the news.

"Have I been that anti-social?" Liza asked.

"Not exactly anti-social, but on the road to becoming a loner. Who is he? Is he in Lower College with us?"

"His name is Simon Watts. My guess is he's in Upper College. Doesn't matter anyway as I'm not marrying the guy." *Hmm, you never know.*

"I think he's in my econ class. Does he have sandy blonde hair, and is he tall and thin?"

"Yes, Yes, and Yes."

"I like his face. He has a smile that makes his eyes twinkle. Nice guy, kind of quiet, I think. He's definitely in Lower College," mused Sarah.

"Maybe you should date him, Sarah," she said laughingly. Liza thought, however, that a new friend might be just what she needed.

Simon and Liza walked into Red Hook to the village diner and had burgers, cokes, and fries. They found it easy to talk with each other and did the usual: where are you from? Brothers and sisters? Major? Hobbies? What are you reading? What do you want to do when you grow up?

"My parents live outside of Philadelphia. I have one sister and a brother who died recently at the hands of a drunk driver." Liza paused as she lost her train of thought.

"I'm sorry to hear that. Your family must be reeling."

Nodding, Liza held back tears and took a sip of coke. Gaining her composure, Liza smiled and said, "Sorry."

Since the swim team was out of town that weekend, Liza and Simon decided to meet at the pool on Saturday afternoon. Letting the relationship unfold in its own way, they didn't rush to intimacy. When they finally moved in that direction, they were both caught a little off guard. It was a Friday night, and Simon's roommate was out of town. By now there was heavy petting, only this night Simon sat up and said, "Liza I don't want to stop anymore. How do you feel?"

She was growing fond of Simon, but she definitely wasn't in love. Not finding any reason not to, she asked, "Do you have protection?" Before he replied she knew the answer. What healthy male with an ounce of ego didn't these days?

Simon had had only one love before Liza; it made him as vulnerable as she.

Liza often thought about Professor O'Flarity before, during, and after sexual forays with Simon. Why? She tried to fight these intrusions, but she couldn't. She assumed she was lulled into this coupling with Simon because he was amusing, nice-looking, and considerate.

Over her four years at Bard, Liza managed to take the three courses Professor O'Flarity taught. Competition was tough, as there were four other girls who started Lower College with her and also managed to keep in lockstep with O'Flarity's classes. No sleeping or snoring in his classes; she was wide-awake, and her brain was open to all he said.

Simon and Liza had never discussed being exclusive, but neither ever strayed. They enjoyed each other's company. One evening, she told Sarah, "Simon and I reach for each other and feel safe in each other's arms?"

For Liza's part she found it easy to be with Simon; he would remember to ask how a paper was coming along, or what would she like to do on the weekend. She didn't have a need to make a lot of friends. She and Sarah were close and did things together, when time and circumstance allowed. Otherwise she wasn't afraid to be by herself.

Thinking about Simon left her in somewhat of a quandary. Her feelings were not as strong as they had been with Steve. They were comfortable with each other. That was the highest approbation she could confer on this relationship. Since the word *love* had not been uttered between them, Simon apparently felt the same.

After graduation, Liza thought they would drift apart.

1974

FIERY TO THE TOUCH

The morning of graduation and a half-hour before Liza's parents were to arrive, Simon knocked on her door, and Sarah opened it.

"Hi Sarah, can you believe we're graduating?"

"Yes and No."

"I know what you mean."

Liza was just coming in the door when Simon smiled uncertainly and said, "Liza, do you have a few minutes to talk?"

"Only about ten minutes, I have scads to do before my family arrives."

Sarah piped up, " I know when to make myself scarce."

Liza said, "Are you sure? We can always take a walk."

"I'll come back in fifteen. Besides, it's so clear today, a walk will do me good."

As Sarah left, Simon pulled at Liza to sit with him on her bed. She had a funny feeling in the pit of her stomach. Facing the window, she saw a flurry of activity: students scurrying with boxes, bags and clothes folded over their arms, as well as the detritus of four years in a small space.

"Liza, I love you." Simon smiled and simply asked, "Will you marry me?" She could see his excitement. He continued, "We could have both sets of parents give us their blessing."

The look on Liza's face said it all, because in the next breath he sighed, "You're not ready, are you?" She thought even that question was kind of him.

She still hadn't spoken. She was thinking, *Yes, but I can't take any more of your time.* She bit her tongue so she wouldn't say, *I'm not worthy of you.* She realized that wasn't the thing to say to someone who has just put his soul on the line. It sounded so empty in her mind. Perhaps she had used him, but she didn't want to say that either. So she took the cheapest way out. All she could say was, "Oh, Simon."

A lot of noise in the hall made by graduating classmates grabbed their attention. Simon said, "Take your time, I shouldn't have sprung this on you. I'll go, and we'll meet up for dinner with our families as planned. We can talk later when you've had a chance to think about it. Sorry, Liza."

"I'm the one who's sorry, Simon."

As Simon closed the door, Liza looked at the clutter that needed to be packed.

By dinnertime Liza had pulled herself together, and everything seemed back to normal, at least to Simon's standards.

The families met at a dimly lit French Bistro. A silver, miniature Eiffel Tower was the centerpiece on each table with a votive candle sitting in

the middle. Liza was grateful; she didn't need everyone to see her misery when she thought about what she had just done to this loving friend.

Simon's family was gracious and full of fun, much like her family before Finn's death. Mr. Watts turned to Jack, "You have mighty pretty daughters." Liza blushed. "And Liza is all the good things Simon has said and more." Liza cringed and blushed even more. *Simon must have shared his intentions with his parents. What must they be thinking?*

"Simon is ever so likable, and we enjoyed his visit," said Jack. That year, Simon had spent a week after Christmas with the Walshes.

The waiter came with the salads. Liza had only a few bites. Distractedly, she moved her food around her plate.

At one point during dinner, Fiona smiled at Liza to let her know she knew how she felt. *Oh, Mom, you don't know how I feel, because I haven't been honest with anyone, including myself.*

The truth was Liza had fallen into bed with Simon but not into love. Truth in this case stole hope. They needed a heart-to-heart talk, which she dreaded. How could she have hurt such a great person? The last thing Simon said before leaving was, "Call me when you're ready."

When Sarah and Liza were finishing loading their parents' cars, Liza said, "Simon proposed, and I said nothing. I'm ashamed of myself. How did I not see this coming?" She took a deep breath.

201

The sky was clear, without a cloud marring its surface.

Sarah stood silently as Liza talked, and when she was finished, said, "I never thought Simon and you would work out. You seemed happy but not in love. I saw more feeling in the way you looked at Professor O'Flarity."

Liza couldn't believe what Sarah had just said. "I'm head over heels in love with him, but he told me that 'some things are not meant to be.' I know I'm crazy to entertain the idea, but I can't live without him. He's never hinted that he has feelings for me, but I know he has them—I just know it."

Sarah, without skipping a beat, told Liza to make sure to stop by O'Flarity's office and invite him for a visit to the City of Brotherly Love.

Liza said, "No can do. It's just not meant to be; I made a fool of myself once; I'm not about to do it again." Deciding she needed a walk, she bumped into O'Flarity in front of the dorm.

"Oh, hello," said Liza.

"Have any job prospects yet?"

Liza replied, "I'll be working at J.B. Lippincott in Philadelphia. I guess you never get down that way."

He looked longingly at her and sighed, "Oh, Liza." With that they shook hands, she didn't think she was deceiving herself when she thought their hands were fiery to the touch. They were both blushing when she turned to leave.

She was sure she'd hear from him now. Wouldn't she?

HE WAS GONE

At Lippincott, a publishing house, Liza was headed to work as a researcher. There were many young women who held the same position as Liza. Simon was headed to NYU to do graduate work. She waited a week before she called and said, "Hi Simon, are you free this weekend?"

"Of course."

She grimaced and said, "Perhaps, I could come up for a visit?" His joy and her hesitation once again said it all.

When the "talk" came, Liza knew there were no words that could make things right. They had returned from lunch at a small Tapas Bar in midtown. He with still an ounce of hope, and she with a ton of dread, they were both nervous.

Sunlight was pouring into his tiny kitchen window, and Simon was standing in the light making tea. When he brought the tea tray into the living room, Liza took it from him and asked him to sit next to her. She smiled at him for a few seconds and then simply stated, "Simon, I love you, but I'm not in love with you. I am so sorry for all of this. I would like us to be friends."

This time Simon was silent. When he found his voice he said, "I'm sorry you won't be a constant in my life." He continued and Liza saw the painful smile when he said, "We still have tonight and tomorrow."

Walking around Manhattan, and eating different foods was something they both enjoyed. Liza hadn't grown up with bagels, but after that weekend they became a favorite of hers. Simon even managed to get tickets to *Once Upon A Mattress*, an irony she recognized immediately.

"I'll sleep on the sofa, Liza, and you can have my bed."

Since she was about to lose a dear friend, she didn't sleep.

Mostly in silence, they walked the eighteen blocks to Penn Station. Once in a while, one or the other made a comment about a store window, the fast pace of living in the Big Apple, and at one point, Arthur Ashe's victory over Jimmy Connors at Wimbledon. Simon mentioned Cher's marriage to Gregg Allman that had lasted all of nine days.

Liza thought his *id* was working overtime to pull that one out.

When parting at the train station, Simon said, "I've got to be honest. It'll be too hard to be just friends."

She nodded. As the train pulled up, he kissed her on the cheek and wished her luck.

"I'm so sorry, Simon." When she found a seat and looked out the window, he was gone.

1975

A GHOST

She wondered every day if Michael O'Flarity would call. Was she obsessed? The five letters she composed all had the same theme, different wording, but she had the good sense not to mail them. Aching for him, she had the remembrance of his hand touching hers, and of his words, *even if I did* and *for now* to keep her attached to him.

###

When home, Liza took regular visits to her mom's closet and communed with her other mother and Finn. It didn't matter that they didn't answer. During one visit, Fiona was in her bedroom and couldn't understand the words Liza was saying in the closet, but she could hear the longing in her voice. Liza was talking non-stop about Michael O'Flarity.

When Liza left the closet, Fiona seized the opportunity and asked, "Liza, what's wrong? Come sit and talk with me." They sat on her parent's bed. Rouge managed to jump up and curl herself on Fiona's side of the bed.

Liza unleashed her tormented soul. "Oh Mom, I'm in love with a professor from school. I don't know if he has a wife or is in a committed relationship. Yet I just know he feels something for me. I can't get my mind off him."

Fiona listened but didn't guide her in any way. She shared two thoughts: "Only the ones involved can settle the affairs of the heart," and after a few minutes: "I know you'll find your way."

Hugging her mom, Liza said, "Thanks Mom, I really ought to be getting back now. I'll let Rouge out." *When will I ever escape the labyrinth of frustration?*

Later she had little recall about that first year in Philadelphia. It was her "wasteland." She was a moribund mess. She drifted from party to party, from book to book, from home to work, and from event to event, except when Sarah visited. Sarah had a job in advertising in New York City. Sometimes she would take the train to Philadelphia, or Liza would take the train to New York. Sarah had started dating a man named Allen Winestock, a financial advisor trainee at a big brokerage firm. By the end of the first year after graduation, Sarah said, "Liza, I'm mad about Allen."

Although they kept in touch by phone, their visits to each other slowed when Allen came into the picture. Mostly, Liza sat at home and pined for Michael O'Flarity.

Working in Philadelphia also, Kate was living with Andrew. Fiona and Jack weren't keen on the idea at first, but gradually came around. On the weekends when Andrew was busy, she would see if Liza were up for going to a movie or a concert. Liza always felt secure in Kate's presence. Her social-

207

working skills came naturally to her. She seemed to anticipate needs before they were expressed.

Having tea in Kate's living room, which was mainly odds and ends of furniture from their mom and dad and other bits from Andrew's parents, Liza said,

"Kate, I want to share something with you."

"Shoot."

"I'm in love with one of my professors from school. I don't know what to do. I don't even know if he's married." Liza looked down at her lap. She noticed the rag rug they used to dance on before their mom had let them redo their bedroom. She was happy her sister had the rug.

Kate listened, didn't make any judgments but smiled and gave Liza a hug. "You'll just have to find out, won't you?"

Liza couldn't help thinking that the people Kate ministered to in her professional capacity must light up when they knew she was approaching.

"So this is why you back away when any man makes advances towards you."

"Every thought I have is of him. In between sentences, when I pause to take a breath, in my dreams, he's like a ghost. I can't touch him, but I know he's there."

1976

DISAPPEARING AT AN ALARMING RATE

On a cold, snowy evening in January, Liza was reading Saul Bellow's *To Jerusalem and Back,* sipping some Chablis, a gift from Jack on her last visit home. "Entertain," Jack had urged her. Liza figured that entertaining herself had to count or the wine would turn to vinegar.

When the phone rang, she assumed it was her parents or Kate, yet deep down she was praying it was Michael. Of course he didn't have her phone number, but he could call information. Her first assumption was correct, as her parents were on the phone. There was a hesitation in their voices, so she knew something was up, and it wasn't good. Liza interrupted her mom when she was asking her about work and said, "Mom, what's wrong?"

After a pause her mom spoke up. "I'm afraid my breast cancer has returned."

"Oh, Mommy," was all she could murmur. Her dad broke in at this point and said that they had an appointment at Johns Hopkins in Baltimore on the following Monday.

"I'll go with you."

"Perhaps it's best at this point if just the two of us go," said Jack. After a few more attempts at banal conversation, they each sent their love to touch across the wires and said, "Good night."

Looking around her efficiency apartment, she realized the only thing she had done with Sarah's help was to paint the walls a pale, pale yellow. Her parents had given her a sofa bed, two brown leather chairs, and a French metal table with two metal folding chairs.

Shaking her head, she cried, "Mommy, no, you can't have cancer again."

Maybe it was time to call God back. Willing to make deals that were too foolish to share, she felt mentally that she was a mendicant on her hands and knees. Fear that her mom might come to rest in that airless closet made her stomach queasy. Not knowing much about cancer, she knew this: its comeback wasn't good.

Calling Kate, she found the line was busy. She must be talking to Mom and Dad. When Liza finally got through, she blurted out, "I'm scared for Mom."

Kate, with a catch in her voice, said, "Me, too."

"What should we do? "

"We rallied round her once, we'll do it again."

Their mom hadn't told Kate anything other than what she had shared with Liza.

"Oh Kate, I need your hand right now."

"I need yours, too. It's so quiet with the snow. Try and get to sleep. We've got to be at our best for Mom.

"I love you. Good night, Mrs. Boobytrap."

"I love you, too. Good night, Mrs. Burgee."

###

The next morning, Kate called and roused Liza. She had thought more on the situation. "Let's take turns going home to be with Mom and Dad. Do you want to go first?"

"Sure. I'll leave Friday from work."

The train rides on Fridays were a time for Kate and Liza to prepare themselves. The news from Hopkins wasn't good. Fiona's cancer was stage IV this time, and the cancer was now in her lungs.

After two months, Jack was losing as much weight as Fiona. Liza had to brace herself each visit when she opened their front door. Her mom's body was disappearing at an alarming rate. To pick up a glass was hard for her. Liza would catch glimpses of their steadfast love for each other. Jack would touch Fiona's shoulder as he passed her, or take her hand and put it to his cheek. At times Liza felt she was intruding. That was never even hinted at, but there was such devotion in their eyes for each other.

I'M SORRY YOU'RE SICK

On an afternoon as the light was fading, Jack brought Fiona a letter and said, "I think it's from your mother."

Reluctantly, she asked Jack to open it. One sentence: *Fiona, I'm sorry you're sick. Mother.*

Jack gave the note to Fiona. "It must have taken a lot for her to write this."

Fiona stuck the note under her pillow. "Jack, please call my mother and ask her to visit." She wished her mother were a bright spot in her life.

Liza went back to the window seat where she had read her stories to Fiona, only now she was reading aloud *A Tale of Two Cities* at Fiona's request. When her mom asked her to read this book, she was puzzled. Of all the books—why this one? Of course she wouldn't question her choice aloud. Maybe it would come to her as she read.

The opening line wasn't helpful. There was no best of times, so the paradox didn't work. No one could do this for Fiona. There would be no trading places. So many double themes...best and worst, light and darkness, hope and despair. They would live these themes till Fiona succumbed to this cancer.

Liza remembered the words of Lucie Manette, "I have sometimes sat alone here of an evening, listening, until I have made the echoes out to be the echoes of all the footsteps that are coming by-and-by into our lives."

Rouge was now eleven and left Fiona's bed only to go outdoors and to eat. She got heavier as Fiona got thinner.

Jack came into the bedroom on a Saturday morning. Fiona watched snow blanket the tree branches outside their window. The sky was gray and when the wind blew, the snow swirled like smoke escaping a chimney.

"Fiona, I've made steps for Rouge to get on and off the bed so she won't disturb you."

"How thoughtful. Shall we try them out?"

"Come on, Rouge. Come on, girl."

Rouge seemed bewildered.

Jack left, came back with a biscuit, and put it on the top step. He coaxed Rouge to the top.

"She's been my stalwart companion. I honestly think she knows what I'm feeling and licks me when she wants to tell me so."

"I can't argue with that. I'm glad she's with you when one of us can't be."

Rouge sat up on the bed and gave one short bark.

214

Jack drove to the house and picked her up, but Mrs. Crosby didn't say anything beyond, "It was kind of you to fetch me."

When Fiona opened her eyes, her mother was sitting in a chair at the side of the bed. She tried her best to smile, and Rouge lifted her head.

"I don't know what to say to you...will 'I'm sorry' do?" Her mother pressed her hands on the side of her dress.

"It will do just fine. Thank you for coming, Mother."

"I became my mother, and the three of you suffered because of it. If I could take back the years..."

"You have by coming here."

"Yes, your father"...her voice trailed off.

"Mother, give me your hand." As Fiona touched her mother's hand, she realized that she didn't remember the last time she had held it. *I must have as a child. Surely, crossing a street.* She closed her hand on her mother's and felt a pulse of grace to this action. "I'm happy for you, Mother. I know it took courage."

"I'm happy that you didn't become me."

Silence engulfed them.

As her mother stood to leave, she bent over and kissed Fiona's cheek. That was the last Fiona saw her.

MY LIFE HAD MEANING

Once when Liza was with her mom, and neither had talked for an hour, Fiona looked at Liza and commented, "Liza, do you remember when we bought Rouge, and the man, I forget his name, told Finn if he took good care of the dog, the dog would do the same for him. Well, it wasn't Finn she took care of, since she couldn't go with him, but she has taken good care of me, as all of you have."

Liza, sitting on the floor petting Rouge while her mom spoke, thought a minute, looked up at Fiona, and said, "Mom, don't worry about Rouge. We love her, and we'll take good care of her."

"I know you will, Liza. You must take care of each other, too."

When Fiona was fast asleep, Liza had to curtail her closet visits. Otherwise she felt selfish. She always cried and didn't want her mom to hear that. Should she put her mother and Finn in her old bedroom? What if her mom wanted to talk with them, to prepare her place with them? Better to let them be.

Throughout that spring, she read to her mom on weekends. Fiona got weaker as Liza read on. Even though they both knew the ending, Fiona wasn't prepared to die until Liza finished. One of the last things Fiona told her was, "I think my life had meaning, and my death will bring medicine a step further towards a cure."

Stricken because Fiona used the past tense, Liza thought about *meaning,* and wondered if she had meaning for her mom.

A GOOD LAUGH

Fiona's brothers, Peter and Liam, had taken to stopping by once a week to check in. Sitting next to the bed, and one of them, sometimes holding her hand, often said nothing. Otherwise they told Fiona about something from the past that had come into their minds. Peter seemed to be making an effort not to stir the Catholic pot.

On one visit, Liam asked Fiona, "Who started the food fight in the kitchen one night when the four of us were eating pie before bed?"

Fiona laughed till it literally hurt. "Can you believe? It was Sally Anne."

"It was worth it, as I don't have much to laugh about these days." Fiona told him more than once. "Everyone is so solemn around me. Thank you for a good laugh."

Coming into the room, Jack asked, "What's so funny?"

They almost couldn't contain themselves. Liam responded, "It was the actual throwing of food. We just didn't do that in our house growing up."

"Sally Anne started it. It wasn't like her," Fiona said.

Kind enough to stop by on his way home, the doctor said he was pretty sure that she had cracked a rib and that tincture of time would be the best medicine. With a smile, a cracked rib, and little time, Fiona quickly fell to sleep that night.

NO RULES FOR DYING

"This wig is too cumbersome. Jack, can you hand me my cap?" Fiona dropped the wig on her night table. She looked around the room that she had shared with him since 1946. At least four times it had changed colors, and a balcony had been added. It was presently a soft blush color. The bureau was now cluttered with brown bottles, pill containers, tissues, an ice bucket, a tan vomit basin, and three vases with yellow roses, her favorite flower, one of which the petals were dried up and falling off.

The one thing that hadn't changed was the bed. Their bed: the bed where children had been conceived, worries dispelled, and laughter plentiful. She couldn't help but notice the dark outline of a bloodstain on their silk crimson coverlet. She ran her fingers across it. The cleaners had failed in their efforts to remove it.

Seeing her children's portraits on the opposite wall each morning made her happy. This room was Jack's and her sanctuary.

Jack carefully placed the felt cap on her head and sat down on the edge of the bed. Rouge took the hint, got off the bed, and settled herself on the floor by Fiona.

Fiona touched her cheekbones, which seemed even more prominent, and her lips, which were always dry and cracked. A scarf over the dressing table mirror was a favor she had asked of Jack, as she didn't need to see herself in the stages of decline.

"Jack, I'm preparing to leave you, and if I make a mess of it, please forgive me."

Jack, swallowing hard, said, "Sh…Fiona, my love, there are no rules for dying." He put his hand to her cheek. "I'm drowning, Fee. There is so much I want to tell you."

"I know. But nothing more needs to be said." A few weeks ago she had reread every Valentine letter he had written to her since the first year they were married. The letters were in her night table drawer, bound together with a yellow ribbon. She coughed. Jack lifted her head and put a straw to her mouth from a glass filled with water. Each year she cried for days over the letters that carried such tenderness and love. But it was much more than the words. It was the everyday with him.

Fiona took Jack's hand to her breast. "I disbelieved the possibility of death the first go-round, but now I accept it. Please accept it, too; let me go, Jack." She smiled at him, hoping the smile was the bearer of many words. "I will go gently." She knew him down to the freckle on his left baby toe. She knew it would take a little more time for him to let go. When had he ever refused her anything?

He slipped off his shoes and lay down beside her. This was once her favorite time of day, when the night seeps in slowly, pushing the day westward. Now it was a reminder of one day less.

"You seem far away," said Jack.

"I'm thinking of you, my love, you. I know that if you were dying, a piece of me would die, too… I'm taking a piece of you with me Jack, and I'll be leaving a piece of myself behind … you were the first man I kissed, and you'll be the last." She was so tired, but at peace. If she allowed him to speak his thoughts, it would break her heart, and she would break down and make a mess of things. Putting a finger to his lips, she closed her eyes.

Through his tears, Jack whisper-sang in a quavering voice, *Goodnight Sweetheart*, "Dreams will enfold you. In each one I'll hold you."

Fiona opened her eyes, smiled and then fell asleep comforted once again by his voice.

FOUR URNS, ONE SHELF

Dad sang to Mom one last time, and Liza didn't know if Mom heard him, but she liked to think she did.

When Fiona lapsed into a coma, Liza, Kate, and Jack were standing bedside. The doctor had come and checked her vital signs and given her a heavy dose of morphine to alleviate pain. "It will be soon. She's ready."

She remained in the coma. Around ten o'clock in the evening of the third day, as the three of them were getting ready for their night vigils, her mouth fluttered ever so slightly, and she was gone. The bedside light flickered, and Rouge whimpered.

Each kissed Fiona and then hugged each other.

Jack removed Fiona's cap and the photo that Finn had had with him when he died fell onto the pillow.

"She wanted all of us with her," said Kate.

Jack nodded.

"Dad, would you like us to leave you alone?" Liza asked.

"Thank you."

When the girls left the room, Jack shut the door. Hearing him sing, *My*

Girl's an Irish Girl—they remained motionless, crippled.

Rouge was the last to leave the room. Her muzzle rested on Fiona's chest. Until the undertaker came, she stayed with Fiona. When Fiona was taken out of the house, Rouge stayed on the floor by Fiona's side of the bed.

###

Fiona's funeral and Finn's were not alike. After watching Fiona slowly wither away, the family felt a sad acceptance. The priest's words didn't bother Liza this time, as she didn't hear anything he said. Glad that Fiona's fight was over and that there was no more pain, the notes they put in her coffin before she was cremated lacked anger.

Liza's grandparents walked in with the family at Fiona's service. The Walshes were surprised after Jack's conversation with Mr. Crosby on the phone.

"Our daughter should be buried in the family plot."

Jack, fragile but determined, held his ground and said, "Fiona belongs with Finn and Sally Anne."

Liza thought, *She certainly doesn't want to lie next to you. The ground's cold enough.*

At the house after the service, Liza saw a tear on her grandmother's cheek and offered her a tissue. A hint of a smile crossed her grandmother's face as she accepted it. Liza saw her own mom's smile in her grandmother's and could almost hear her mom say, "My darling daughter."

Gazing ahead sternly, her grandfather held his chin high. He and Mrs. Crosby stayed in a corner of the living room, beside the tall case clock, as they had when Finn died. Liza went out of her way to offer them food. Her grandfather shook his head quickly not looking her in the eye, but her grandmother took a cucumber sandwich and said, "Thank you, Liza."

Her grandfather glared icily at both of them. Liza felt as though she had been slapped. *After all these years,* she thought, *I'm still not a part of the family to him.* She slipped away and found her dad.

"Liza, sorry, I don't have the energy to take on your grandfather. Help me say goodbye to friends who are leaving." Taking her arm, he stood along with her and Kate at the front door and once again went through the motions, each holding a river of tears at bay. Sitting next to Jack, Rouge touched his pant leg.

Her grandparents were the last to leave. Her grandfather tipped his hat as he went through the door, still not focusing on anyone. Her grandmother, however, said each person's name and gave each a hug. She even gave Rouge a pat on the head.

Fiona's ashes sat between Sally Anne's and Finn's in the closet. Once when Liza came home earlier than her dad had expected, she found him in the closet. "Do you visit the closet regularly?" asked Liza.

224

"Your mom brought me in after Finn died. It's nice to know they're safe in here. It's a confessional of sorts."

Grinning, Liza said, "I feel the same way."

The next time Liza was with Kate, she asked her whether she was a closet regular. "Yes," Kate replied.

"You realize we have a mausoleum in Dad's bedroom?"

"Yeah, but it's too soon for us to divest ourselves of the dead. Let's focus on Dad instead of the closet."

Liza's visits to the closet were longer now, and she took Rouge in with her. It didn't seem as lonely that way. She sat on the stool with a tee shirt of Fiona's in her lap. Rouge laid her head on the shirt, sniffed and looked around. After not finding Fiona, Liza knew Rouge would leave. She could hear her lie down on the floor on her mom's side of the bed.

Immediately after Fiona's death, Rouge stopped eating. The vet told Jack, "This happens when dogs are particularly close to a person who's died. If you could become a reason for Rouge to live, then she might be okay." Looking Rouge over, the vet commented on a little rhyme by Robert Frost. "The old dog barked backward without getting up I can remember when he was a pup."

Jack went into a routine to lift Rouge's mood, taking her for long walks, sitting on the floor, petting and talking to her for long spells at a time.

225

Slowly, Rouge came around but still insisted on sleeping on the floor by Fiona's side of the bed.

Rouge saved Jack as much as he saved her.

Although Kate and Liza gave most of Fiona's clothes to Goodwill, each managed to find a few keepsakes. Liza kept a navy linen blazer, which she loved because it carried Fiona's scent. She wore it many times. When she got a stain on it, she sent it to the cleaners. What had she been thinking? Fiona's scent, a mixture of Ambush and Ivory soap, was now gone. She could have had her mom's essence for a long time but thoughtlessly purged it from her jacket. Maybe it was time to separate herself physically from the dead. Maybe it was time to shut the door on the mausoleum closet. She wondered if that were possible.

That winter, Rouge died of old age. She was cremated too, and her ashes were placed in an urn in front of Fiona's.

Fours urns, one shelf.

Jack's demeanor was painful for the girls to watch. The loss of Rouge seemed to be the last straw. He used to have a purposeful stride; now it was more of a weary shuffle. He grew so quiet that the girls hesitated before speaking to him, afraid to disturb his cloistered thoughts. He would go from room to room in the darkest part of the night as if looking for Fiona, Finn, or Rouge. Perhaps he was looking for himself, too.

1977

A WILD LOVE CHASE

In 1977, her last spring in Philadelphia, Liza saw a way of making contact with Michael O'Flarity. When she received her *Bardian Alumni/ae News,* in it was a farewell acknowledgement to him, and a wish for good luck in his new position at Claremont-McKenna College in LA. In a split second decision, she was ready to fasten her seatbelt and head West. She called Kate to tell her that she was thinking of moving to LA and why.

Kate, with a smile Liza could feel over the phone said, "Go get him, Mrs. Boobytrap."

By hook or by crook, she would find a job. She called the *Los Angeles Times* to enquire about job openings. There was an opening in the Opinion section and the newspaper was asking for three written opinions from applicants. She bought the *LA Times* for a week before deciding what to write. Their articles covered the gamut from political opinions to optical fiber used to carry telephone traffic.

Liza's first opinion carried this headline: "Star Wars." Lead: "Who hasn't seen it?" Her second opinion noted: "Bacteria In Lab Makes Insulin." Lead: "What's the future of gene splicing for other purposes?" The third opinion was "The UK celebrates 25 years with Queen Elizabeth on the throne." Lead: "Can the monarchy survive another 25?"

A week after she had sent in these opinions, Liza received a call from the Editor, Ron Sochow, asking her if she could come for an interview. She could not suppress her reply, "You bet." When she hung up, she was mortified. *Bumpkin, I'll bet that's what he's thinking.* At any rate she was thrilled to have an interview and a few days later felt confident answering the questions posed.

In early middle age, Ron was tall and sturdy with dark brown hair and an Alfalfa cowlick. His amber colored eyes with minute flecks of brown floating in his irises were fascinating. He paid attention to Liza's every word.

Trying to sit still, and not showing how nervous she was, Liza asked him, "Why do you like working here, Mr. Sochow?"

Scratching the side of his face, he smiled and said. "Well" he hesitated, "I like the activity, the hum of the place, the deadlines, the possibilities, but most of all I like getting to the truth of the matter and sharing it with the public." He became distracted as a plane flew past the window and its shadow darkened the room for a second. "Everyone has secrets when you come down to it. It's up to us to find out if the secrets should be told."

"I never thought of it that way, but it's something I'll ponder if I get to work here." She immediately liked him. So much like her dad. "In fact, I'd love to work here, Mr. Sochow."

When the interview was behind her, and she was flying home, she became pessimistic and decided she didn't stand a chance. The woman in the seat next to her wanted to talk; Liza wanted to sleep away the frustration she felt about the failed interview, and the undoing of her plan to be near Michael O'Flarity. *Am I on a wild love chase?*

A week later, she received the call telling her that she had the position if she wanted it. "Want it! Are you kidding?" She exclaimed. "It's a dream come true."

Liza gave *Lippincott* a month's notice and impatiently waited to head west. Before she left Philadelphia, she did another daring thing. She sent Michael O'Flarity a note congratulating him on his new position, telling him that she, too, was moving to LA, and wondering if they could get dinner somewhere, as they would both be new in town. She told him that she had landed a job at the *Times*, and if he thought it doable, he could contact her there. She mailed it to Bard, knowing they would forward it.

"What if he rejects me? What if I'm being a fool?" She asked Kate. "What if he's married? None of the girls at school thought he was."

Kate simply stated, "I guess you won't know, if you don't go and find out."

"You're right, Kate; California, here I come."

Jack was happy for her, but in his eyes, she saw how her absence was another scar was forming. Knowing he wouldn't even hint at his distress made it all the more difficult. *Am I being selfish, or headstrong?* She loved Jack dearly; he was her dad after all. Yet her desire for Michael O'Flarity was as strong as the magnetic North Pole; she could not shake herself out of his field.

She had to do this. There was no turning in any direction but his. But was it the right direction? Her desire was a limitless blue sky no matter the weather.

###

"Dad, think about coming to LA for a few days and help me get settled
Happy to oblige, he tried hard to be upbeat and succeeded for her sake.

Exploring Highland Park, Liza decided she could walk to work since it was neighborhood close to the *Times* office. They found a few take-out places, Villa Sombrero, and Langer's Deli, Ralph's Grocery Store, which was called a Groceteria, a movie theater, and Ivers Department Store.

"I'll be glad to buy you a car," Jack said.

It seemed pointless, as she would take public trans when she needed a car and didn't need the parking and insurance hassle hanging over her. "Thanks, don't think I'll need one, but if I do, I'll let you know."

"I've been looking through the rental ads in the paper; there's an apartment in Highland Park, unfurnished, and the price looks right," said Jack.

Getting out of a taxi, as they approached the building Liza commented, "Wow, talk about an oversized stucco box." After the inside tour, which took all of two minutes, Liza said, "This will work. I really like the east-facing window in the kitchen for morning sun." Jack read over the contract and Liza signed it.

After procuring furniture, Liza took his hand and said, "Dad, I couldn't have done this without your help. I'll call you every Sunday, and we'll catch up."

"Oh no you won't. I'll call you. You can't carry that kind of bill. Coast to coast is expensive."

Two beautiful oriental carpets, which were in storage, were to be a present from Jack for Liza's new home. The dominant color was a robin's egg blue, and Liza was thrilled to have them. She had a vague recollection that she had played on them as a small child.

Jack smiled and said; "They were in the living room and dining room before your mom redecorated when you were about five." Both felt surprise that she remembered them.

"When I return home, I'll send them."

The last morning of Jack's visit, he handed Liza an envelope. She recognized her mom's handwriting on the front of it.

"I just found letters to each of us in Fiona's bed-side table from a few months before she died. I couldn't go through her things right away; it was too painful. Sorry I didn't find them sooner—here's yours." He picked lint from his sweater, "Read it when I'm gone. With the deaths of Finn, Fiona, and even Rouge, I felt that I had won the lottery when I found the letters. Each time I read mine, Fiona gives another piece of herself to me. I hope you'll find the same thing."

"Oh, Dad!"

Taking a cab to the airport, they made small talk. Liza waited for her father to board before she left. Standing quietly as was their habit, she felt a sadness creeping up her spine as she said goodbye to her father.

REGRET IS A CHEAP EMOTION

After her taxi ride home, she ran into her apartment, threw off her jacket, and opened the letter.

December 29, 1976

Dearest Liza,

I imagine you sitting in the closet talking with the four of us. Because I think maybe Rouge is with us, too. It was too hard for her ever to leave my side. I know the closet is a place to let the sorrow dribble out of you, but we both know I'm in a better place. So, I'm hoping that will be helpful for you. You have been a daughter that every mother would wish for. You inherited your mother's kindness and her ability to see the best in others. Not only was I happy to have you for a daughter, I was also happy for Kate and Finn to have you as a sister.

My darling, I know you're in love with a man who doesn't know of your longing to be with him. I think you are old enough now to write a letter or do something to have him know of your feelings. That way you can put this matter to rest one way or another. Although I'll not have a chance to meet him, I do know he must be special to have won your heart. If he's married, I pray you will do the right thing.

235

More than anything I wish for you to be happy. Not an easy wish for Dad, Kate, and you. This sorrow has got to end, so that the three of you will get on with the business of living.

It is Jack I worry about the most. He has a tendency to keep his feelings to himself. If you will talk to him about all of our deaths, I think it will be helpful to both of you. In case you've forgotten, he has the best smile in the world. It hasn't been in evidence for a long time.

Perhaps the closet wasn't the best of ideas. I pity the last person alive that has to make the decision of what to do with all the urns. It is too much of a burden to pass on to grandchildren. Maybe the ashes could be taken to Cape May and scattered on the water. So when you are up to discussing it, the three of you need to take action regarding this matter. With or without the closet, I hope to remain in your heart.

How to end a letter of this type is a mystery to me. How lucky for me that you came into my life just when I had lost my beloved sister. Now I will hope that luck will come your way in the form of Michael O'Flarity. If not him, then perhaps another man who will turn your heart and head in a new direction. Just remember that regret is a cheap emotion.

Back to the ending— I'll just say good night, sweet Liza. Think of me sleeping peacefully with Sally Anne, Finn, and perhaps Rouge. You have my love, Mom.

Liza sat for a while feeling blessed. Imagine her and her mom both having the same idea about Michael. Getting the okay signal that what she had done was the right thing. Now it was the waiting game. Could she manage that?

Her mother's photo from junior year at Chestnut Hill was in her underwear drawer. This way she would see her as each day began. Her mom's letter went under the photo for safekeeping.

PLAY IT SLOW

Liza had been in Los Angeles for two months and hadn't heard from Michael. She was finally reconciled to the phrase, "Some things are not meant to be." *Have I moved here for nothing? What was I thinking?*

Walking to the bus one morning, she saw an attractive man coming out of a neighboring building, walking in the same direction. He smiled and said, "Good morning." She smiled back and wished him a good day. The same thing happened the next day. On the third day he said, "Hi, may I walk with you?"

She thought *Why not?* And said so. This was her chance at a new beginning. Funny how much information can be shared in a ten-minute walk. Larry Moore had graduated from UC-Berkeley Boalt and had just taken a position with O'Meany & Mihar doing insurance litigation. Within a week he had asked her out to dinner. Over Saturday night's dinner, Liza found out he had been raised in Ardmore, a stone's throw from Bryn Mawr; they had lived in neighboring communities growing up.

When Larry listened to Liza he cocked his head ever so slightly as if hearing what she was thinking, too. He had had a brother die in Viet Nam, and Liza knew from the anguished forming of words to tell his brother's story that time had not become his friend yet. When a solitary tear escaped his eye, Liza reached for his hand and said, "I know."

238

She didn't tell him about Finn then because her wound was beginning to close ever so slightly and she wasn't ready to pry it open. It was Larry's moment and she listened.

After that first dinner together, they made plans to grab a bite to eat and see a movie on Sunday night, *The Tin Drum,* an award winning German film. During the movie, he reached for her hand. She had forgotten what human touch was capable of. She thought to herself, "Play it slow, Liza, and see where this takes you."

UNCERTAINTY IS A CRUEL CONSTANT NAGGING OF THE SOUL

When she collected the mail Monday afternoon at work, she received a postcard with a photo of Stevenson Library at Bard. *Could it be?* Michael O'Flarity supplied his phone number and asked her to call him. After seven years...

She felt the old excitement that she had felt when she was in his classroom and in conference with him. *So much for Larry.* Should she call Michael that day or wait a few days? The words didn't change, but each time she read it she found her mind filled with different possibilities. When she walked to the water fountain, a colleague kidded, "You sure have a bounce in your step." After the longest thirty-two minutes, she dialed the number.

Michael answered the phone. When he said, "Hello," she thought she wouldn't be able to speak.

After clearing her throat several times, she managed to identify herself. "Hi Michael, it's Liza." Playing with the paperclips on her desk, she couldn't stop her heart from somersaulting.

"I wondered if you'd call. It's good to hear your voice."

"Yours too." *I just said Michael and not Professor O'Flarity.* She blushed.

"I'm between classes right now. Could we meet at Tanellies on Friday night at eight?"

"I'll be there."

For the four days she waited, she couldn't stop smiling, and couldn't concentrate on work. More than once she told herself to pull it together. Joy flitted around her insides.

A colleague caught her giggling for no discernable reason. In her apartment she danced with no music playing. Not giving it a second thought, she ate burnt toast. Songs she had forgotten were sung in the shower every morning. She felt herself on a swing, going higher and higher, just thinking of him.

On Friday night, when she stepped out of the taxi, she saw him standing with his hands in his pockets. He walked over to her, kissed her cheek and said, "We have a lot of catching up to do." Liza took his offered arm and smiled till she thought her face would break.

The restaurant had posters of Italy around the walls. Their booth had a poster of the Ponte Vecchio in Florence. Votive candles flickered on red and white checked tablecloths that finished the décor.

Seated, they looked at each other for a long minute. The lighting was dim enough that she hoped he didn't see her burning cheeks.

"You can't imagine my surprise when I got your note. I'm really glad you sent it."

"I am, too."

Michael talked some about Bard and then about his new job. "I can't believe our luck moving to California at the same time."

Liza smiled. "How did you manage having so many adoring female students in your classes?" Liza asked.

The waiter interrupted by filling the water glasses. They locked eyes on each other.

When the waiter had gone, Michael said, "You were the only one who made me think twice about my obligation in the classroom."

"You have no idea the turmoil I've suffered since the first day in your class."

"Yes, I do. I've felt the same way. Something about you pulled at me."

Between courses, Michael took Liza's hands in his.

After they finished a meal of Linguine Carbonara, accompanied by Chianti Classico, Michael ordered a small lava cake to share and a bottle of Prosecco. He made a toast. "I might be presumptuous, but I'm going to toast our future together."

Liza raised her glass; she had no words because she had no breath. Falling, falling, more in love with Michael as each second passed.

Back at her place, standing in the hallway, Liza asked, "Would you like a nightcap?" He declined, and she could feel her body stiffen and a quick forming fog moved through her mind.

"I have dreamed of this meeting for a long time. There were times at Bard where I just wanted to hold you. When you wrote the story about the professor and the student, what I really wanted to write was *someday*."

242

Running his fingers through his hair, he said, "There is, however, something I need to share with you, if we are to continue seeing each other, and it's something I want you to think about carefully. I'm married. Well, separated."

"Did you say married?" She stared at Michael and the long tunnel like hall behind him.

"I haven't lived with my wife for ten years. She had an affair, and I didn't have it in my heart to forgive her. The man she had the affair with died. She was devastated losing him, and I was devastated losing her." He took a deep breath. "She was the second loss in my life. My first love left me for another man, too."

Liza could feel her face fall and her insides rive as Michael continued.

"My wife and I never divorced. We have lived separate lives." He held the top part of his right arm with his left hand. "Before you ask, I have dated some, but I've never let anyone touch my heart after my marriage disintegrated." With that, his hand brushed her cheek, he smiled sadly, and walked down the corridor. Turning back, he said, "Think carefully; I'll call you soon."

Sitting in her kitchen, Liza's mind was a pinball machine, thoughts going every which way. *What have I gotten myself into? No, it's okay; we can handle this. Michael will get divorced and then we'll marry.* Sitting down, she realized she was perspiring. *Why would two women leave him? Things happen. Perhaps they were never meant to be, but I was. Where's Kate when I need her? Mom wants me to do the right thing.* Uncertainty is a cruel constant nagging of the soul.

A KISS ON THE CHEEK

Liza woke to the sound of the phone. *I hope it's not Larry!* When she realized that she had forgotten about Larry, her heart quickened while thinking, *what to do?*

"So, Miss Liza, where would you like to go tonight?"

Make no decision until you have time to think how to handle this.

"Larry, I'm in the middle of something. May I call you back later this morning?"

"Sure, call me at the office. I'll be there till late this afternoon."

"Will do."

Where is my head? Larry is a great guy, and they were beginning to have feelings for each other. How to explain to him without hurting him? Wasn't that a joke? Can't be done. She thought of the saying her fifth grade teacher, Sister Benavenuda, used to use, "Tell truth and shame the devil." When Liza studied Shakespeare in college, she found out these words were spoken by Hotspur to Glendower in *Henry IV*.

She called Larry back and asked him to come to her place for dinner. It was time for a candid talk with him that wouldn't amount to an assault of his heart.

###

Larry and Liza hadn't had but a few dates. Though it wasn't a breakup, it was a situation that still needed an explanation. She told him, "When I met you, I had just about given up on the love of my life and thought I should move on." Over a steak and a salad, she explained everything, so he wouldn't try and fill in pieces when he left. "It's been seven years of wishing and hoping."

Trying to smile, he said in a dispirited voice, "I can't compete with that. I'm glad he called now, rather than a year from now. Thanks for taking the truthful route. I didn't have the courage to do that with my first love, and I've always regretted it." He hesitated and added, "I admire you."

After a minute of silence, Larry started talking about the wine they were drinking. It was a California red, which was not a staple in her parents' house. They were French all the way. Sometimes, not often, a German dessert wine might appear.

The conversation moved to books and their jobs. When they both knew it was time to say goodnight, they wished each other well, and in her heart, Liza was hoping that she would see him with another woman before he saw her with Michael.

He kissed her on the cheek and walked down the dimly lighted corridor.

A HUNGRY KISS

Wednesday came, and Michael hadn't called. Liza became anxious, and by Friday she was panicked. She called in sick at work that day, and remained in a chair looking out her living room window. The sky was clear with no clouds, and the sun moved from east to west as it does every day. Around noon she ate a ham sandwich, which she didn't bother to dress. She followed this with a glass of milk. Plopping back into the chair, she began to cry. *What was wrong? Everything seemed so perfect. How could he do this to me? I thought we understood each other.* She was becoming unraveled by a dark anxiety and withering from within. Her brain was riding the highway of sleeplessness and there was no place turn off or park.

On Saturday night, Michael went to Liza's apartment with a bouquet of roses. Liza, who had been crying steadily, was now sitting in her dark living room. She opened the door and choked, "I thought you were dead."

"I've been such a fool. Can you forgive me?"

"Tell me why."

"Am I asking too much from a young girl like you? You have your whole life ahead of you. I've already lived half of mine. I'm still married. You must be absolutely sure before we move ahead."

"We can work this out. We can!"

"If you allow me to stay tonight, you won't be able to rid yourself of me. Let me turn on the light. I need to see your face."

The light revealed her reddened face, and from her blue eyes he recognized a lust, a lust for him that he hadn't seen since his own college love affair. All he could murmur was, "Oh, Liza, I'm so sorry. Forgive me?"

"I'm yours, Michael, till death do us part."

She didn't want that night to end, so she took his hand and led him to her bedroom. After lighting the sandalwood candles she had hoped to use a week ago, she stood in front of him. He asked her to stand still and close her eyes. He then asked her to raise her arms, and he lifted her sweater, ever so slowly dragging the tips of his fingers over her skin as he continued. He undid her slacks slowly and gently pulled them down while once again slightly grazing her thighs with the tips of his fingers. When he undid her bra, she thought she could stand this no longer, and no longer stand without responding. By the time her underpants were off, with Michael using the same slow method, she was sure she would faint. Following his lead, she slowly undressed him. Their eyes met and they kissed. It was a hungry kiss that left no room for doubt.

Sunday morning came, and she awakened to Michael's blue eyes taking all of her in. "I wanted to find you, Liza."

"I wanted you to find me." As Liza uttered these words, she remembered Françoise sitting on her towel so proud of being able to hide and saying these same words.

Besotted with one another, they were longing in the middle of having. In the beginning, they would fall into lapses of silence afraid that the spell would be broken.

248

At last Liza got up, put on her robe, and began to scramble eggs. As they ate breakfast, Liza shared personal things about her mom, Kate, Steve, Simon, Finn, and her mom and dad. She shared her most personal secret: "No one knows who my father is because my mother died giving birth to me, and she wouldn't say who he was."

The morning light washed over them as it filled the room.

He told her many things; it was as if he were letting the air out of his chest and ridding it of the carbon dioxide locked within. It was time to be filled with fresh air. Liza was that air. He told of his parents' deaths, his sister who lived in Kansas City and of his first love, who had hurt him deeply, and finally after ten years being able to begin again with Shelly. Closing his eyes for a minute, he continued. "Leaving my marriage pushed hurt so deep inside me, that when I dated other women later, some of whom I had admired and had cared for, I could never commit to them. When I saw you sitting in class the first time, something clicked inside of me. I was frightened of the feelings you had evoked in me."

"Why didn't you call me when I lived in Philly? You have no idea how I longed for you to call."

"I wanted to, but my mother suffered for years from cancer. She never recovered from Dad's death, and the cancer was the final straw. I felt love and duty bound to help her die. For the last part of her life, she was a lost soul." Michael reached for Liza's hand. "I didn't want to start anything with you till I knew I could carry it through. I thought of you often, you have no idea." He kissed her cheek. "A while back, when I was in New York for a

249

conference, I saw you ahead of me on a subway platform, and you were with a fellow I had seen you with at Bard. I thought, let things be. When your note was forwarded from Bard, I knew then that maybe, maybe we were meant to be."

"I feel as though I've known you a long time."

DOUBT CAN BE A PRISON SENTENCE

Five weeks after meeting, lying in bed on a lazy Saturday, they both thought it time for Michael to file for divorce. Michael confessed that he wasn't sure where his ex-wife, Shelly, was living.

Liza sat up quickly and put the quilt around herself, "How can that be?"

"We separated, and she moved to Idaho, to be near her parents. The last time I sent her a Christmas card through her parents, it was returned. I found out that her parents had died, and I didn't think much more about it."

"Is there anything else you need to share with me?" Fear lurked in her words and in the little synapses that made connections in her brain. *Why am I just finding this out?*

"I'll hire a private detective to find her." Feeling the sun on her hair that was coming through the transom above the door warmed her.

If Liza had second thoughts, she didn't voice them. After all, his explanation was reasonable. He hadn't intended to marry ever again. She lay back down, raising the quilt, and he slid under with her.

Michael hired a private detective, Andy Parlett, who usually worked with the police. After two weeks without any report from him, Liza asked

Michael, "Does it worry you that we haven't heard from Andy? It's bothering me."

"Everything will be okay. I love you; isn't that enough?"

"Honestly, I'm having doubts. I mean it is enough, but I want to marry you and have five little Michaels running around."

"It will happen. Give Andy a chance to find Shelly. Nothing, and I mean nothing, will stand between us— I love you."

And so they waited, and finally, after three weeks, Andy found Shelly in San Francisco working for an attorney. She was still single but had a child ten years old.

The thought crossed Liza's mind that this child might be Michael's, but she decided to wait till after he had had a chance to see Shelly. *First he's married, then he doesn't know where his ex is, and now maybe a child. Shoo these thoughts from your head. He has done nothing wrong. He loves you unconditionally.*

Doubt can be a prison sentence, when you can't think clearly.

###

Because Michael's teaching schedule, and Shelly's personal life didn't allow him to fly to San Francisco immediately, Liza tried not to talk about Shelly. Whatever the mess was, he would untangle it. Ten days seemed forever.

The first few days, everything suggested normalcy. Playing scrabble in her apartment one Sunday afternoon, Liza suggested to Michael that they talk about their wedding.

"Perhaps we should wait till after my trip," said Michael. "We don't know yet when the divorce will be final."

Liza blanched, and uncertainty poked around her intestines. Not wanting to appear anxious, she concentrated on her letters, F, F, I, Y, H, T, A. Ah, taffy, that would give her fourteen points. But, just as she was about to lay the tiles on the board, she saw the letters could also spell faith. Yes, but faith was worth only eleven points. Right now her world was dependent on faith, so she played those letters.

That Tuesday at bedtime, Michael kissed Liza goodnight and turned on his side, facing away from her.

"Is anything wrong?" asked Liza.

"Nope, just a little tired, that's all."

"Okay, sleep well." Uncertainty, again!

On Thursday night, Liza stayed at work to catch up on some opinions she was having difficulty writing. After nine, when she finished, instead of calling Michael to pick her up, she hailed a taxi. When she arrived home, Michael wasn't there. Finding a note on the table that read, "Went for a walk," caused her thoughts to fly round her mind, like bats echoing, *Something's wrong? What am I missing?*

Around ten-thirty she heard his footsteps in the hall. Biting her lip, she opened the door. Greeting her with a kiss, he took hold of her hand and led

253

her straight to the bedroom. *Maybe everything will be all right.* Only a small piece of a scary dream lingered, when she awoke. She tried to catch it but it quickly dissipated.

The sky spoke of rain when Liza dropped Michael at the airport on Saturday morning. Liza hoped that all would be resolved. *Am I jealous? No! A smidge? Maybe?* After all, Michael and Shelly had been apart for ten years. And yet her time with Michael amounted to a little over three months. His time in San Francisco was lunch with Shelly and meeting a college buddy, Sam, for dinner. After spending the night at Sam's, he'd catch the first flight home.

Back in her apartment, determined to keep busy, Liza started cleaning. She vacuumed, dusted, and washed the insides of the windows. After lunch, she broke her promise to let her dad do the dialing and called him.

"This is a pleasant surprise. I hope nothing's wrong," said Jack.

"Nothing's wrong. I thought it high time to tell you I've been seeing someone." The power of positive thinking was foremost in her mind.

"That's wonderful news. When do I get to meet him? What about Thanksgiving?"

"Hmm, maybe Thanksgiving, if that's okay with you. Michael's away for the weekend, so I'll check with him when he returns." Liza could still hear the sad catch in Jack's voice. "Dad, how are you? Really!"

"One day at a time. I try and keep myself occupied. I see your mom everywhere I turn and in everything I do. There's a grief group that meets on Wednesday nights; I go when I'm having a hard time."

"I'm sorry I'm not closer to spend more time with you."

"Enough about me, I'm so happy for you. Do you want to tell me about him?"

"I'll tell you this much, he's a college English professor. I could go on, but I don't want to fill you with my bias regarding him. You'll just have to make up your own mind."

"In that case, I can't wait to meet the man who has stolen your heart."

Had she been rash telling her father about Michael? What if Shelly won't give him a divorce? Was she willing to live with Michael without marriage? The thing about destiny is that it moves us along. *Que sera, sera.*

SAFETY IN SILENCE

Wanting to be a vision of loveliness, Liza chose a pale blue dress and a cream sweater to greet Michael at the airport. He had told her that this dress was his favorite.

Of course she arrived a half-hour before his plane landed. Watching siblings fight over a toy, while the parents paid no attention to them made her uneasy.

The wide grin Michael displayed as he came into view settled her stomach. He put down his bags and kissed her and picked her up.

Disentangling herself, she said, "Darling, we're in an airport."

Putting her down, he whispered in her ear, "I can't help myself. All is well."

Now, she wanted to pick him up. Instead she took his free hand and they walked to his car in unbroken silence. She remembered Fiona saying that there's safety in silence.

Because of the no-fault divorce law in California, after twenty-two days, the divorce was final. Liza and Michael celebrated with a dinner at home. Sitting in the kitchen while Michael prepared veal scaloppini, Liza felt herself a poster for dazzling happiness. Whenever he moved past her, he would put an olive to her lips or kiss her, or just stop and smile, and then go back to the task at hand.

"A lot of preparation has gone into this meal, Mr. O'Flarity." She watched him light a candle on the table and carefully set one gardenia to float in a glass bowl.

Liza had seen the Champagne chilling in the fridge. A melody of desire played throughout her veins. While eating their salad, Michael leaned across the table and said, "Liza Walsh, I can't even explain properly what I feel for you. My heart is swollen because of you."

"Oh, Michael, I know, I know."

When dinner was over, before dessert, Michael asked, "Liza, will you stand and close your eyes for a minute."

Could this be the moment? Delighted that Michael had opened the window a crack, she tried to slow her breathing. Then the strains of Rachmaninoff's *Rhapsody on the Theme of Paganini* surrounded her.

He went back to where Liza was standing. Placing both her hands in his, he said, "Liza Walsh, will you marry me?"

Entranced by the music, the perfume of the gardenia, and a small breeze kissing her uncovered neck, Liza opened her eyes and squeezed Michael's hands. She nodded. With that he placed a ring with a diamond surrounded by small rubies on her finger.

"This ring was my mother's. We can, however, buy one just for you if you don't want a ring that had belonged to another."

"I couldn't find a better ring. I love that it belonged to your mother."

257

They forgot about the dessert and champagne, but they would never forget this night.

In the morning, after another round of lovemaking, Liza held her ring hand aloft so that the sun's rays could catch fire within her diamond and throw little prisms throughout the bedroom. "I'm never taking this ring off."

"I certainly hope not. Together forever."

"Wait a minute," said Liza. She remembered the champagne in the kitchen and made mimosas. Sitting up in bed Michael accepted the drink. Liza held her glass up and said, "Together forever."

By the time they made their way to the kitchen for brunch, Liza asked, "Michael, what do you think about spending Thanksgiving with my family? We could share our news then."

It was decided: Thanksgiving with her family, and they would take two extra days from work so Michael would have a better chance to get acquainted with them.

"If for some unknown reason things go awry, I'm still going to marry you!" He said. "It took me too long to find you, and I have no intention of letting you slip through my fingers. Have you told your father my age?"

"Stop worrying."

BUDS OF DESIRE

On the plane to Philadelphia, as the sun was setting and ringing the clouds, she decided it was time to tell him more about Finn, as he would see photos of him around the house. Yes, he had read her paper of loss, but this was the first time she really went into detail about the tailspin that followed Finn's death. Since she couldn't conjure up Finn, she tried to present him in a way that Michael would understand the Finn they were missing. The man they had recently found and was taken from them.

Jack had taken Fiona's photos and put them in a drawer. Someday he would take them out. For now, however, he was so stricken with loss when he looked at them that he would lose his ability to speak.

"I remember the story you wrote, and I thought to myself someone close in Liza's life has died. I hear that depth of insight, now. I'm sorry that I won't get to meet Finn. If you'll tell me about him when you think of him, somehow he will become a reality for me."

"Michael O'Flarity, there are no words for what I'm feeling about you in this moment."

After telling him about Finn, she told more about her mom and dad. During their second night together, she had told him about her mom's recent death. He had held her while she tried to find words that told this part of her family saga.

"You must know I have trouble thinking of anything but you," he whispered.

"And I'm head over heels in love with you," she replied.

"Words seem so small and thin compared to what I feel for you."

Loving that Michael said that, she snuggled into his side and said, "Let's share our news at dinner one night."

He took her hand, and they flew the rest of the way in silence while their insides became buds of desire opening to full bloom.

Jack, Kate, and Andrew were at the airport to meet them. If Jack were surprised by Michael's age, his face didn't give it away. Turning her head, Liza thought, "If only Finn and Mom…"

As the men carried the bags upstairs, Liza could tell that Jack and Michael were going to be okay when she heard them laugh, and Jack say, "Liza looks so happy, I can't ask for more than that." Lisa knew her dad was putting his sorrow in storage for the few days of their visit.

For dinner, Jack had provided lemon chicken, fried baby shrimp, spring rolls, vegetable chow mien, and fried rice from a local Chinese restaurant. Her mom's touches graced the dining room. The large watercolors above the sideboard were dominant: one a field of poppies in France and the other a hillside in Tuscany. The two corners opposite the door to the kitchen each had a white wooden pedestal holding a marble sculpture. *Mom's with us.*

The talk drifted to the economy. "Do you think Carter can handle the energy crisis?" asked Jack.

"I'm more worried about inflation," said Andrew, "and the war in Afghanistan." Jack, Andrew, and Kate seemed to ask a lot of questions to satisfy their curiosity.

"What courses do you teach?" asked Kate.

After Michael had enumerated these, Jack asked, "Where was home before LA?"

Tired from the flight, Liza asked "Can we play *Twenty Questions* tomorrow?"

"Of course, I hope we haven't been too nosy," said Kate.

Michael chuckled. "Not at all, isn't this what families are about? You want to make sure Liza is okay. In my book she's super."

On a street lined with yellow elms, red maples, and orange sassafrases stood Kate and Andrew's Tudor style house. Each street in the community was a paint box of colors. Along with the chimney smoke, Liza and Michael were happy to have a taste of autumn again. With a turkey in the oven, Kate, Michael, and Jack spent that morning preparing a sweet potato dish, wild rice and lemon, and the stuffing for the turkey. Liza and Andrew rolled out piecrusts and made a pumpkin and an apple pie. The sun poured through leaded glass windows making ripples of light on the table. The cabinetry and table were maple, and the walls were a wheat color. Liza, getting up to look for cinnamon, almost stepped on their golden retriever, Honey Pie,

261

who blended into the wall. She stopped, petted her, and said, "I miss having a dog."

With a bemused expression, Michael said, "My mom had a miniature poodle after my dad died. I believe FeFe helped her when she was dying."

Jack smiled ruefully thinking of Rouge. He needed to change the subject so as not to spoil the moment. "Anyone read *Rumors of Rain*?"

"I just finished it," said Michael. He explained to the rest of us that the central character, Martin, a self-centered, rich South African businessman, found his life changed drastically when he and his son, who had returned from the Angolan war, visited the South African farm where Martin had grown up.

"Just think, in a matter of days, his lifetime security was destroyed with only past values to guide him," Jack commented.

Michael replied by sighing and shaking his head slightly. "Society on the edge of collapse and all that that entails. Also, where do your loyalties lie when self preservation is involved?"

"Definitely a political storm was brewing from the beginning. So why rain in the title?"

"I thought about that… rain washes things…cleanses them."

"So who's going to wash up this mess?" asked Liza.

"My pleasure," said Andrew.

###

Dinner was set for late afternoon, and Kate was excited at being the hostess. She tried to remember the little things that Fiona had done to make the day memorable, such as headbands with turkey feathers for each to wear. Having driven to a farm near Paoli, Pennsylvania to secure the feathers, Andrew and she had made the bands.

In all the excitement of the day, Kate forgot to turn the oven off for the last hour that the turkey was supposed to be resting, and it came out of the oven overdone. Resigned about her mistake, she was able to scrape off the burnt parts, laugh at herself, and carry on. Andrew diverted everyone's attention from the bird to all the other dishes made by family members and their guest.

When Liza saw how her sister had handled the situation, she was once again in awe of her. Her mom's china, Spode pheasant plates, on Kate's table caused her heart to skip a beat. She hugged Kate and whispered, "It's good to have Mom with us."

Michael offered information about himself and his family. Each felt a connection when he talked about his mother's illness, and his father's heart attack.

Jack in a melancholy voice said, "Each of us has moments when we're pierced by pain… but then it lets up for awhile, so we can go forward." He saw that everyone was looking at him. "Sorry."

Liza, sitting next to her father, touched his arm and thought, *if you ever love again, the pain will peel away. Mom would want that.*

263

Michael continued, "I had the good fortune of moving to LA at the same time Liza did."

Liza kicked Kate gently under the table.

"So Michael, do you do any writing?" asked Jack.

"I wish I did! I think about it, but I don't seem to have the story that would punch one in the gut. The story that encompasses the frailty of our natures."

Lisa interjected, "Yes, but you know how to bring out the best in other's writings."

Before they finished, Jack invited everyone to dinner the following night at the Merion Cricket Club.

The burnt turkey was a blip in the family's eyes. This family was safe harbor.

ALL IS WELL

The next night, Michael admired the old world elegance of the Club's building designed by Frank Furness.

"Wow, what a view." The lights from the clubhouse shone on the lawn and cricket greens. Michael asked, "Do all of you play tennis? Cricket?"

"We do play tennis, and Andrew and I play golf," said Jack. "Do you play?"

"No, my sport was cross country. I still run when I get the chance. Although now I seem to walk more."

"Liza, how's your job? Enjoying it?" asked Kate.

"Fine. It's not as easy as I thought it would be. I can't just mouth off with an opinion; it has to be grounded in truth. I have to do a massive amount of research."

"I would think you'd have to be passionate," said Jack.

"Yep, and I have to make the reader care about what I'm saying …and I need a solution." Liza laughed, "Not always easy."

"She nails it every week. People are writing more often than not how much they like her opinions," said Michael.

After a delicious supper the waiter came with a bottle of champagne.

"What are we celebrating?" asked Kate.

Andrew stood and proposed a toast to the girl's mom and dad for raising two beautiful daughters. Michael tapped his glass and said, "Hear,

265

hear." Andrew went on to say, "Jack has given me permission to marry Kate, and marry Kate I will, if she'll have me." Her countenance said it all. She jumped up and kissed Andrew unabashedly.

Jack raised a glass, "To Kate and Andrew."

Everyone around neighboring tables clapped and raised their glasses to them.

With that, Andrew slipped a ring on her finger—her first question was, "When did you talk with Dad?" Jack and Andrew both smiled and wouldn't divulge the meeting place or time. The others would learn later that the only place found for privacy was the bathroom at the top of the stairs. The family joke was that Kate's destiny was decided at the Walsh Powder Room Conference.

Andrew would finish his residency in the spring and join an established practice in Villanova. Kate asked Liza to be her maid of honor, and Andrew's brother, Frank, would be the best man.

"What do you think about Bermuda in May?" asked Kate.

"Sounds good to me. Who would object to that?" said Liza.

Kate and Andrew would be married on the beach by an Episcopal minister. Kate and Liza would fly to Bermuda beforehand to scout the location and finalize details.

All went back to Jack's house infected with the joys of the moment. They wanted to be together the entire time. Lying on their beds, the girls were so wrapped up in the excitement that when they realized it was 2:00 AM, Kate whispered, "Goodnight, Mrs. Boobytrap."

Liza got up, kissed Kate on the cheek, and said, "Goodnight, Mrs. Redmond."

"Oh Liza, I'll really be Mrs. Redmond."

Michael and Andrew slept in the twin beds in Finn's room.

Liza fell asleep remembering Kate saying she had a really strong feeling about Michael; he seemed to be part of the family without any hoopla.

Liza told Kate, "I've never been happier."

Kate countered with, "What, you didn't think we noticed? You know, you and Michael resemble each other. You even walk alike."

Liza made only one trip to the closet that weekend. This time, with a joyful voice, she told the assembled urns, "All is well. I'm okay as well as Kate and Dad. Well, Dad is taking baby steps." Marriage is on the horizon for Kate and me. She wanted her marriage to be a tapestry of everyday occurrences that was sewn with love. She and Kate had had the best possible role models in their own parents.

JEWEL LIKE LEAVES HID THE PATHWAY

Summer returned on the Saturday after Thanksgiving. Liza and Michael decided a walk after breakfast would be delightful. Shedding their coats the minute they stepped out of the house, Liza could smell the scent of burning leaves along with the pungent fragrance of chrysanthemums planted in the porch pots. The air was crisp, but the sun was strong as they ambled towards the town of Bryn Mawr. She jabbered on, saying that the Welsh name, Bryn Mawr, meant *great hill*. She wasn't sure why she was so loquacious that morning, except that she wanted to share everything about where she had grown up.

The leaves undressing the trees fell in a lazy sort of way, unprovoked by wind. With the sound of crisp leaves being crushed underfoot, they made their way onto Lancaster Pike and the seven-block stretch of stores. She had always loved the old pale pink bricks of the shops that fronted the street. They seemed to gather light within themselves.

They stopped in front of a jewelry store, and she was reminded of what she had forgotten to tell Michael last night. "Let's not tell our news now. It's Kate's time to be in the spotlight."

"I've been thinking, would you mind if we were married at City Hall? I don't want all the pomp and pageantry," said Michael.

She stopped and looked at him. *What, the biggest day of my life?*

268

"When I was younger, I had the traditional wedding, but at my age..."

"I didn't know you felt this way."

"You understand?"

Seeing their reflections in the store window, she tried to gauge from his facial expression if he understood what he was asking of her. *Surely he must know what this means to me.* She felt like a punctured balloon.

They had to step back when the alarm sounded at the fire station. The old station sat between two shops. A firefighter stopped traffic so the engines could make their way into the street. Michael turned to her and said, "I hope no one's hurt."

"Actually, I am. I really want to have a wedding with my family present. We've been through a lot as a family, and I don't want to do this without them."

Passing the six-foot, carved brown bear in front of the hardware store, she recalled when her dad would hide behind the bear and using his bear voice, talk to Kate, Finn and her. The girls would squeal in delight. Finn would raise his eyebrows and say, "It's just Dad pretending." She didn't have it in her to share that story right now.

"Of course you want your family, how thoughtless of me. Forgive me. What was I thinking? My sister wouldn't forgive me if she weren't present. A beautiful bride, that's what you'll be."

"Thank you, Michael."

Are we near the college?"

"Close. Do you want to see it?"

"I wouldn't mind a stroll around it.

The whistle call from the train making its way from Rosemont Station to Bryn Mawr didn't seem so forlorn now. It was a two-minute ride. They cut across a small park where the jewel-like leaves hid the pathway. Liza kicked at the leaves as she walked along feeling like a kid again.

The campus was empty. The gray buildings were a striking contrast to the gold crowns worn by the tulip poplars and sycamores. They almost seemed arranged to her under the bluest of skies. *Nothing gold can stay. Wasn't that what Robert Frost had said?*

When they reached Merion Green and were sheltered by evergreens, Michael said, "Let's sit for a bit." They sat on the ground. She wrapped her arms around her knees, but Michael unwrapped them and laid her back on the ground. He began kissing her, and all her cares floated away on the overhead clouds as she kissed him back. God how she loved him! When she opened her eyes, she saw a picture of her wedding dress forming in a cloudbank.

Michael, now stretched alongside of her, was leaning on one elbow looking so lovingly at her that a spasm of joy ran through her innards.

"We should head back," she said.

Michael helped her up. They continued their pilgrimage, taking the long way round to Kate and Andrew's house. Leftover turkey was for lunch.

1978

THE INTEREST OF OUR JOY

After Kate's wedding in Bermuda in April, on the plane home Michael said, "Liza, what do you think of Florence for our honeymoon?"

"I was thinking the same thing."

"The poster!" they both exclaimed.

He grinned, "I remember looking at that poster our first dinner together and thinking you and I would go there one day."

"Gosh, I'm not sure what I was thinking. I was sure I was dreaming the whole time. I worried I might wake up. But now, I'm thinking we could live on the interest of our joy forever."

###

Liza thought it high time that she met Michael's sister Patrice, a marketing analyst, and her husband, Alain Lepan, who owned a small, four-star French restaurant in Kansas City called *bouche a nourrir.* They had two children, Addie, five, and Adam, three.

That May, Liza and Michael planned a trip to visit them. Overhearing Michael talk to his sister many times, she understood their great affection for each other.

Each thought driving 1,500 miles from LA to Kansas City would be a wonderful experience. "I think we can do five hundred miles a day," said Michael. "This old Benz will last another fifteen years."

Not caring if the car broke down, she said nothing. She was a beacon of dazzling happiness; nothing could dim her feelings.

Remarkably, Liza and Patrice resembled one another.

"Liza, we could be sisters. Your mouth is shaped like mine," said Patrice.

"Well, we each have blonde hair. At any rate we look as though we both have Irish ancestry," said Liza.

Immediately, they were taken with each other.

The Lepan children appeared typical for their ages. Addie said anything that popped into her head. At one point, she asked, "Do I have to go to Dada's restaurant with you? The food's awful, and I want a peanut butter and jelly sandwich."

Alain said, "No problem." He took the peanut butter and raspberry jelly to the restaurant with him, and when they were served succulent lamb chops with a cherry glaze, Miss Addie was given her sandwich. She asked the waiter, "Why don't you smile?"

The dismayed look on Patrice's face made Liza wonder, what her own children would be like.

Adam, a foil for Addie's bluntness, batted his long eyelashes and smiled angelically.

While Michael and Alain took the children to the playground, Patrice and Liza had some time to themselves. The two were sitting in the kitchen, which seemed modern to Liza with its stainless steel counters and black cabinets with frosted glass fronts. A wall of windows facing east overlooked the back garden. The sunlight splashed the grey walls, making them almost golden.

"I'm so happy to see Michael so happy. An early on love affair that ended abruptly really hurt him. He never told us why. But I guess you know that," said Patrice.

Liza nodded. *Don't ask specifics, Michael told you what he wanted you to know.*

"During his year abroad, our dad died. Michael was adrift for a while. When he married Shelly, the family rejoiced, thinking we had our old Michael back." Patrice stopped and turned to face Liza. "When they separated, Michael retreated into himself. If he dated other women, he didn't tell us." She drummed her fingers on the table. "He had also taken care of our mother over the years. You are the first woman we've met since Shelly."

Liza smiled, "I'm glad we're here. Families are important." She had a strong sense that a man who was a good brother and son could only make a good husband.

On their way home, she asked Michael, "What do you think about getting married in Kansas City and having the reception at Alain's restaurant?" Michael was delighted.

When they returned to California, Liza called her dad and said, "Dad, we're getting married."

"That's wonderful, darling. Your mom would be so happy."

Jack thought of what Fiona whispered in his ear before they left the altar. It was a poem by Emily Dickenson.

It's all I have to bring today—

This, and my heart beside—

This, and my heart, and all the fields—

    And all the meadows wide—

1979

CLOSE TO HUBRIS

In January Kate, Andrew, Jack, Patrice, and Alain flew to LA to hold an engagement luncheon for Liza and Michael at the Botanical Gardens.

Liza watched as Kate and her dad were drawn in by Patrice's smile. All trooped around The Huntington Library Art Collections and the Botanical Gardens, especially admiring the Japanese Garden, occupying nine acres at the base of a canyon. While walking through the walled courtyard, with its rock and sand plot, Michael turned and said to Liza, "I have never been happier in my life." It was at times such as this that Liza's heart would feel so full that it would hurt. She would feel an overwhelming sensation of too much love. She wondered if that were even possible. At times she would have to stop and collect her breath and herself.

To settle ideas for their wedding, they gathered at the *Rose Garden Tea Room and Café* to have lunch. A dappled light fought its way through the overhead canopy of entangled vines. The scent of the roses was one of the things Liza remembered most from that day; the other was the sheer jubilation. All had brought their day planners, and the first thing they did was to choose the sixteenth of September for the nuptials. Liza said, "I think we have more than enough time to put this wedding together." She gave Michael a wink and they turned to Alain and Patrice.

"May we be married at your house with a reception at your restaurant?" asked Michael.

Alain and Patrice caught each other's eye and in a split second both nodded in agreement. "We'd be honored. But let's do the whole thing at the house," said Alain.

"The garden should be lovely then." Patrice said, "We might have to do a few things to spruce up the house and garden."

Alain agreed.

The prairie style house, with its open floor plan, will provide an exquisite setting. "I think it's perfect as is," said Liza.

Patrice said doing a few things would put her into the wedding spirit. "I can't wait to get started."

"Kate and Patrice, if you'll be my attendants you can buy cocktail dresses of your own choosing." Liza and Kate both laughed remembering the hideous orange marmalade dress with a row of brown lace around the bottom that Kate wore in the wedding of a college friend. In turns they spit out the story, at times not being able to do anything but double over with laughter. Kate had to wear brown fishnet stockings, and carry dyed orange carnations. When calm returned, Liza asked Patrice and Alain if Addie could be their flower girl and little Adam their ring bearer.

"Of course. I'm sure they'd love it."

The wedding party grew to fifteen people. Besides the nine of them, Liza wanted Sarah and her husband Allen to share in their happiness. She also invited her aunts and uncles.

Liza didn't remember what they ate for lunch that day. It hardly mattered. Having her family together like this, Liza thought, *I must be dreaming.* At one point, she looked over at Kate and Andrew and saw them give each other a knowing look. Liza piped up, "Okay you two, what's up?"

Kate smiled demurely and patted her stomach. "I'm happy I may choose my own dress, as I'll be six months pregnant in September." Cheers and more cheers.

Jack, who had a small workshop in his basement, said, "I was looking for a project. I'll restore the crib I made for you, Kate."

When the plans were finished, Liza walked with her father to the door of the café. "Dad, Mom's here. I just know she is."

"I hope you and Michael will be as happy as your mom and I were."

Liza and Michael saw the family members off at the airport. What a glorious weekend they had enjoyed. When they got back to Michael's apartment, they opened a bottle of champagne from Jack.

"I promise I won't go crazy when you leave the cap off the toothpaste," Liza said, toasting Michael. "I promise not to lose it when you use my razor," Michael replied. After a few bouts of "I promise not to," Michael changed the tone with "I promise to kiss you every day we're together."

In her heart, Liza felt a pang close to hubris when she suggested, "Nothing can ever come between us." But then she thought that if you don't think that way in the beginning, you probably don't stand a chance when something hard comes along. She couldn't keep her finger in the dike of her heart any longer and her feelings kept gushing out of her. "You are my everything." She didn't care if what she said sounded corny.

1980

TOGETHER FOREVER

It was time to let go of the two apartments, a waste of money, and to buy a small house, a reasonable goal. Moreover, the idea of being in a beach town near LA was something they both wanted. In June, they found a house in Hermosa Beach. A craftsman style cottage on 10th Street built in 1914, the house had two bedrooms and one bath. One of the bedrooms was such a strong yellow they felt a need to put on sunglasses as soon as they entered it. The other bedroom, a pale pink, would be perfect as library/study/guestroom. Liza and Michael both turned to each other at the same time and said, "This is it."

In the weeks following, a contractor removed all paneling from the living room and dining room and put up plaster walls. At Liza's direction, he painted every room a dusky beige.

"I like that we brought the outside colors of the beach inside with the paint we've chosen," Liza told Michael.

The kitchen was small, with just enough room for a table and three chairs. The best part was the deep porch that reminded Liza so much of Cape May, including a front yard, a small plot of grass that was surrounded by a white picket fence. The house would be ready in August.

Liza could think herself back at the Cape May cottage and feel the breeze and smell the salt water. Whenever she went to the house by herself, she wandered the beach for a bit, sat down on the sand, closed her eyes, and saw Cape May in her mind's eye: Rouge running in the surf, Finn holding hands with Sophia, both laughing, a few steps in front of her and Steve. Or she

282

saw her mom and dad walking the beach barefoot, each with a glass of wine in hand.

It was a happy remembrance wandering around with Finn and Fiona. Details she had forgotten would stream through her mind like an old 8-mm. movie. Even some of the clothes they wore then were as vivid as they had been that summer when they were all together. Her mom would have on her favorite blue shift and flip-flops; Finn would be barefoot in cutoff jeans.

How Liza wished that her mom and Finn could see their new house. Somehow, it began to feel right talking to them outside the safety of the closet. When she got to the point of tears, something always seemed to startle her and bring her back to the present. Most times it was a caucus of cormorants, the screech of a Western Gull, or even a tugboat whistle; then she would mosey back to the house to see how the work was progressing.

Before leaving each time, Liza took measurements for curtains, shades, or furniture. *This will be our little sanctuary.* She and Michael planned to put the two oriental rugs in the living and dining rooms. The rugs were a little out of character with a beach house, but she couldn't part with them. Things like this didn't faze Michael, who said, "Decorate how you like." She tried to take him at his word, but she showed him things she was about to buy, just in case he had an objection. He never did. Together they walked in dreams.

###

The end of July was extremely hot that year, and the house wasn't ready as promised on August first. There was a plumbing problem, and the kitchen tiles didn't arrive on time. They would have to wait until after the wedding before moving in. While this delay was somewhat of a nuisance, it seemed to be best in the long run. Michael had a conference to attend in Boston immediately after the honeymoon.

They were standing in the half finished kitchen on a Sunday afternoon. A storm had come up. Liza felt as though they were in a little boat being rocked about relentlessly by the wind. She smiled and said, "Our marriage means more to me than this house being ready."

"Come here, you." He carried her into the empty bedroom. At least the new carpeting had been installed. "Since we can't leave till the storm passes, I say we christen this room."

"There'll be no arguments from me, Mr. O'Flarity."

###

Until the house was ready, Michael moved in with Liza. "Michael, you must hang a few of your paintings so that my apartment feels like it's ours." He chose three, and it took them a Saturday afternoon to hang them— first here, then there.

It was an overcast day, so they turned all the lights on, trying to have each painting catch the right light.

"Oh well, we'll only be here a few weeks. And then together forever."

"Together forever," she repeated.

It was a tight fit, but neither seemed to care. Michael's furniture went into storage.

FREE RANGE OF INTIMATE FEELINGS

After the wedding an announcement would appear in the *Los Angeles Times* and the *Philadelphia Inquirer*.

Liza had a small Hallmark pocket calendar, which she was crossing out the days till the wedding. Wanting to have a personal touch, she decided to hand write invitations to their families.

Before the wedding, Michael had another conference to attend, this time in Philadelphia; Liza was able to go with him. She would go on to Jack's house, and Michael to his conference. Patrice flew to Philadelphia, too.

Hoping to find suitable dresses for the wedding, Kate, Liza, and Patrice set off for the small shops on the main line. They found all three dresses in a boutique in Haverford: Liza's a creamy silk suit, Kate's a knee-length, deep, garnet red silk dress with an empire waist, and Patrice's a garnet tea length sheath.

After their shopping excursion, they went back to Kate's house. Andrew, outside weeding, stood up to greet them. "Wait till you see what we bought," they teased him. They donned their dresses and danced around the yard, singing *I'm Getting Married in the Morning*. Andrew applauded, and Honey Pie howled as they twirled and sang at the top of their lungs.

###

The week was going faster than Liza had anticipated. *How could it be Wednesday already?* They would fly tomorrow to Kansas City for the wedding.

The wedding came off without a hitch. While Addie decided at the last minute to dance down the steps, Adam was the perfect ring bearer. The assembled guests chuckled, but Liza barely noticed. The only person she saw was Michael at the bottom of the hall steps. As she walked down the steps, her heart did the talking. *This is really it.*

When it came time to exchange vows, Liza softly answered, "I will." Michael did the same."

Asked by Michael if the house flowers could be gardenias, Patrice had made sure they were placed in the rooms in profusion. Noticing immediately, Liza touched one and said, "You remembered everything." A tear found its way down her face. She was a free range of intimate feelings, which she wasn't worried about containing.

The restaurant's sumptuous catered feast started with caviar and ended with a beautifully decorated wedding cake, which to the delight of the guests was chocolate. The feast was served on the long table on the patio under an arbor strung with lights. With guests in sweaters, it was warm enough to sit outside. A string quartet played at the bottom of the garden, and the music seemed to float around everyone. The best part about this wedding: it belonged to Liza and Michael.

Liza couldn't stop thinking, *I kept my eyes on the prize for eight years, and in this moment I understand the meaning of bliss.*

###

Their plane to Florence left the next day, so they practiced that night and the following morning calling each other Mr. and Mrs.

In Italy, it rained most of the week, but their spirits weren't dampened. Michael had been to Florence years ago and wanted to show Liza everything the city had to offer. They visited all the usual tourist destinations: the Uffizi, the Pitti Palace, the Duomo, and a host of other churches. When they walked through the Palazzo Vecchio, Liza was taken with Eleonora di Toledo's rooms, which were decorated with scenes of virtuous women. "Michael, look at this one of Penelope, waiting faithfully for her husband to return." She kissed his hand. "That will be me."

In little out-of-the-way restaurants they found romance, had gelato every afternoon, and sank into bed at night, arms enfolding each other and loving each other as if each time might be the last. They couldn't get over their great fortune of finally being together permanently.

On the flight home, Michael declared, "I think we should return every ten years on our anniversary."

"Yes, please," was Liza's reply.

"Oh, by the way, did you send out wedding announcements before we left?"

"Kate said she would take care of it the minute she got back home."

They slept most of the way back, content to start this new chapter together.

###

Back in Hermosa Beach, the house wasn't quite ready, so they went back to Liza's. The move was put off for two more weeks. This time it had to do with a leaky roof.

"We don't want any setbacks once we move in. I'm glad this is being fixed now," said Michael.

"I'm tired, Michael. I know you have to pack for Boston. Mind if I turn in?

"Enjoy the honey heavy dew of slumber, my love."

"I love it when you talk Shakespeare to me. Wake me when you come to bed—I'm just happy that this is your last conference till spring."

"Have I ever told you that you smile sometimes when you're sleeping?"

Liza blushed, "It could only be because of you. Don't forget—wake me when you come to bed."

###

The sun made it difficult for Liza to see. "Perhaps we should think about getting a new car when you return. This one has seen better days."

Pointing to the dashboard she continued. "Knobs are missing, and the gas gauge stays on empty. It's too hard for me to figure how far we've been and when it needs a fill up."

"I hate parting with it. It's one of the last things that gives me any connection to my father," said Michael. "After he died it stayed in a garage till I could drive it."

"I know that's important; so maybe I should think about getting one on my own as I'm always afraid I'll be stuck on some dark road by myself, or the brakes will fail on either of us."

"That's a thought. Let's look when I return."

With his hand on Liza's leg, they rode in silence for a bit.

Looking to her right, a large sign pointed the way to the airport.

"It's a clear day. Smooth flying."

Pulling up in front of the airport, Liza decreed, "Husband, parting is as you know sweet sorrow. Your return will be a sweeter happiness."

"Liza, my love, *'stir with the lark tomorrow'*; it will be me singing you awake."

"Do you think other newly weds are as silly as we are?" asked Liza.

"I hope so!" said Michael.

ALL YOUR SORRYS DON'T MEAN A THING

Standing in the kitchen with light slowly sliding down the far wall, Liza dropped her bundles and mail on the kitchen table. She glanced out the small window above the sink at the three pigeons pecking fallen acorns among the hammered gold leaves. *Michael will be back this afternoon… my husband.* The thought made her giddy. She put some eggs on to boil to have egg salad for lunch.

As Liza opened a letter from Clare, a photo fell to the floor. She picked up the photo and saw that it was a younger Michael. *How odd.*

September 19, 1980
Dearest Liza,

I am ashamed and sickened at what I am about to tell you. I have no doubt that you will find it impossible to forgive me. I can't even face you. I tried calling several times for several days but no answer. You must still be in Florence on your honeymoon.

Diane has measles, and Sam is at a conference in Seattle so I'm taking the coward's way out with this letter. I am so sorry, Liza. I should not have kept the promise your mother demanded of me the day she died so many years ago. She made me swear to her that I would never reveal the father of her baby. She was my closest friend, and I felt obligated to keep her secret. She and your father loved each other dearly. She became pregnant by mistake and didn't want him to

291

have to make a choice regarding his graduate work in England and taking care of a wife and baby. She knew he would choose her and you. So she broke up with him. He didn't know this reason. She told him she had met someone else. He was devastated and heart sick. So was she.

By sheer accident, I saw your wedding announcement in *The Philadelphia Inquirer*. It had been left on a commuter plane I took from Philadelphia to New York.

When I saw Michael's name, I wondered could he be the same Michael O'Flarity that I knew as Mickey, when your mother and I were at Chestnut Hill. When I next read that he had attended LaSalle College in Philadelphia, I felt a sickness that has not left me. Hoping against all odds, I called LaSalle's Alumni Office and was told that after his fellowship abroad, he then taught at Bard College. That's when I was sure. Oh, Liza, Michael O'Flarity is your father. In all God's universe, how you managed to find each other is beyond comprehension. There was a second when I thought maybe I could ignore this, but when you have had a chance to understand what I have revealed, I know that you would not want the truth kept from you. The photo of Michael was one that your mother kept on her desk at school.

I can only imagine the pain this will cause both of you, and if I had told everyone sooner who your father was, this tragedy could have been avoided. I hope somehow you and Michael will come to terms with this situation. Liza, I am so sorry. I'm here should you want to talk. Clare

###

Liza dropped the letter and her hand flew to her mouth. "No, No, No!" she groaned. Picking it up, she exhaled, and reread it. *This is a mistake, this has got to be a mistake.* Staring at Michael's photo, she reread the inscription on the back, "To Sally Anne, all my love, Mickey." She felt as if a captive bird were frantically beating its wings in her chest. Surely, her heart would give way.

Trying to find a loophole in Clare's story, she kept going over everything in her mind. How could this possibly be true? Liza's heart was splintering. Aloud, she said, "If it's true, I'll kill myself."

Sitting down on a wing chair, she held her stomach, and then got up, walked around the living room, and sat again. In less than an hour, Michael's plane would land at LAX. An intense pain behind her right eye throbbed as if a snake were puncturing a nerve there and slowly sending out a poison to blind her. *No medicine can fix this!*

A crumb of hope lifted her thoughts. What if she never told Michael? *If I don't get pregnant* was her first thought. Her next one was, *I'm desperate.* Twenty minutes till Michael landed. Her insides were churning.

I'll call Clare! Her hands fumbled through her address book. *Clare's mistaken.*

In a tremulous voice, Clare said, "Liza?"

"How dare you? All the times you could have told me, and you continued lying. My mother was dead, and I was alive. Did you ever once think about me?" Clare started to say, "Liza, I'm so sorry," but Liza forged ahead. "The announcement said the honeymoon would be a ten-day trip to Florence. You could have called Dad…" *What does Dad even mean, now?* "You should have been here to give us the horrible news. At this point though, I'd rather not see you."

While Clare spoke, "Your mother begged me; I had to honor her wishes. I wanted to tell you many times, but," Liza ran her fingers along the second shelf in the bookcase, then touched the flame colored chrysanthemums that sat by themselves on the top shelf. Michael had told her that chrysanthemums symbolized fidelity.

"We're married Clare, married!"

She heard sobbing, and Clare's garbled words. "Nothing I say can undo this. I'm so sorry. Forgive me."

"Why should I forgive you? You've lied so much. So many times you could have told Mom or me. Do have any idea of the pain you've caused?" She tried to breathe. "Tell me, Clare, is there a snowball's chance in hell that what you've written isn't true?"

"It's true, Liza. I'm so sorry."

In a bitter voice Liza said, "All your *sorrys* don't mean a thing to me. Goodbye, Clare." She dropped the receiver and let it dangle to the floor. She heard Clare say, "Liza, Liza?"— And then a click. After a minute, an automated voice said, "Please hang up," followed by a shrill noise. She

294

slammed the receiver on its cradle so hard a small bit of the mouthpiece chipped and fell.

How could she ever forgive Clare's loathsome lying? A small voice inside of her said, "Keep it together. Wait for Michael." Her right foot jiggled. Looking at the leg that she seemed to have no control of, she stood and started pacing again. When she straightened one of Michael's abstract oil paintings on the wall, she remembered that it was the one they had spent hours on deciding where to hang. Placing her cheek against it she thought, *Gone, it will be gone, too.*

Smelling the burning eggs in the kitchen and hearing the popping of the shells, she entered the room and looked at a shell stuck to the wall while her shoe snapped a piece on the floor. She turned off the burner and walked out of the room. A wave of nausea overtook her; she sat back down in the wing chair. The thought of suicide lingered on the edges of her blackened mind.

Michael's keys jangled in the door.

What will we do? Oh, my love!

He opened the door, dropped his suitcase, and with extended arms said, "Liza, my wife."

Liza fought down the bile in her throat and running into his arms. Instead she put her right hand in front of her.

He stopped, "What's wrong? You look like you've seen a ghost."

"Were you ever called Mickey? Did you date Sally Anne Crosby?"

Michael's lips parted as if to say something, but he stopped and looked curiously at her.

Liza spoke again, only more insistent, slower and louder this time. "Did. You. Ever. Date. Sally. Anne. Crosby? Were. You. Called. Mickey?" With tears rolling down her cheeks, she gasped, "Answer me, Michael."

Bewildered, he said, "Yes."

As she handed the letter to him, the photo slid to the floor.

Michael reached down, and his eyes widened. He took his glasses out of his pocket, sat down across from her on the sofa, and began to read. His face went from flushed to ghostly in a matter of seconds. His forehead turned into a racetrack of lines. All he could murmur was, "Oh, Liza." Staring at each other, she thought of that day in his office when she was his student and he had said, "Oh Liza, even if I did have feelings for you, some things are not meant to be." If only she had known then what that phrase would really come to mean.

Finally, Michael spoke, " Liza, this can't be true, yet I am Michael O'Flarity, and your mother was Sally Anne Crosby. It's the photo I gave to her. But she left me for another man. He must be your real father." He brought the top of his fist to his mouth and blew through the tunnel of fingers.

"Michael, do you really believe that? You loved my mother. Was she capable of leaving you for another man?"

Hanging his head, he murmured, "No." He got up and asked, "Do you want a drink?"

Liza shook her head.

He poured himself a glass of whiskey neat, took a large gulp, and sat back down.

Although she knew what Clare had said, she wanted to hear from him why they broke up. She looked at his tear-stained face and asked the question.

"Your mother told me she had met someone else. I didn't believe her because we were so much in love. Yet she was adamant about not seeing me when I went off to England." He took another swallow of whiskey. "Now I understand. Your mother wouldn't tie me down." His voice cracked. "Only what she didn't understand was that I would have tied myself to her, come hell or high water." Catching his breath, he continued, "I should have fought harder for her. I had too much pride. Pride, one of the seven deadly sins. And now I've robbed you of your life." He put his head in his hands. She heard him weeping. When he looked up, he said, "We need some time to think this through. I can't bear not being near you. Let me hold you."

"More than anything I want to crawl into your lap and have you love me, but we both know it would be wrong."

He took another swig of whiskey and said, "We just need time to make sense of this."

Liza was not conscious of twirling her engagement and wedding rings until Michael looked at her hand. She stopped the twirling and took them off. Reaching across the glass coffee table, she handed them to him.

"Please don't do this, keep them. They belong to you."

She remembered that morning in bed after he had proposed; she had held her hand in front of her and told him in a solemn voice, "This ring will never leave this hand." *My God... these were my grandmother's rings.*

"You are my life. I will fight for you as I didn't fight for your mother."

From the window behind him, a full moon floated between two buildings. In minutes, Liza thought, "The moon's light will be snuffed out by the east building, like a candle when a feast is over." Neither moved to turn on a light. Michael approached her.

"No closer! Losing the mother I didn't know, losing the mom I knew, losing my brother, and now you, my beloved husband..." She threw her hands up. "What's the use of going over everything? It won't change a thing. I don't blame you. I just can't handle this." *I just want to die!*

"What if we..." She stopped him mid-sentence. "There can be no *what ifs*! We would always know that you are my father." Her heart reached across the table, but her hands stayed in her lap.

Michael closed his eyes. "Maybe we should call Clare."

"I did that; there's no mistake. Think of all the times people have told us we look alike."

With a stricken gaze, he asked, "Do you want me to leave?"

"I will always love you, but it isn't about want anymore. It's what has to be."

Michael stood and cried, "I don't want to, but I'll do as you ask. I'll call you later to make sure you're okay. I plan to stay in your life." He walked over to her and tried to touch her cheek, but Liza turned her face away.

DARK CORNERS

Sitting in her bedroom before Sam came to bed, Clare wondered if Liza would ever forgive her. Sick at heart, she couldn't tell Sam about it. This was what she would carry to her grave; this was the biggest scar that would mark her heart.

Liza's call had made her feel as though she had been dropped out of an airplane with no parachute. The pain in Liza's voice and her hateful words played over and over in Clare's mind. The owls were swooping and eating at her. Should she go to Liza and tell her how sorry she was? She knew that would be fruitless. Give her time to take it all in.

No one had exposed her lie at the hospital, and a few years ago her conscience had eased up. Hadn't she passed the statute of limitations on lies? She knew the funny thing about lies: they lurk forever in the recesses and dark corners of our psyches, waiting for the indisputable truth to call them into question and expose the duplicity we had thought so safely hidden.

Clare was also reminded of the long arm of coincidence, a device used to move a story along. Dickens was a master at it. Yet, here, in reality, she was the pivotal piece around which this lie had spun.

The magnitude of the problem that she had created was enormous. Her lie was uncovered. Ashamed, she had persuaded herself a letter was her only way out. Could there be no forgiveness now that the rubber band of a lie had finally been stretched to the breaking point? Never meaning to hurt anyone, she had wanted only to be faithful to her best friend. Praying that the light of Liza's mercy would shine upon her, she huddled under the quilt on their bed.

NOTHING LEFT

Liza flipped on the kitchen light and turned off the ringer on the phone.

She looked at the eggshells on the floor. She realized that she hadn't eaten lunch or diner. Eviscerated, that's how she felt. There was nothing left to her. *This will end my suffering.* She reached in the cabinet over the sink and took out a bottle of Tylenol. Rummaging through the junk drawer she found a piece of paper and wrote, "I can't live without you." She looked at the Tylenol and thought she might mess up and not die. Opening the knife drawer, she reached for the first knife. It was serrated. She sat down on the cold linoleum, ripped both wrists, and watched the blood spurt to the floor. She lay on her side and waited. Looking out the kitchen window, she saw the moon again.

UNKNOWN TERRITORY

Walking for a time, with no place to go, Michael felt like a bull that had been stabbed by a matador. He paused when a traffic signal changed from yellow to red. Where was he—somewhere in unknown territory. He then remembered he needed certain things, his schoolwork, some clothes, and other necessities. For Liza's sake, he decided to go back and get them. Tomorrow it would be worse. Retracing the last block, he saw a landmark that he recognized. He sprinted towards Liza's apartment, hopeful that she hadn't gone to bed yet. The last thing he wanted to do was wake her.

When he reached the apartment and unlocked the door, there was a single light on in the kitchen. Michael called out, "Liza?" That's when he saw her and the blood by the leg of the table. "Liza!" he cried out again. Her face looked like white marble. The one-sentence note lay on the table. He felt for her neck pulse. It was faint. He thought, *I'll cradle you to sleep my darling, and then I'll use the bloody knife on myself.* Aloud he said, "Blood has not taken your loveliness. My God, what am I doing? Liza, wake up! I'll fight for you. You must live." He took the towels by the sink and wrapped them around the ragged wounds. He then called 911. He found the letter from Clare still in the living room and stuffed it in his pocket. After unlocking the door he went back to Liza. *Live, Liza, live. My God, let her live.*

When the ambulance arrived, Michael stood aside and watched the medic remove the towels, wipe the blood, spray the wounds with something he

303

was unfamiliar with, then bind her wrists with gauze and hook her up to an IV. He seemed to take a long time. Liza moved slightly.

Riding in the back of the ambulance with a medic, Michael kept his hand on Liza's arm. *Live, Liza, live.* That's all he could think.

The medic told Michael that Liza was lucky because she had made horizontal cuts instead of vertical ones. She was going to live. He also told Michael that he was in shock.

Sitting beside her, Michael shook. He heard the siren; he saw the flashing lights through his fingers. *What had the medic just said about shock?*

At the hospital, Michael called Liza's father and told him the grim news. Jack would get on the first flight to LA. Michael kept vigil by Liza's bedside until she awakened several hours later. When she saw him, she turned her head away from him.

"I will leave, but I am going to fight for you; I won't lose you, too." His eyes focused once more at his lover, now daughter, and his heart turned over as it had three times before. A strong antiseptic odor invaded his nostrils.

Until Jack arrived, he was determined to wait. He sat outside her room, moving constantly to change positions in the chair. *Did my subconscious know?* He was jittery after several coffees. There was a wide window at the far end of the corridor. The pink ribbons of dawn were floating across the sky, and Jack would be here soon.

When he saw Jack and Kate rushing down the hall, he rose. "She's alive," was all he could muster. He handed Jack Clare's letter. What could life possibly hold for him or Liza now? He looked at Jack and then Kate, shook his head slowly, turned quickly, and left.

WHAT HELL MUST BE LIKE

Kate and Jack sat with Liza, who was sleeping. After reading the letter, Jack looked down at his daughter. He held the letter out for Kate. When Kate had finished reading, she winced without saying anything. Sitting like caryatids for hours, they held the weight of Liza's sufferings on their shoulders. They forgot about food and time.

Early in the evening when a nurse came in to check on Liza, she asked them to stand in the hall while she ministered to her. They stood stock-still. It was hard for them to talk, as each was a hurricane of feelings.

After a few minutes, the nurse came out and said, "You can go in now. She's weak, but she wants to see you."

Leaning over Liza, Jack kissed her and whispered, "My darling girl, I love you so much."

Kate went beside Jack and touched Liza's cheek.

With a window behind them, they both sat in chairs to the right of Liza's bed. They could hear the white noise of the internal workings of the hospital. Liza opened her vacant eyes, glanced at them, and then closed them again. She did this several times. Finally, Jack went to get coffee, and when he returned Liza seemed more alert.

Kate asked, "I'm not sure how to comfort you, Liza. What will you do?"

"I want to move back home and live with Dad."

"What about Michael? He loves you."

"And I will always love him. Yet right now, I think it's best for us to keep apart." She watched the moon glide across the sky as she had done the night before. It was a waning moon now.

"Are you sure?" asked Kate.

"I'm not really sure of anything. I am so empty, and yet my thoughts churn and churn so that they make little sense. I want to sleep, wake up, and find out that this whole thing was a nightmare."

"We'll get you through this. I promise. Take your time, but don't make any decisions about Michael yet. You could be a source of strength for each other."

"My beloved sister, I've known what it is to be truly loved. It's been ripped away. I've seen my father naked. I've made love to him. How can I erase that? How can he? And Clare—the gall, I hate her. How could she have done this to us?"

"I don't know, Liza."

Liza started to sob, and Kate held her.

"Things will only get worse if you don't take care of yourself."

Liza fleered, "That's funny. Could things possibly get worse?"

"From where you're sitting, nothing looks good. In a way, this is another death for you. Think how long it took you to recover from Finn and Mom's deaths. Only now you have a chance to have two live fathers. Michael is in pain, too.
You can't forget that."

"I can't handle it. I just can't handle it."

"What can I do to help you?"

"Take me home. I can't stay here. Now I know what hell must be like."

"How about asking for a leave of absence from work and letting the dust settle?"

"You mean ashes, don't you?"

Two days later, Liza was discharged from the hospital into the care of her family after a psychiatric evaluation. The doctor thought it best that she start counseling as soon as possible.

Upon returning to the apartment, Liza saw that Michael had removed all his belongings. She was grateful for that. Now if she could just find a user manual to guide herself.

GLUEPOT OF PAIN

Kate called Michael and tried to tell him as tenderly as possible what Liza wanted to do. Three times she mentioned that Liza would come around. Time was what she needed. As Liza listened from her bedroom, she wondered if that were true.

Kate was quiet for a minute. She then said, "I understand, but a little time and distance would help. Could you help in that way for now?"

Liza heard Kate hang up.

"He understands. You need to know, however, he's not going to lose you. He'll fight with everything in him not to lose you," said Kate.

Liza didn't respond. *My heart is a gluepot of pain, and the glue is setting quickly.*

Kate turned on the radio and they listened to the *Academic Festival Overture* by Brahms over their soup. His *German Requiem* followed this Overture. Kate turned off the radio. When dinner ended, Liza excused herself, went to bed, lay on the edge of sleep, but never made it there.

IN ALL GOD'S UNIVERSE

Before they locked the apartment and gave the keys to the Super, Jack hugged Liza and said, "I understand how devastated you are. I will help you, and if you never want to speak of this again, we won't. I love you." That said; they headed east.

Kate flew home, and Liza and Jack drove a U-Haul back. No talking, music only.

Even though it took them nearly a week, Liza later remembered very little of the trip. She hurt all over as if a dog were gnawing on her bones. She just wanted to sleep, and that's what she did. When they arrived home about seven PM on the eighth of October, it was still light outside, and the sky was a fresco of pinks, salmon, and oranges. Confused for a second, having just awakened, she asked Jack where Rouge was.

"You're not fully awake. Rouge is in the closet with Mom and Finn."

The closet, thought Liza. She wanted to hide in the closet.

Jack opened the front door for her and said, "We'll unpack tomorrow."

Liza headed straight to the closet, almost closed the door, pulled out the stool and began. She looked at Finn and Fiona's urns and said, "I'm sorry to wake you sleeping souls." Then she turned to her mother and said, "How dare you kept my father from me all these years? How dare you made Clare promise to keep such a secret? Why? Why? Why?" She wanted to smash all the urns, but Jack knocked on the door and asked her if she were okay.

"Yes," Liza replied feebly.

"I'll pick up some pizza and beer and be back quickly," said Jack.

When she regained her composure, she picked up Finn's urn and held it in her lap. *I feel tainted and lonely. Was that how you felt?* Clare was right. In all God's universe, how? How could this happen? Angry with God again, she wondered could there actually be a God who would allow this? Or was it simply a matter of the Devil being the stronger? She had been taught one thing, but who really has the patent on good and evil?

With her inner tirade running out of steam, she left the closet and went downstairs to set the table. After they had finished eating, Liza asked her dad, "I need help as soon as possible. A counselor...psychiatrist... can you find someone?"

"Of course."

He went upstairs with her and kissed her goodnight at her bedroom door. "Sleep well."

Since the arrival of the letter, Liza had cried herself to sleep every night. The tears weren't washing away her misery, only leaving faint traces of grooves in her cheeks.

TREE OF LIFE

Located in a house in Bryn Mawr, Dr. Frawley's office was decorated with Asian antiques, French furniture, and many trinkets. Liza had a hard time looking at him. About forty with dark hair and dark eyes, he wore a tweed jacket and horn rimmed glasses. She felt naked as she told him what had happened but tried to keep her emotions in check. Staring at the pattern in the rug, she saw it was Persian with a navy blue central medallion. A tree of life pattern was recognizable, and she thought, *How appropriate*.

Dr. Frawley started slowly. "You must be in terrible pain, Liza."

"I'm not sure I want to live," she replied. "Death would be a kindness."

"Are you thinking of committing suicide again?"

"No, it would kill my dad...and others. I'm afraid I was unthinkingly selfish."

When her hour was up, Dr. Frawley suggested, "Perhaps we should meet more often. How about coming twice a week to start?"

In a few weeks, Liza talked about Michael, but she still wasn't ready to see him.

Dr. Frawley tried to get her to see how important it was for her sake as well as his to unravel their feelings together. After all, the doctor said, "Michael has been dealt some cruel blows, too. I'll be glad to orchestrate a meeting of the two of you in my office." The drapes in his office were closed, and the table lamps didn't really help to brighten the room.

Maybe not such a good idea. She didn't want to be the subject of an anonymous book, or a case study in a medical journal. If she and Michael were ever to reconcile in some way, she wanted it to be a private moment. Not a moment where she felt stung again by a wasp of longing.

NEVER ANY MRS. ANYBODY ELSE

Wanting to help, Kate and Andrew hoped it would be good for Kate to spend one night a week with Liza. Kate came over around five and took Liza out for dinner. After dinner they would return to the house and get ready for bed.

For Jack, it became a night to see friends or go his grief meeting.

Once as Kate was undressing, she asked Liza if she wanted to feel the baby kick. Liza smiled and nodded. She reached out, put her hand on Kate's stomach, and waited. She didn't have to wait long. The baby's kick seemed so strong. *I hope your journey through life won't be a series of burdens, little one.* "Does the baby kick a lot?"

"Mostly when I need a rest. It's good to see you smile."

"I want to smile, but somehow my mouth can't always do the gymnastics involved."

"What are you thinking about Michael?"

"I know that what my mother did, shutting him out, was wrong. I know that I can't do the same thing. I'm just not ready yet. Can you trust me to know when the time is right?"

"Of course."

When they finished talking, Kate reached for Liza's hand and said, "Goodnight, Mrs. Boobytrap."

Liza responded, "I guess I'll always be Mrs. Boobytrap, and never Mrs. Any Body Else."

314

Kate replied, "Don't be so hard on yourself; you'll always be my Mrs. Boobytrap, even when you're married with three children."

Liza whispered, "Goodnight, Mrs. Burgee. Thank you for being secure shelter."

SKATING ON BLADES OF HOPE

Two weeks before Christmas, Kate gave birth to a baby girl. She and Andrew agreed the baby should be called Fiona. Somehow, within a week's time, Fiona became Fee.

Earlier, Kate had asked, "Liza, would you help me out for a few weeks with the baby?" Liza had said, "I'd love to."

She enjoyed bathing and dressing Fee, but her favorite time was singing lullabies and rocking her to sleep. There were times when she held the baby with joy, and other times she felt sad thinking that her dreams of children were unlikely to be fulfilled. When taking care of Fee, Liza felt more like her old self. One morning she told Kate, "It's good to feel needed."

Wanting to provide a Christmas tree for Kate and Andrew, Liza and Jack drove to Meechum's Christmas Tree Farm and walked among the scented avenues of spruces, firs, pines, and cedars. The sweet balsam smell and shafts of sun filtered through the spires and extended arms of the trees. Liza felt it a sacred space, one she could easily surrender herself to. She hadn't felt this alive for a long time. When she found the perfect tree, Jack lay on the ground and sawed away. Placing it on a wagon, they took turns pulling it back to where they would pay. The air was crisp with a hint of smoke coming from a fire pit near the checkout stand. They stood still for a long minute just breathing in the day before paying.

Returning from the tree farm in Devon with a seven-foot scotch pine, they delivered it to Kate and Andrew's back porch.

At home, Jack made a fire and Liza made tea. Jack pulled out the ornaments that Fiona had so carefully packed after the Christmas before she died.

Together they decided which ornaments they should give to Kate, and which they should keep. They laughed, smiled, and cried as they remembered the different origins of each. The paper chain that Liza and Kate had made in 1962 was faded and falling apart. Liza held it a minute and dropped it in the fire. "In a few years Fee will make us a new one." Skating on blades of hope, she wanted everything back to normal.

Christmas day was joyful. Dressed in red velvet footie pajamas, with her chubby, cherub-like cheeks and wisps of soft brown hair framing her face, Fee was a gift to all. Although passed around frequently, she remained sleeping quietly for the most part.

Opening the ornaments, Kate was deeply touched and overwhelmed. Sitting in her and Andrew's living room with a fire crackling behind her, she fingered the angel ornament that Fiona had given her when she was six. "Mom

317

had bought it for me because she said that I had been such an angel helping with my baby sister." She touched Liza's arm.

Fiona had painted Kate's name in gold on the angel's skirt. The *e* had worn off, so it was now Kat, the angel. Holding the angel to her chest, she smiled.

Liza hoped Michael was spending the holidays with his sister. Had he told them everything? She prayed he wasn't as worn down by loneliness as she was.

1981

A DIFFERENT WORLD

Watching the ball drop in Time's Square on TV was how Jack and Liza rang in 1981. A year ago her world had been so different. Jack toasted to a better year for both of them. Clinking glasses, Liza wondered if that were possible.

At the beginning of January, after three months of therapy, Liza told Jack she wanted to go to work again. "Dad, do you know anyone at *The Inquirer*?"

Thinking about it, he said, "Yes, I do know one of the editors. I'll see what I can do."

A few weeks later, a job opened up at *The Inquirer*, and Liza applied to an editor named John Reiner. Her old boss Ron gave her a glowing letter of recommendation and said that he wished she were back at *The Times*. Not only was she a good reporter, but also she had such a sunny disposition.

When Liza read this, she thought, "That's what being in love does." She tried to smile the day of the interview. Mr. Reiner's office was gray with chrome furniture. The walls were hung with newspapers, framed in black, from famous editions. She couldn't take her eyes off the one behind his desk. *KENNEDY SHOT TO DEATH.* Lead: *Johnson Sworn In As President.* Reiner kept on talking about the paper. *Closure must be easier when someone was actually dead.* No more writing an opinion column. She'd be an education staff writer.

After a few days, Mr. Reiner called and offered her the job. She could start the following Monday, January 18. How could she work for *The Inquirer?* It was the paper that had printed her wedding notice. But—she needed to be busy.

She heard her dad having a long talk with Michael that week saying, "I think she's making significant progress." Funny, she thought herself on the third rung from the bottom of a very high ladder.

IN FLUX

When Liza came in from work a few days later and was looking over the mail, Jack passed on Michael's words. "I'm happy for her to be working."

This time Liza turned to Jack and said, "Please ask him if it's okay for me to call him."

That night after dinner, Jack said, "I'm calling Michael now." He went to his bedroom and shut the door.

When Jack finished, Liza headed for the closet. She picked up her mother's urn and whispered, "I'm letting Michael back into my life. What you did was painful." When she came out, her dad was waiting for her in his bedroom. She kissed him and said, "Good night." She could feel the veins in her heart stretching ever so slightly.

Waiting till the weekend, and hoping for fewer interruptions, on Saturday morning Liza pulled the phone from Jack's room into the closet and dialed Michael's number. She sat on the floor. It was mostly dark inside the closet. A small beam of light fell over her shoulder from the inch-wide crack of the open door. She was still angry with her mother and wanted her to witness the anguish involved.

"Hi, I'm sorry that it has taken me so long. How are you?"

"Worried about you," said Michael.

"I'm working at the *Inquirer,* as I'm sure Dad…Jack has told you. Nothing exciting, but it keeps me busy."

"I'm teaching only two courses this semester. My heart isn't in it. Is the doctor helping you?"

"I guess; at any rate he's not hurting." Twisting her hair around her fingers with her free hand, Liza choked back tears, remembering her first day in his class, and the start of this impossible situation.

"What type of relationship do you want with me?"

Liza thought for a moment and said, "Maybe just phone calls for now. Is that okay?"

"Whatever will get us through this."

"I want that too, but it might take longer than you want. Can you help me by waiting?"

"I'll do anything for you. Just ask."

They began to talk on a regular basis. Their conversations got longer with each call. Liza did the dialing, Michael the waiting. Still a bit shy, they each thought themself a blemish on the other. Both were hoping time would cure all. Yet time wasn't hours passing anymore; it was more a chipping away at an amalgamation of hurts and thoughts.

In time Liza began to feel comfortable on the phone with Michael. Thank goodness that her dad and Kate had encouraged her to let Michael back into her world. Even though she appreciated the fact that Michael hadn't given up on her, she couldn't face him yet. More inner fortitude was needed before this meeting could happen. She had to get to a place where she wasn't thinking of Michael sexually. She had dreams. Sometimes, she woke up crying because her subconscious was tempting her with Michael the lover, and rejecting her for being an incestuous woman.

When she shared these dreams with Dr. Frawley, he assured her she was still in flux about all that had happened. "In time you'll be able to fight back because you were innocent. You didn't seduce a man you knew to be your father. You must trust yourself. You never would have done such a thing." Now, she had to work with the knowledge she had. "See the coupling as accidental on your part as well as Michael's."

Dr. Frawley's words helped, but her insides were still sore.

After one such session, Liza called Michael and was trying to frame a question but was fumbling for words. She kept rearranging herself in the closet. Her mother's urn was on her lap. The light from the bedroom seeped in.

Finally, Michael said, "Liza, is there something you need to ask me?"

She bit her lip, and softly uttered, "Do you dream about me sexually?"

When he hesitated a second too long, Liza countered with, "It's okay, I dream of you, also. Dr. Frawley is working on this aspect of our relationship in treatment. Perhaps you would benefit from seeing a psychologist or someone who will lay these issues bare, so we can move on.

"I'll do anything to get us to the point of squaring our relationship. Someday, I hope I'll see myself as your second father."

She was glad that Michael didn't want to take Jack's place in her life, Liza knew it was too late for that.

They sighed some, they laughed some, and they still cried. Maybe one day they could see themselves as father and daughter.

When Liza shared this with Kate, Kate smiled, held up crossed fingers, and gave Liza a hug.

Another time Liza was talking with Michael, and, unrelated to anything they were speaking about, she asked, "Do you ever think about marrying again?"

He took his time answering, "No. Do you?"

It was her turn to pause, "I can't imagine it ever happening. It's taking all my reserves to keep going each day. I don't think there can be a next time."

"I get it, but you deserve a good man to love and marry you. You're young. I'd like to be a grandfather some day. I don't want to frighten you. I just want to be a part of your life, a viable part. Mostly, I want to see you happy."

"Thank you. You're further along than I am. You're a good man, Michael." She rubbed the back of her neck. "If only Clare's 'good' intentions hadn't gotten in the way. I'm still so angry with her. I don't think I'll ever forgive her."

"It's so complicated; your mom placed a heavy load on her shoulders, but—you have to decide what you'll do about her."

"Aren't you angry with her?"

"I'm afraid I'm more angry with your mother for keeping you from me. We loved each other so much."

Liza wanted to say, *You loved her more than me?* Her better angels kept her quiet.

With Dr. Frawley's help Liza was making small strides. In the beginning she almost thought he was judging her, thinking that she was feeling too much guilt over something that had been out of her control. When she questioned him about this, she received an answer that put her mind at rest. Hence, she was better able to listen to him. He explained, "You have to understand the difference between guilt and shame. You are using the terms interchangeably."

With time, Liza was able to express the unspoken guilt she had harbored over her mother's death, and the shame she carried over her sexual relationship with her father. She also felt guilty about not allowing Michael completely back into her life. She was feeling anxious living with these troubling emotions.

Dr. Frawley talked about Clare and the guilt and shame she must be carrying. At some point he hoped Liza would be able to understand why Clare had felt it necessary to lie for so long. Not condoning Clare's actions, he wanted Liza to try stepping into Clare's frame of mind.

Only forgiveness will bring peace, and yet I can't find it in myself.

At Liza's suggestion Michael entered therapy. Liza could tell when they talked that he was able to intellectualize his feelings and knew with certainty he had done nothing intentionally to hurt her.

One Saturday morning ten minutes into the phone call, Michael asked Liza, "Do you think at some point I could move to Philadelphia to be closer to

326

you?" He cleared his throat. "I'm carrying so much guilt over the pain you're experiencing."

Sitting in the closet, Liza began crying. "It would be nice," she said. "Just not yet." She touched her mother's urn and shook her head slowly.

"Please don't cry. I'll wait."

Hearing him take a deep breath," she said, "I'm tired Michael, sleep will help. I'll call you soon." She mouthed the words, "I love you, take care." A faint scent of Ambush came from one of her mom's dresses. She gathered every garment one at a time to her nose and sniffed. Finally, she found one that had gotten mixed up with another hanger and realized this one carried Fiona's scent. *I miss you so much, mom.*

Going to her room, she fell into a deep sleep letting her subconscious play havoc with her dreams.

SOME JOY BACK

"Liza, I think an Irish Setter puppy would bring some joy back into this gloomy house. Remember how much Rouge did for your mom at the end?" Jack had found a breeder in Paoli, and they would go on Saturday morning to choose their puppy.

At the McCleary Setter Farm, there was a small, thin bitch in a pen with twelve offspring. Liza climbed into the pen and sat down; within seconds one little bundle of brown fur climbed into her lap. That was that. She turned to her father and said, "This is the one."

Jack smiled and said, "That's the same way Finn chose Rouge." This time it was Jack who turned to Mr. McCleary and said, "I know this dog will take good care of my daughter."

Thinking of everything, Jack had even bought an Irish dictionary to find a suitable name for the wee one. When they read that *Mona* meant *little noble one,* they thought that perfect, and so Mona it was. Liza smiled more that day than she had in the last few months because Mona made the house sing with glad barks.

"Dad, thank you for thinking of this. It's so good just to hold something."

Her dad gulped, turned from her, and said, "I know. So you won't mind sharing her with me."

"Oh, Dad, we are a sorry pair."

Before going up to bed, they took Mona outside. They made a nest of an old blanket in Liza's bathroom and put a clock that ticked loudly under the blanket.

Liza and her dad each gave Mona one more snuggle against their necks before placing her on the blanket.

"If she wakes, I'll hear her and take her out," said Liza.

"If you need help, wake me."

Liza woke to the sound of faint puppy whimpers. Jumping up, she lifted Mona out of her nest. She tiptoed downstairs and went into the backyard with the puppy. It was a clear night, and stars were sprinkled in every direction.

"Hurry girl," she urged the puppy. Liza's feet were freezing: she had forgotten to put on slippers. As she lowered Mona onto her nest, she thought better of it. She climbed into bed and let the puppy lie on her chest. She imagined the heartbeat as Michael's and fell quickly back to sleep.

A routine was established that night, one that she and Mona could both live with.

What high-spirited dogs setters are, and strong willed. There were many mornings when Mona grabbed one of Liza's shoes and did not give it up without a chase.

"Dad, what is it about dogs? Joy lives in their barks, tails, licks, nuzzles, playfulness, and even their naughtiness."

"And," said her dad, "they never resist a hug."

When Mona was housebroken, Liza thought the puppy could sleep next to her on the floor as Rouge had done with Fiona, instead of on her chest. After all, she was growing into her skin. The vet said she would weigh about sixty pounds at maturity. Mona had other ideas. Waiting for Liza to fall asleep, she would jump onto the bed with her. Although Liza knew this was a bad habit, she couldn't fight those big orange brown eyes. After a week, Mona gave up any pretenses and started out on the bed. She would snuggle up against Liza's legs. They both liked the new arrangement. Every morning when Liza woke up, Mona had her muzzle across Liza's feet. Liza had only to say the magic words for Mona to lift her head: "Food, glorious food." Upon hearing these words, Mona jumped off the bed, bounded down the stairs, and sat waiting to be served her meal.

WRAPPED IN SILENCE

The first Thursday afternoon in February, Liza was interviewing the Director of the WINS program when she began having back pain. Thinking she must have pulled a muscle, she dismissed it. Her back was still bothering her when she was eating dinner. "Dad, I've had this pain in my back all day."

He suggested, "Try using the heating pad tonight." He took another sip of wine. "I can't think having Mona in bed with you is helping your back. You're probably scrunched up."

Mona's eyes won again over Liza's back pain that night.

The following morning when the pain persisted, she made an appointment with their family doctor. He thought she had strained her back and gave her a prescription to ease the pain. *Perhaps this pain can supplant my other one.* She was to take these pills for two weeks to see if she felt better.

As the pain hadn't subsided at the end of two weeks, Liza returned to her doctor. Dr. Swain, though much older, reminded Liza of Finn; he had the same grimaced face that Finn had used with family before Viet Nam. Yet when the doctor talked to her, his voice had gentleness to it. She felt at ease in his presence. "Liza, I think you should have a CT scan, just to be safe."

She didn't want to think about the possibilities, so she asked, "When can that be done?"

"Now. I'll call ahead and they'll be ready for you."

A few days later, Dr. Swain called and told Liza that her CT scan indicated a need for a bone biopsy. She asked him if she should be worried. He said he'd be better able to answer that when he saw the results from the biopsy. The biopsy was performed that afternoon.

In a panic for these results, she waited two eternally long days. Dr. Swain called again, this time to tell her that she had multiple lesions in her backbone and ribs. He then ordered a mammogram and biopsy of her breasts. Having to wait two more agonizing days for all the results, she now knew she had bone cancer, but could she possibly have breast cancer too?

###

On Friday, February 19th at four-thirty, Liza and her dad went to see Dr. Swain. The two of them sat motionless in his small, windowless office. Dr. Swain didn't soften the news. She had not only bone cancer but stage IV breast cancer.

As he spoke, she felt what was left of her insides shrivel. How many times had this doctor been the bearer of such bad news? She wanted to put her hands over her ears and repeat and repeat, *La, La La*. Liza now understood how Fiona must have felt. Was it really possible that Jack and Kate would lose yet another family member? So many choices to be made, but at that moment she couldn't make any. She wanted Jack to make it all go away. No matter how she looked at it, she was facing a death sentence.

They were to meet the following day with Dr. Watkins, the oncologist who would handle her case. She understood what Stage IV breast cancer meant, and she knew that bone cancer was painful.

332

On the ride home, she and her dad didn't speak—each paralyzed by the news. What could they possibly say to each other? Jack reached over and held her hand. When they entered the house, Jack held Liza, tears running down both their cheeks. Mona was waiting with a bark and a wag. Liza got down and hugged her. More tears.

"Would you like some tea?" asked Jack.

Liza turned from Mona and said, "I don't think so, Dad. I think I'm going to lie down. Please call Kate and tell her."

When she went upstairs, Mona followed. A closet visit before she went to sleep might help. Mona walked in behind her and lay by the stool. Liza looked at the shelf and said, "I'll be joining you soon enough. I won't be able to put the smile back on Dad's face, and I'm sorry, Mom, that I didn't understood the full weight of the cancer you lived with for so long." *Do I really want to hear what the oncologist has to say?* Part of the time, she stared at the urns, her mind a complete blank.

When she left the closet, Kate was waiting in their bedroom. Kate held her as the blue twilight made its way into the room through the slats in the blinds. Liza lay down on her bed followed by Mona, and Kate lay down on her old bed. Kate said, "Liza, give me your hand."

When Liza's hand slipped out of Kate's, Kate rose and whispered "Sleep tightly, Mrs. Boobytrap."

"You, too, Mrs. Burgee."

Liza could hear Kate tiptoe down the stairs. She heard Kate's words to Jack "No, I'm not. We have to get on top of this for Liza's sake."

"May I go with the two of you tomorrow to the oncologist?"

"You'll have to ask Liza."

"What time is the appointment?"

"Two o'clock."

"I'll be here at one, and if Liza doesn't want me along, she'll have to say so. Dad, do you ever think our family is cursed?"

"I don't know what to think anymore."

"Should I call Michael?"

"That's Liza's decision. See what she says tomorrow."

Getting up, Liza walked to the window. She knew Kate was kissing Jack, and she heard, "Goodnight, Dad." With her thumb and forefinger, she opened a wider space between two slats. Kate climbed into her car. The car window was cracked, and Liza always slept with a window open. Hearing a keening sound first, she then saw her sister hit the steering wheel with the palm of her hand and dissolve. Liza managed to stifle her scream. Mona, who had been at the bottom of her bed, got up and stood next to Liza at the window—so much anguish and nowhere to escape.

Liza awakened with the sunrise. Trying to gather her thoughts, she lay still and thought of how brave Fiona had been, how she had set the bar high for Liza to follow. Liza was determined to follow her courageous example. That would be her goal. A small victory—but a victory nonetheless. She would listen to the doctor, but she was pretty sure she wasn't going to undergo chemotherapy, or hormone therapy, or whatever else had been mentioned yesterday. She didn't have it in her to fight anymore.

334

Kissing Mona's head, which was on her chest, she remembered Fiona's second bout with breast cancer, and she knew about Elizabeth Kubler-Ross's work. Liza thought that she didn't need to deny impending death; she was dead to herself already. Anger and bargaining were out; she had tried to bargain with God when Fiona was so sick, and she had gotten nowhere. She was still angry over Fiona and Finn's deaths. Depression, well that was easy, as that's why she was seeing Dr. Frawley. So she might as well jump to acceptance and be done with it. Liza wanted it to be over. How can Michael become a part of her dying? He hadn't been given that opportunity with her mother. She must do this for him.

Kate and her dad needed to feel a part of the process, too. Although Liza had been too afraid to act in college, she was now ready to give the performance of her life, and she was determined not to screw it up. Wait to tell Michael. *It seems the shadow of misfortune follows me everywhere.*

###

A packed waiting room greeted them. So Kate and Liza sat in chairs across the room from each other, and Jack stood by a side window looking out. Both women paged numbly through magazines.

Finally, a nurse took them back to Dr. Watkins.

Shaking their hands, Dr. Watkins remarked, "Unusually warm weather for February." He had a gracious demeanor and a warm smile; his office, however, was as cheerless as Dr. Swain's. The pale gray walls were

335

hung with prints of dogs in different stages of hunting: crouched in the weeds, on point, carrying the bodies of lifeless birds.

Recently, when Mona had come in with a songbird in her mouth, wagging her tail and so proud of her work, Liza had felt distress. Mona hadn't chewed the bird, but it had died anyway, either of suffocation or possibly panic. "I'll be as dead as these birds," Liza's thought when Dr. Watkins began to speak. He talked about the different types of treatments: systemic therapy, hormone therapy, and chemotherapy. "Is your mother still alive?"

"My mother died in childbirth, and my mother's sister died in her late forties of breast cancer."

Dr. Watkins thought a moment and spoke quietly, "There's a good chance that your mother would have had breast cancer, also."

Liza wasn't going to waste anyone's time. Listening politely, she then said, "I don't want to go through the pain of chemotherapy. No one in my family needs to watch me waste away." When she gathered her thoughts, she spoke again. "I understand the seriousness of this disease. I'd like to be kept as comfortable as possible and stay at home."

When she finished, Jack started to protest, "Liza…" Liza silenced him with a raised palm and continued. "Can you keep me comfortable and possibly give me a rough idea of how much time I have left?"

"Yes, it is possible for you to be kept comfortable; you can receive radiation therapy to kill cancer cells in the areas that are causing pain, and you can start with small doses of morphine and increase the dosage as needed," Dr. Watkins said. His phone rang, but he didn't answer. "As to time, I can never

336

be certain, but I would think in terms of a few months. I also think you should take some time to reconsider your options."

Liza asked when and how to schedule the radiation therapy.

"Immediately," he told her. "My nurse will help you schedule a program tailored to your needs."

Standing first, Liza said, "Thank you, Doctor." Shaking his hand, she turned towards the door, not looking at Kate or Jack. *This part is so hard on them.* From the moment she left that office, she started to visualize her funeral, which changed each time she imagined it. She realized in a flash that with a death sentence, the mind doesn't stray far from that reality.

Jack and Kate followed her down the long corridor. The floor creaked.

"Please don't make this any harder than it already is," Liza said as she climbed into the car. "I can't go through a protracted illness. I'll need your help and courage to get through this as it is." When she didn't say anything else, neither did they. It was late afternoon, and the curtain of night was lowering itself. She caught a whiff of the winter honeysuckle by the front door and wondered why she had never really appreciated the scent when it was truly delightful in the dead of winter.

As they entered the house, Mona ran around them exuberantly. They stood in the kitchen, dazed.

Liza thought about Fiona and the letter she had left for her... the closet. "In the letter Mom left for me, she wanted us to disband the closet. We can't leave it to Fee or any other grandchildren. So I'm hopeful you'll follow

337

Mom's wishes. I'd like you to take all of our ashes to Cape May on a warm spring day and scatter them on the water." As their eyes began to water, she continued. "If Mona ran along the beach as Rouge did, I think that would please Mom, Finn, my mother, and even Rouge. Please do this." She took one of each of their hands in hers. "It's time." Having said this, she felt lighter and more peaceful.

"Your hand is so cold," said Jack.

"The tea will warm me."

Kate made peppermint tea that seemed to revive them.

Needing to lift the silence that had now enclosed them, Liza said, "Kate, tell us about Fee and how she's growing."

Kate took a long minute to compose herself. She sang Fee's praises and shared her feeding, sleeping schedule, cooing sounds, and funny faces.

"I'll clean up, and you'd best be getting back to that sweet baby," said Liza.

Kate kissed Liza and Jack and stopped when she got to the door. "Liza, I'm here for you."

"Thanks, Mrs. Burgee."

When the door shut, her dad went over to her, looked into her eyes, held her hand, and said, "I want to make everything better for you. Maybe we can guide each other through this."

Liza stepped into Jack's arms and whispered, "Thank you, Daddy." They remained that way for a minute before separating, trying to smile at each other. Wrapped in silence, they began going through the motions of every day minutia.

Taking a measure of the kitchen, which had been the hub of family activity when all were alive, Liza thought, *This house will be too big for Dad. I should probably get him thinking about selling. Not just the closet, but also this entire place is a mausoleum. Maybe if he's not surrounded by memories at every turn he might meet a woman he could spend time with. Maybe it's none of my business. Maybe he needs to work this out for himself.*

STRUGGLING FOR AIR

Liza got a small tablet of paper from her bedroom and headed to the closet. She wrote:

1 Burial at sea – done

2 No prolonging of life – done

3 Talk to Michael – yet to do

Mona nudged her nose through the crack in the door and came in. Liza thought, "Oh, my goodness, Mom chose to be read to so she wouldn't have to talk, and it gave me something to do. What book? Well, there are plenty of books I've been dying to read." When she realized what she had just thought, she didn't laugh. She had lost her funny bone when she lost Michael. Then in a flash it came to her.

#4 Ask Michael to read *A Hundred Years of Solitude*

#5 Ask Kate to help make a small quilt for Fee

#6 Dad - What to ask of Dad? Think more about this

#7 Clare - I should open my heart to forgiveness

After dinner, Liza called Michael. In the beginning, she tried to be chatty, but

Michael picked up an unusual timbre in her voice.

"Is anything wrong?"

Be straight with him. Just say it. "I have Stage IV breast cancer. It has already spread to my bones. I have a few months to live."

Liza imagined Michael trying to make sense of what she had just conveyed. She pictured him paralyzed. Stopped in his tracks.

After a lengthy pause, he said, "I want to be near you especially now. Please say yes."

"I'd like that."

"Tell me how you feel and what you're thinking."

"Except for radiation I'm going to refuse treatment. Radiation will kill the cells that are causing pain in my back. I'm already on a low dose of morphine."

She shifted her bottom on the floor of the closet. "How do I feel? Feeling hasn't been in my vocabulary for a while. Mostly, I'm empty. I think about the sickness that's devouring my body, and in a way it's a blessing. I'm tired."

"I would trade places..."

"I know that." She paused to catch her breath. "To think that every day you live is a day closer to death, and you think you'll have years to prepare. I was given time to do this and yet these next months will fly by, and I'll breathe myself out of existence. I don't want to dwell on the dying, but I can't seem to focus on the living part. So whatever small thing you can do to ease the way I'll be grateful for."

341

"I'll do my best."

They sat in silence and realized that not talking was a small thing they could do for each other.

Finally, Michael asked, "Is Jack around?"

"Yes, but I have a request. Will you start divorce proceedings? Will you do that for me? I believe we need closure on this matter."

He murmured, "I'll do it for you."

"Hold on." She laid the receiver on the floor. She knew Michael was trying to resuscitate his own heart.

Her dad followed her to the closet. He picked up the phone, stood next to Liza with his hand on her shoulder, and held the receiver between them so Liza could hear the conversation, too.

"Liza said it was okay for me to come and be with her. Do you have any suggestions where I might stay?"

"Finn's room."

"Are you sure?"

"I think all of us need to help each other. So please, stay here. When do you think you'll arrive?"

"As soon as I can cover my two classes for this semester. I'll call when I have everything settled. Thanks for being so kind, Jack."

"This hasn't been easy for you, Michael."

###

When Michael first saw Liza, the surprised look on his face gave his thoughts away.

"Yes, I've lost weight. It's the disease."

Liza saw the scars in his eyes as he looked at her. She wanted to feel his strong arms around her. She didn't want sex. That wasn't part of her vocabulary anymore. She just wanted to feel again. Feel anything, again.

When they arrived at the house, Michael asked, "And who is this?" as Mona greeted them.

"That's my pal, Mona. I'm so tired. Do you mind if I slip upstairs now?" Mona followed, and they made a quick trip to the closet.

Funny, she hadn't noticed Fiona's robe before, hanging on a hook at the back of the door. Perhaps Jack had put it there. Liza put it on and wrapped it tightly around herself. Wanting to wear it, she thought for a second and realized it would conjure so many raw images in Jack's mind that she took it off.

"Goodnight," she called down the steps, turned and went to bed thinking about her two fathers. How kind of Jack to open his house to Michael. Maybe Michael would help Jack in the healing process, as both were struggling for air.

The morphine that Jack gave to Liza was in pill form, and the dose she was taking was slowly increasing. Liza woke with the sunrise every morning. The morphine made her a bit spacey, but her dreams were works of wonder. Never had she seen such brilliant colors, or remembered long forgotten scents from childhood, and the beach roses at the Cape May cottage.

343

Knowing Jack was still wondering if they should try to persuade her to prolong her life or to agree to what she wanted made her sad. She counted on Michael to know that she had suffered enough and that she should be allowed to die quietly. In the end, she believed that Jack would agree with Michael. Poor dad— always being asked to let a loved one go.

Lying still, she thought about what she could ask Jack to do. *Perhaps something to do with breast cancer. How could this have happened?* This was the first time she had allowed herself to do some soul searching. If only—she knew she was at some fault here, skipping yearly checkups because she had traded the pill for a diaphragm. Many things had interfered with her doing routine matters of health, and all had been major. After her breakup with Simon, she had been determined somehow to be with Michael. Was her determination her downfall? So much for answered prayers. Knowing that what's done is done, she turned her mind back to something Jack could do. She also wondered how you die. Does a light go out? Is it painful? Like Fiona, she'd probably go into a coma first. Would she still be conscious of people in the room, or in essence would she be gone even to herself? What could Jack do? What about God?

Mona lifted her head from Liza's feet and looked at her as if to say, "Isn't it time to eat?"

Liza said, "You're right, girl, enough of this tomfoolery. Food, glorious food."

###

344

When she entered the kitchen, with Mona trailing behind, Jack was making pancakes for Michael and asked Liza if she wanted any.

"Just one, please. Dad," *I don't know what to call them.* "Michael, Dad, I think since I'm not feeling too bad, I'd like to go to the Barnes Foundation this afternoon. Maybe Kate and Fee will come too. What do you say?"

"Capital idea," exclaimed Jack.

"Count me in," said Michael.

"I think you'll enjoy the Impressionist and Post-Impressionist paintings housed there. My favorite is Monet's *The Boat Studio.* Do you remember Dad when Mom would take us there, and sometimes Violette de Mazia, I think that was her name, wouldn't open the doors?" Liza chuckled. "She was a real character. I forgot, the Renoirs. If you see nothing else, they are sumptuous. I could go on, but better if you decide for yourself. Let's go after lunch."

Kate with Fee in a Baby Bjorn had arranged to come around ten and work on the quilt. While they were working on it, if they had to pass thread or a patch of material, their fingers might touch, and they left them there a second or two longer than necessary. At times like this, Liza wondered about the next world. Would she be able to watch over Kate, Jack, and Michael, Andrew, and

Fee? Could she influence them in any way? Would she talk to those who had gone ahead of her? She thought, "Why not?"

Growing tired about eleven, Liza went upstairs for a short nap before lunch. Strength came in spurts, while weakness came in droves.

This museum had always put a smile on Liza's face when she went with Fiona and Kate. It did so this day, also. She looked up with pleasure at the hinges and locks that adorned the walls, she marveled at the magnificent collection. She wanted to lie down in Monet's *Boat Studio* and float away in peace. After forty-five minutes, she felt like a paper doll, flat and lifeless. Sitting down she said, "You two finish the tour. I'm quite content to sit here."

Before they entered a second room, Liza overheard Jack say to Michael, "Let's hurry through the rest of the rooms. I don't like leaving her for long."

They started for home and Michael, full of enthusiasm, said, "I couldn't agree more that the Renoirs are spectacular, and I really like his vibrant use of color. I'd never realized that children played such a prominent role in his work."

Jack piped up and said, "The Cezannes will always be my favorites."

The golden fingers of the sun touched their shoulders as they boarded the train. Even though the ride was only nine minutes, Liza fell asleep.

###

Walking up the front steps, Liza said, "I'm really beat. Michael, would you read to me when I wake?"

"Sure."

She leaned into the winter honeysuckle and took a long whiff. She was determined to breathe in its wonderful scent for the rest of her days.

###

When she awakened, she heard Michael clear his throat in the living room. Liza called to him. She could hear a tripping sound as he scrambled to the steps. As he entered her bedroom, she handed him *One Hundred Years of Solitude*.

He sat across from her on Kate's old bed. Michael's eyes met hers and he whispered, "I'm so sorry for all of this." She saw how hard this was for him but thought it best that he purge himself of any lingering thoughts that would nag him later.

"I wish I could turn everything around, and I mean everything." He waited a moment to collect himself again and continued. "I will be with you till the end. Thank you for letting me."

"We won't talk about this anymore, because I believe we already know what's in each other's heart. Your being here is the best medicine for me. Thank you."

A soft, golden peace accompanied the blue tinge of twilight that settled within the room and their hearts.

And so Michael began reading, and Liza began to immerse herself in the magical realism of this novel. She compared her struggles with those of Jose Arcadio Buendia. At the end of chapter two, she fell asleep.

###

That same night Jack stopped by her room to see how she was doing. She tried to smile but didn't have it in herself to do so. "Dad, I think I need to increase the morphine now. Just a little bit. I still want to be present to all of you."

"Oh, my darling, don't worry about us. We need to make sure your pain is controlled. I'll talk to Dr. Watkins tomorrow morning."

The clutter of medicinal paraphernalia on her bureau reminded her of her mom, but the gardenia on her bureau was all Michael.

THE LIMITS OF REALITY

With a fire crackling in the fireplace and Liza reclining on the sofa with a blanket over her legs, she and her dad were reading in the living room when she put her book on her lap and said, "Dad, do you think you could do two things for me?"

He answered, "Of course, my darling."

"I know this will be difficult for you, but could you sing me to sleep when the time comes? It would mean so much to me." Liza pulled her blanket up.

She watched her dad slump in his chair and then quickly sit up straight. "And I have another idea...I wonder if you would raise money for breast cancer research in Mom's name?"

"I'll do my best to sing for you. As for raising money, I will pour my heart and soul into it, but you must know I'll be doing it for you, too."

"Could you start soon, so I can share in the progress you're making?"

"Sure."

"Thanks for your love and care. I believe no matter what happens after I die, I'll be in a better place." Liza smiled, and Jack tried desperately to smile, but a wave of loss undulated throughout his body.

###

As Michael descended the stairs, the doorbell rang, and he answered it. He signed for the package and went to the living room.

Dejectedly, Michael went over to Liza and said, "The divorce papers have arrived. Do you want to look them over?"

Liza knew there was nothing to look over. She also knew she couldn't look at Michael as she would fall apart. Rubbing her hands together, she felt the zipper like scars on her wrists. Quickly, she put her hands under the covers. "Just tell me where to sign."

Opening the envelope, Liza saw Michael's face turn ashen. His eyes were so wet he could hardly find the places for Liza to sign. He headed for the kitchen. Liza could hear the faucet running. The tall case clock chimed the hour. Upon returning, he took a deep breath and with effort took a pen from his pocket and pointed to where Liza should sign. He was close enough that she picked up a hint of Lifebouy soap, a scent that she had associated with sex. Now, nothing stirred her. She felt sexless. After signing the papers, she said. "I'm going to nap here by the fire. It's better this way, Michael."

Kate arrived in the morning, needing more material for the quilt. Liza, still in bed, smiled and said, "I've got an idea." Slowly, she got to her feet and opened her closet, taking out different articles of clothing from the many cotton, silk, and wool dresses and skirts.

"Do you really want to use these?"

"I can't think of anything better than to have Fee wrapped in pieces of my life."

She and Kate cut squares. A wobbly card table was set up in the bedroom. Scraps of material were scattered on the floor. The wind rattled the windows, and fleecy clouds floated across the sky.

"Kate, do you have anything you need to say to me?"

Kate, with all her knowledge of human interaction, didn't disappoint. She stopped sewing and whispered, "I think we've said everything over the years. Thank you for being my sister. Thank you for loving me."

"I'm sad to leave you. Of everyone I love, I feel I have let you down the most by not prolonging my life."

"Don't think that. I don't like what you're doing, but I do understand that you've had enough. I hope you'll get a long deserved rest, Mrs. Boobytrap."

They both smiled. Liza was glad that she had put one more thing to rest.

As was her habit now, Liza awakened at sunrise. She lay still and thought about Sarah and how to tell her. Perhaps a letter was best. It took her a while to frame the words; she hoped she did so without being mawkish. At the end of the letter, she asked Sarah to call her. Were her words clear headed enough under the influence of the morphine?

351

Her room was beginning to smell more like a hospital, and the gardenias that Michael replaced periodically were losing their strong scent for Liza. She had to go to the bureau and hold a flower close to her nose now. Which of the senses was the last to go? She guessed sight. But maybe it's all at once. Did it matter?

Thinking it would help her to concentrate as much as possible, she asked Michael to prop her up with four pillows. Sitting in the chair in front of the window, he began reading.

"It was as if God had decided to put to the test every capacity for surprise and was keeping the inhabitants of Macondo in a permanent alteration between excitement and disappointment, doubt and revelation, to such an extreme that no one knew for certain where the limits of reality lay."

God figured prominently in the solitude. Liza stopped Michael when he read that sentence and asked, "Do you still believe in God?"

He was quick with his answer. "Sometimes yes, sometimes no. It was easy to leave the Catholic Church, but not so easy to leave God. Perhaps that was the gift of Catholicism. Ambiguity is such a funny word, because it also means inexplicable." A heavy sigh escaped him.

"Now that I'm dying, I think about it a lot. I don't understand a God who tests some people beyond their limits. What's the point? If there is a God, then I guess we wouldn't be capable of understanding divine thought. Yet we were taught that we were made to His image and likeness. I want both my feet in the same camp. I want to die at peace with my beliefs."

352

"Oh Liza, I can't help you, but you know that." Mona came in from outside, jumped up on the bed, and rubbed her cold fur along Liza's side.

"Michael, I've been thinking about something. Did you ever give my mother a locket?"

"I did. I put my picture in it."

"It was in my mother's hands when she died. I wore it everyday till I lost it. Had I not lost it, you might have recognized it and made the connection." She put her hand to her neck. "There was no picture in it. Clare must have removed it." *Our wills and fates do so contrary run...*

They were quiet for a few minutes, and Liza broke the silence with, "Please read."

When the light faded in the room, Michael looked over at Liza.

"I'm fading, too. Please don't turn on the light," she said.

Liza felt weaker each day, and she knew her time here was slipping away faster than she had expected. Not wanting dinner the night before Sarah arrived, she forced herself to eat. She wanted to have as much strength as possible to see her dear friend.

Kate came over to help Liza change into her bedclothes. Jack would have helped her, but she didn't want him to see how thin she was. As Kate helped her put on her pajamas, Liza asked her to tell Jack and Michael that she wanted a small dose of morphine the next morning. She hoped to be at her most alert for Sarah. Before Kate was able to ask her if she needed anything else, Liza was asleep.

PART OF HER JOURNEY WAS OVER

Morning had broken, and Liza woke with a start but couldn't remember the dream. Looking over at Kate's bed reminded her of the many nights they had confided in one another. The *Laura Ashley* wallpaper still pleased her. They had chosen it in high school when Fiona had told them they could redecorate their room. The trim was a *Pearl Ash* paint. It had held up well, and Liza still liked being in this room.

Turning her thoughts to Sarah, she knew this would be a hard meeting, but a necessary one. Even though she wasn't sure about the afterlife, she wanted to be sure about tying up loose ends in this life.

Sarah ran up the stairs when she arrived. Liza saw the practiced smile on her face and the first of spring daffodils in her hand. "Hi!" Sarah said slightly out of breath. Mona jumped off the bed to give Sarah a proper greeting: licking her hands and sniffing her skirt.

Liza perked up. "Hi, yourself. How was the drive?"

"Uneventful."

"The daffodils are so joyful, and their scent is so strong. I always think it's because our noses have been stuffed with the cold winter and now finally our senses awaken again." *Are there better scents ahead for me?*

Michael appeared in the doorway with Sarah's bag. "Do you girls need anything? Would you like the shade drawn? It's so bright in here."

"And so dark at night." The words had slipped out before Liza had time to catch them. "The light's fine."

"I'd love a Coke, if you have one," Sarah answered.

Liza said, "That sounds good. I think I'll have one, too."

Sarah went to sit on the other bed, but Liza asked her to sit on the bed with her. They hugged; Sarah broke down and through her tears said, "I told myself I wouldn't cry. So much for promises." Mona tried to get back on the bed again.

"Not now, Mona. It's okay. I really do understand. So, start with little Liza and tell me all." She looked at her dear friend and believed she was a witness to her own life.

After Sarah shared anecdotes about little Liza, Liza realized she was growing tired, and hoped Sarah wouldn't feel awkward if she fell asleep.

Sarah said, "Wow, that drive made me sleepy; mind if I lie down and take a nap before dinner?"

Determined to make dinner a festive occasion, Jack invited Andrew, Kate, and Fee to join them. Jack was going to invite Liam and Peter, but Liza thought better of it. They would have to wait a day or two.

With a concerted effort Liza ate in the dining room with everyone. She managed with Sarah's help to put on jeans and a turtleneck, which made her look like an upholstered toothpick—at least it was her thought as she looked in the mirror. While dressing, she knew she would have to keep the conversation flowing, or it would be stilted with long moments of silence. She thought of several things. President Reagan calling the USSR an "evil empire" seemed like a good opening. *We could also talk about popular music or the newest fad, mobile phones*, she thought.

At table, after a blessing given by Jack, Liza opened the conversation. "I just read an article about the world's first automatic mobile phone system being launched in Oslo. Can you imagine walking around with a phone?"

"Seems crazy," said Michael. "Apparently they're heavy, and you have to be in places that get reception."

"Think how far the car has come. My father used to crank to start his first car." Jack said. "The phones are heavy now, but I can only imagine in a short time they'll get lighter and lighter."

Like burdens, thought Liza. *Okay, move on. Don't spoil this night.*

The candlelight on the table and the dimmed chandelier cast a peaceful glow on the gathering. She realized that she would not have dinner again with all these loved ones. Maybe they would meet in the hereafter. She realized that now she was the one being maudlin, not the others.

Unable to eat anything, she slipped pieces of food to Mona, who accepted them without question.

357

She saw Michael look at her plate and smile. She managed to smile back.

When plates were cleared, Kate came in from the kitchen with a Baked Alaska. Liza held back the tears, then managed to get up and go to her sister. "Thank you." She whispered in Kate's ear, "A perfect ending to this night."

Seated, Liza ate as much as possible, two little spoonfuls. The conversation was loud and lively. Every once in a while, Fee would interject with a cooing sound or brandish a wide smile.

Liza was relieved that the conversation flowed, and that there were no references to her illness. With her head on Liza's feet, Mona stayed under the table.

After an hour at table, Liza excused herself; Sarah did as well and helped Liza get ready for bed. Liza was so tired that she'd have to wait till tomorrow to ask Sarah if there was anything she needed to say to her. When Liza was settled, Mona jumped up and snuggled in beside her.

"Wow, that's some arrangement," said Sarah.

Liza awoke, and Sarah was still sleeping, so she got up slowly. She was weak and feeling nauseated. She peered into Jack's room. He wasn't sleeping, as she had feared. Mona tagged along as Liza went into the closet. The closet was different that morning. Someone had been in there since her last visit. The urns weren't where they usually sat. They were mixed up... the sequence wasn't right. After rearranging the lot, she thought better of it and put them back as they were. Either Kate or Dad had done this for a reason, or they were preoccupied when they returned them to the shelf.

Liza said a prayer for herself, hoping she had the strength to die. Whom she was praying to she really wasn't sure. In the back of her mind, she knew why she had come in... this was to be her last visit. No more. She kissed each urn and bowed her head. She had to go on by herself now. Liza closed the closet door. That part of her journey was over.

Bracing herself against the walls, she made her way back to the bedroom. Wanting to talk with Sarah, she hoped she could muster the energy to do so. Believing she was nearing the end, she opened her heart to silence.

Michael brought a tray with French toast and orange juice. Jack entered the room behind Michael with a tray of food for Sarah. The two men settled down, Jack at Liza's desk and Michael on the floor leaning against her closet door while Sarah ate, and Liza pushed the food around her plate.

Mona was trying to mooch food from the two of them. That gave them something to talk about. Each one admonished her and told her to lie down. She continued her begging anyway. Michael remarked, "She certainly is stubborn."

"She's Irish, after all," replied Jack.

Everyone laughed—the kind of laugh that relieves tension.

The men left the girls to meet in private. The day was overcast, hinting of rain.

Sarah turned on the overhead light and then sat across from Liza.

Lisa smiled at her friend. "Is there anything you need to tell me?"

"I'll think of you every day while I'm raising your namesake. How lucky we were to find each other as roomies at Bard. She thought a minute. "I don't know what you believe at this point, but I hope we'll meet again in the next life."

"I'm afraid that's my struggle at the moment."

"I wish I could help you. I hope that you are at peace when you die."

"Thank you, my friend. You are easy to love."

Liza put her head on the pillow and closed her eyes.

The four of them ate lunch in Liza's room. Liza took only one bite. She asked, "How has fundraising going, Da… ?"

Jack and Michael paid no attention to her slip. "I'm happy to announce that FiLi Foundation is being formed as we talk. I'll provide the seed money, and we'll go from there."

"That's wonderful," she replied.

Jack asked Michael and Sarah to be on the board and to help make decisions as to the recipients. "I'll ask Kate to help, too."

"If you wouldn't mind a suggestion, how about a trust to assist families who are at the end of their insurance, so this illness doesn't take them into bankruptcy? When I was getting radiation, I heard sad stories at the hospital."

Everyone agreed.

Liza said, "I'd like to say goodbye to Sarah now." When the men left, Sarah moved to sit on the bed with Liza. Holding hands, they both began to sob.

Liza said, "Our tears say it all. Now go, and smile when you think of me."

Sarah leaned over and gave Liza a gentle hug, picked up her overnight bag with shaking hands, and tried to smile as she left.

A POULTICE FOR CLARE'S HEARTACHE

How hard it is to die even when you want to, Liza thought. Jack came in to give her morphine. As he was calculating her dose, he looked at her and asked, "A little more than last time?"

Liza nodded.

Mona jumped onto the bed, and together they dreamed. Liza thought she saw Fiona and told Jack and Michael about it during dinner.

Jack thought that was a good sign and told Liza so. He hoped Finn would appear, also.

After dinner, Liza asked Jack if he needed to say anything to her.

Jack, looking so pale and thin himself, said, "What to say to a dying daughter? Oh, Liza, what a sad journey we've shared. I would trade places with you if I could. I have always thought of myself as your father." The whites of his eyes were spider webs of red. "I'm now happy to share the honor with Michael. I hope your death takes you to a better place, where there will be no more sorrow for you ever." With that, Jack took Liza's hand and held it till she fell asleep.

###

Liza knew she had to put her heart in its rightful place; she had to deal with Clare. She had to forgive Clare for Clare's sake. She wasn't sure if she meant real forgiveness on her own part but perhaps saying the words to Clare was the best she could do. She asked Kate if she would write a note for her. Haltingly, she suggested some of the words Kate might say.

When Kate was finished, Liza signed her name. She didn't read it, for she had no doubt that Kate's words were a poultice for Clare's heartache. She wondered if anyone closed her eyes for the last time and made peace with all of life's hurts. My mother wasn't at peace with Michael, and Mom was not at peace losing Finn. Liza thought she would take Clare to the underwater grave with her. So be it.

Liza began to withdraw from everyone, awaiting her uninterrupted sleep. Each day a piece of herself was whittled away from inside her heart. That night, in her room before she had another dose of morphine, Jack asked her if she wanted to see her grandparents.

Liza thought about it and said, "Why? I have nothing to prove. Grandfather will always think of me as the bastard child of their wanton daughter. Kate can help me with a note for Grandmother. You may tell them after I die, but that's up to you. I do want to say goodbye to Uncle Liam and Uncle Peter." She noticed the moon through the leaves of the tree outside her window. "Please turn out the light, Dad." The moon seemed a good thing to

363

concentrate on. She remembered the moon when her mom had given her mother's ashes.

###

The following morning her uncles came. Everything was happening so fast now. *Maybe everyone knows instinctively when death is imminent, even those who suffer a heart attack*, she thought.

Trying to rally for their visit, she was capable of nodding or shaking her head. How they tried to be upbeat for her, and she cherished them for that. They talked about her mother, bringing up half forgotten anecdotes. The night she hid her father's car keys. So unlike her, but he had forbade her from going to a skating party. She went anyway, and Fiona thought she'd be okay if she got back by three. At four Sally Anne looked at her watch. She ran home as though the wings of Mercury were attached to her shoes. They were not fast enough. She was severely punished and two days later hid her father's keys. The funny part was she hid them where she thought he might have left them— in plain sight. They each secretly delighted in his fuming, while looking for his keys. Every once and a while, it seemed as though Sally Anne stepped outside of the religious container where her father had carefully placed her and her siblings.

Almost asleep in the middle of Liam's telling her about his eldest daughter's new job, she heard him cracking his knuckles while he was talking. That was the last thing Liza remembered before falling asleep.

GOING HOME

Volunteering with hospice, Myra Shields was a kind, middle-aged woman. She asked Liza if she had any questions and if she understood what was happening to her and also told her that they would make her as comfortable as possible.

"Yes, I understand."

Becoming restless, she couldn't get comfortable. Her legs were beginning to swell. From watching Fiona, she knew she was close to quietus.

Michael peeked his head in around four that afternoon to see if she wanted him to read.

She was awake and said, "Let's finish this book." Since neither had read it before, they were surprised to find incest among the Buendia family.

As he read this, Michael began laughing. Liza picked up on it, and laughed to the point of saying, "Stop." Neither of them could. Finally Michael said, "In all God's universe of books, how did you manage to pick this one?"

"A fitting end, don't you think?" She asked Michael.

With that declaration, Michael read the last paragraph of the book:

"Before reaching the final line, he had already understood that he would never leave that room, for it was foreseen that the city of mirrors (or mirages) would be wiped out by the wind and exiled from the memory of men at the precise moment when Aureliano Babilonia would finish deciphering the parchments, and that everything written on them was unrepeatable since time

366

immemorial and forever more, because races condemned to one hundred years of solitude did not have a second opportunity on earth."

Liza wasn't hungry that night. Calling Kate she suggested they finish the quilt the next day. After a fitful night's sleep she was still desperate to finish it. Kate came and did most of the work. Liza managed to sew a few stitches to the last patch in the corner. The material was from the dress she had worn when she had met Michael on their first date.

Putting down her needle, Liza said, "I don't think my life had meaning. Mom's did, but mine didn't. This thought has been nagging at me for the last few weeks."

"Oh, Liza, your life has meaning for everyone in this family. You're only twenty-eight. You're so brave. You're giving us the strength to accept your dying."

"I hope you're right." She wobbled back to her bed and lay down.

Kate bent over Liza, gave her a kiss, and laid the quilt on top of her.

Liza managed to say, "Thanks, Mrs. Burgee."

Removing the vase with the dead gardenias from the bureau, Kate tiptoed out of the room.

These last weeks had been especially hard on Liza, with the long hours of sleeping, the leg pain, her fractured thoughts, and sometimes incoherence. She knew she was sleeping more. She had finished what she needed to. Another small victory, but was she was ready for the way of all flesh? The end had seemed so fast for Fiona.

In one of her clearer moments, Liza told Jack, Michael and Kate that if she understood what was going on, she'd try and raise her little finger to let them know she could hear them.

The next morning when Myra administered the morphine, Liza was hallucinating about a car with wings in the room. She also saw a painting on the wall that wasn't there. Asking Michael about it, she sat up as though nothing was wrong with her and said, "Tell Clare I forgive her." And lay back down.

Michael, not wanting to agitate her further, told her it had been difficult to get the car into the room and that he'd tell Clare.

Liza slept a few hours, and when it was time to administer the morphine again, Michael had trouble rousing her.

Returning that night, Myra told the family that it was time for them to take turns sitting with her, to be with her when she died.

Liza raised her right hand and touched her forehead and then her heart, her left shoulder, "O my God I am heartily sorrow…" and her hand fell to her side. Within seconds, she lapsed into a coma.

###

Kate sat on the edge of the bed and kept Liza's mouth moist. As she had done when Liza was little, she brushed her hair.

Michael saw that Liza's face was peaceful. He asked Kate if he could sit with her for a while. Kate and he traded places.

Keeping watch at the bottom of the bed was Mona, her head resting next to Liza's legs.

Around seven in the morning, Myra returned and checked Liza's vital signs. They had dropped considerably. She asked if the dog had to be on the bed.

Jack and Michael both answered, "Yes!"

Kate was called to come back.

Seeing that Liza's breathing was labored, Michael hoped that she would hold on till Kate came. When Kate entered, Michael saw Liza's finger twitch.

Michael had ordered gardenias, and Kate, having met the florist at the door, handed them to Michael. He broke a flower off the plant and held it under Liza's nose.

Jack touched Kate and Michael's shoulders and said, "I promised Liza that I'd try and sing. I'm not sure I can. Help me."

"I can't carry a tune, but I'll do my best," said Michael.

"I'll try," countered Kate.

"Do you know the hymn *Going Home*?"

Michael nodded, "Some, but not all."

"I do," said Kate.

Jack said, "Wait a minute, I have the words in my office." When he came back, he handed a sheet to Michael, who shared it with Kate.

Mona, who knew that something was amiss, sat up and listened to the three of them.

All three found their voices and softly sang this old Negro spiritual:
Going home, going home,

I'm just going home.

Quiet-like, slip away-

I'll be going home.

It's not far, just close by;

Jesus is the Door;

Work all done, laid aside,

Fear and grief no more.

When singing stopped, Liza exhaled her last breath.

Leaning over, Kate kissed her hand and left the room.

Jack kissed his daughter on the cheek and whispered, "Sleep tight, my darling girl." He also left the room.

370

Watching the bright yellow sunlight make its way into the room, Michael sat on the bed and held her still warm hands. Bending down, he kissed her scarred wrists. He and Mona stayed with her until the undertaker came.

Acknowledgements

Thank you to John Page Williams, my husband, and Nancy Osius Zimmerman, more than a friend in need, who read this work at least fifty odd times and was always encouraging. I am eternally grateful.

It all started with four generous women who came on a near weekly basis for several years to read for chocolate ginger cookies: Nancy Osius Zimmerman, Cynthia Doster, Dee Clark, and Robin Noonan. They saw what I couldn't and were gracious in sharing this knowledge. Thank you dear friends.

Writers along the way gave me so much valuable feedback and bolstered my confidence. I appreciated that they had knowledge and shared it. All have a vocation in helping fledgling writers. Ann Hood, Sigrid Nunez, Jill McCorkle and Barbara Rogan may I never forget the wisdom you imparted. Your senses of humor aided in the process so much. Thank you.

To Deborah Schneider, an agent of substance, who read my first draft and give me an analysis that helped to point me in the right direction. Thank you.

To Mark Gottlieb who showed faith in me as a writer.

Dr. Stanley Watkins kept me on track with medical information. Thank you.

Anthony B Wolff, PHD, psychologist and clinical specialist answered questions I had about Finn and his personality. Thank you.

Michael Waitz gave me editing advice, which I found valuable. Thank you.

Lei Hu and Rosanna Oh, are two writer buddies that I met at conferences and they shared insights into the character development and overall feeling of the story. Thank you.

These friends and relatives took the time out of their busy lives to read and give helpful suggestions. Thank you. Kelly McCaskill, Madlyn Donegan, Maggie McCullough, Sue Schanz, Judy Dorfleur, Gigi Redmond, Jennifer Kirchnick Duffy, Becky Wilson, Sue Renfrew, Jeralyn Jacobs, Freddy Struse, Gale Wakins, Jan Ferguson, Debbie Goodwin, Deborah Book, Clayton Bond, Deb Fortier, Gillian Pommerehn, Jin Lee, Cynthia Scruggs, and Wendy McIntyre.

Kelly Belle spent hours with me to ready this yarn for publication. She has my admiration and thanks.

Made in the USA
Middletown, DE
16 January 2020